The Island Experiment

Kepos Chronicles Book 3

Erica Rue

ISBN: 1-945994-54-1
ISBN-13: 978-1-945994-54-8

Editing by Jessica Hatch of Hatch Editorial Services

Cover Design by Sanja Gombar, fantasybookcoverdesign.com

Published by Tannhauser Press
tannhauserpress.com

Visit ericarue.com for more information.

For Jacob and Valen

For Jane

The Island Experiment

1. BEL

Belen Sangha rubbed her cheek where the Ven had carved its mark. That day the Vens had boarded the *Calypso* felt like a lifetime ago, but it had been less than two weeks. The fresh scar felt smooth and tender, even if she couldn't see the shiny pink spiral that marred her brown skin.

A buzzing sound caught her attention. She looked around the lab, searching for her prey. It was in here somewhere. She'd come down into the basement of the Mountain Base to upload the datacore, but she'd gotten distracted when she realized she wasn't alone. Something was down here with her.

She saw movement out of the corner of her eye. She tracked her quarry across the room, but lost it again when it landed out of her line of sight. Bel deftly wove her thick, dark hair into a single braid down her back to keep it out of the way while she hunted the insect—a red-striped stinger, as Evy, a young Aratian girl they'd befriended, had called it. She'd checked the lid of the container when Evy had shown her the angry red bug, but it had escaped all the same. It must have hitched a ride down here with her.

She wondered what Evy was up to now. The Aratian settlement, with the Vale Temple at its center, had been the site of their major battle with the Vens. After the battle, most of the Vens were dead. Most of the colonists were alive. She still couldn't believe it, and a momentary pang of jealousy rose up inside her. She wished things had been different back home, where her colony had been wiped out by the Vens. She had survived and ended up at StellAcademy, just to get stranded out here on a summer internship gone wrong.

She shook off the thought. The price Kepos paid for victory had been high, and there was nothing she could do about the past. With the information on the datacore, maybe she could find a Ven weakness to exploit and do something about the future. There had been a reason she risked her life to download that data before the Invader was destroyed.

Bel was in one of the basement labs that Sam had barred all colonists from. Sam, once a researcher on Kepos, had uploaded her consciousness into the Mountain Base computer, merging with its AI in order to better protect the colonists. The lab equipment had long been stored away, leaving the workbenches in the center of the room bare. Surprisingly comfy chairs bordered the empty tables. There was a large screen at the far end of the room displaying the words *Upload Complete*. Bel had just finished uploading the contents of her manumed into Sam's systems. She turned her wrist and read the same confirmation message on her manumed. The device was more than just a communicator; she'd been able to download a portion of the datacore onto it before Sam destroyed the Ven ship. She hoped she'd gotten enough to get some answers.

"That's the last of it, Sam," she said.

The AI responded, "Zane has already given me his translation program. It will take some time, though." Bel thought her voice wavered at the end. Was Sam starting to sound more human, or was it Bel's imagination?

She heard the basement door open. Zane Delapont and Professor Elian Oberon had finally arrived. Zane's blue eyes found her immediately, and his smile gave her goosebumps.

"Sam is going to translate the datacore using your program. She adapted it," Bel said.

Zane nodded, but he didn't look happy.

"What's wrong?" she said.

"Can you handle that task, Sam? It will be pretty demanding on you," he said.

"Yes, I can. I will use the data you already have to extrapolate a greater vocabulary, though there will still be words I will be unable to translate, or that I'll translate incorrectly," Sam replied.

Zane turned to exchange a look with Oberon, and that's when Bel saw it. A large, dangerous-looking bug with a red stripe and pulsating abdomen had found its way onto Zane's back.

"Don't move, Zane," Bel said. "The red-striped stinger is on your back. It might sting or bite." She looked around until she found something that she could use: a thin, metal panel leaning against one of the tables.

Bel quickly positioned the metal sheet to flick the bug away, but it took to flight. When it landed on a table, Bel scooped it into her empty water bottle. She would release it outside later. And maybe throw out the water bottle afterward, just to be safe.

"Is it venomous?" Oberon asked.

"I don't know. Evy found it, but I never remembered to look it up. It looks like it has a painful sting at the very least."

"I won't argue with that," the professor said.

"Sam, do you have a database of all the organisms on this planet?"

"Yes," Sam said, giving her access.

Bel searched by a number of criteria, including the order and family she thought the insect might be in, but even its striking color did not yield any results.

"Sam, it's not in here," she said.

"This database contains all approved species," the AI replied.

"That doesn't make any sense. It can't be all of them." As soon as Bel said it out loud, something clicked. "You said 'approved' species. This is one of Jameson's experiments, isn't it? You mentioned them in your audio logs." Jameson, often called the Farmer by the colonists, had been a terraforming researcher, like Sam, but he had brought the colonists to Kepos and wiped their memories. He had made himself a king—no, a god—that is, until Sam had stopped him.

"His unofficial experiments were not permitted to be released in the testing area," Sam said.

"Well, permitted or not, it's here," Bel replied. "What's the testing area?"

The screen went blank for a moment before a color-coded map of Kepos appeared.

"This looks like a map I found back on the space station," Zane said, peering at it. "There's more detail here, though. The colors represent the planet's different biomes, and those little triangles must be Kepos' research bases."

"Then the gray area is not for testing," Bel said. "Is that where he released them?"

There was a pause. "All of Jameson's nightmare experiments were confined," Sam replied. Bel found her answer annoying and purposefully opaque.

Oberon was frowning. "What do you mean, *confined*?"

Bel studied the map while they waited for Sam's reply. She was slow today.

The mountain region turned from red to gray at a certain point, but that was quite far from the base itself. Evy hadn't gone off too far during her bug hunt. Plus, the mountains wouldn't be considered a confined area. At that thought, she glanced at the lower edge of the map and saw a blip of gray. She reached forward and zoomed out, revealing a gray patch, floating in the sea.

"An island," Bel said. "He put everything on that island."

"Nothing on the southern island has the capacity to escape," Sam said. "They were not designed to be as hardy as some of the creatures we seeded on the mainland. Jameson never would have come back to start a colony if he thought what he put on that island could escape."

"What's on the island exactly?" Zane asked apprehensively.

"I never knew them all, but you could go through his own records."

"Can you show us what you do know?" Oberon asked.

Sam granted them access to another section of the database. "Here's Jameson's catalog."

There were only a few dozen entries in this one. Some of them were only sketches, but among them Bel found a picture of the red-striped stinger. She read its description.

"This little guy," she said, giving her water bottle a small flourish, "is called a percussor insect. He won't kill you. You will, however, experience extreme pain at the site of the bite for days and sensitivity that can last for months."

"Are you certain you've correctly identified the insect?" Sam asked.

"I know bugs, Sam, and this is it. The things from the island aren't confined. How could he ever think they would be?"

"Jameson was smart, but arrogant," Sam said. "He probably thought he could control them. I imagine he had some fail safes in place to prevent this, but he died before he could finish whatever he was planning."

Died? Bel thought. *You killed him.*

An old maxim her mother used to repeat popped into her mind. *Life finds a way.* Bel was angry that a scientist would be so careless and then bring these people here, but Jameson wasn't a regular scientist. He seemed to think he was some untouchable god, and for just a moment she was sad he wasn't around to see how truly wrong he had been.

That's when Zane spoke up. "Bel, check the 'approved' database for that fake plant thing that attacked Lithia."

After a minute of scrolling, Bel said, "Nothing's coming up, but I may not be searching for the right thing. I never saw it in person."

Zane tried a few more searches, but found nothing. "I'm willing to bet the angler worm is another one of his abominations. I'll check the nightmare list."

"Nightmare list. I like that," Bel said.

"Angler worm?" Sam asked.

"Yeah, beautiful, creepy flowers that grab you and pull you into the ground if you get too close. There's a little tree in the middle."

"I had no idea he actually engineered it. Many of the creatures in his logs were only theoretical. He tossed out a lot of ideas and worked almost constantly. This is very bad. If the things on that island are escaping…"

"Here it is," Zane said. "*Capitella florianna*. A flower worm." The sketch showed what the worm looked like underground. It had a thick central body, with its head rooted firmly in place by tiny, abundant hooks. Its midsection diverged in many directions, breaking the surface of the earth in order to display its captivating blooms. Its tail also broke the surface, though just barely.

"The ones I've seen have longer above-ground tails," Zane said. "Like small tree trunks."

"This was just a sketch. I guess we can expect some variation. What else is over there?" Bel asked.

"I don't know, beyond what's in Jameson's catalog," Sam said. "I wasn't a part of his experiments. After a while, I fell out of favor and he found others to assist him. Much of it, though, he preferred to do alone."

"I don't think you can deny that the nightmares from the island are making their way here to the mainland," Bel said.

"You might be right," Sam said, "but I don't know how to stop them. Jameson's the only one who did. I'm certain he had a way of controlling them, or he never would have started his colony with those creatures in his backyard."

Oberon had been swiping through the database entries. He let out a single, humorless laugh. "Is this supposed to be a dragon?"

Bel looked over his shoulder at the image. It was a lizard, about the size of a small dog.

"No wings," Zane said.

"But it breathes fire." Bel summarized its description. "It produces and spits an accelerant, then ignites it with its bifurcated tail." She looked up. "So, like striking two pieces of flint together." This was no sketch or digital rendering, but a real picture of a dragon. The idea that, like the angler worms, a fire-breathing creature could escape its confines and infiltrate the mainland set her teeth on edge.

"What are we going to do, Oberon?" Bel said.

Oberon wouldn't even look at her. He closed his eyes and massaged his temples. "This is not something we caused, and therefore, it's not our concern. We should focus on heading home. I've spoken to Victoria about taking the Ven ship."

"We're leaving? We can't leave without helping them. Plus there are still a few Vens running around."

"Bel, it will take some time to figure out how to fly the Ven ship outside of the atmosphere. Victoria and Benjamin are working together to figure out how to destroy the last of the Vens," he said.

"If we even can," Bel said. She didn't much care for Victoria, the leader of the Ficarans, but if she was working with Benjamin, the current Regnator of the Aratians, Bel would consider that a win. The two groups of colonists, the Ficarans and Aratians, had finally come together to defeat the Vens. She hated the fact that the Vens were still out there, a perpetual threat.

Zane chimed in. "We don't have a choice."

"Any sightings?" Bel asked.

"No, but people aren't doing a lot of exploring right now."

"Neither should we. This whole situation is a mess that we're no longer a part of," Oberon said.

Bel crossed her arms. *Vens. Dragons. How could Oberon just leave these people to their fate?* "And when the dragons make their way here to the mainland?" She couldn't believe Oberon would leave them to the mercy of a genetic engineering nightmare.

"Bel, please—"

"She's right, Oberon," Zane said, stepping forward. "We owe it to these people. We helped them defeat the Vens, but there's still more good we can do here."

Bel smiled and grabbed Zane's hand. Warmth flooded her body. When she looked up at Oberon, some of that warmth receded. He looked completely drained.

She could see him thinking about it, weighing his responsibility as their teacher and his role in the present colonial upheaval. "What makes you think we can solve their problems for them?" he asked. "What right do we have to intervene? That kind of hubris on the part of one man got them into this."

Bel tried to interrupt, but Oberon powered on.

"Their issues existed long before we arrived, and when the Vens were the primary threat, it made sense to help. We may have been responsible. But now? We have a chance to leave and get them real help. Even though we're outside the Bubble of Alliance-protected space, I may be able to talk some of my contacts into an evacuation, or at least get them some supplies. Sam can tell the colonists about the island and the dragons, and they can make their own decisions."

Bel examined the bags under Oberon's eyes and felt her own shoulders sag. Maybe he was right. If there was a chance to get these colonists the kind of help they needed, shouldn't she support that?

"The professor has a point, Bel," Zane conceded. She felt him glance at her. "If you really think we can get someone to come back out here, that might be the best option for the colonists."

"I do," Oberon said. "It won't be easy, but—"

"And if they refuse to leave?" Bel asked. "They wouldn't be the first colonists outside the Bubble to refuse." She had grown up in a colony outside the Bubble. Even the threat of the Vens couldn't always convince people to move to a safer location.

"True, but they'll at least have the choice. Jameson didn't give them that when he brought them here and erased their memories."

Bel nodded, but frowned nonetheless. What kind of choice was it actually? They had just fought for this land and won. The colonists deserved a little peace and quiet after everything. She didn't think that many would be eager to leave, though, even if they understood the truth of the universe beyond Kepos.

2. LITHIA

Lithia Min leaned casually against a Flyer near the entrance of the Mountain Base. Though the views were beautiful, the nature sounds were drowned out by mechanical whirring and shouting from one side of the landing pad to the other. The morning was warm already, and sweat was beginning to form on her forehead, but she couldn't go inside yet. She pulled her long, black hair into a ponytail to get it off her neck and shoulders, hoping that would help her cool off.

She stared at her manumed, pretending to read. It was a skill she had practiced many times, moving her eyes across the page and pausing occasionally to look up with a pensive expression. She had been perfecting the art of eavesdropping her entire life. The hard part was not reacting as she overheard Victoria's frustration.

Victoria, the Ficaran leader, and Colm, her second-in-command, marched out onto the landing pad. From what she'd gleaned of their conversation, there had been a disturbance back at the Aratian settlement while the last Flyers were being loaded with Aratian supplies. The delivery of food supplies was a big part of the deal that had established the alliance between Aratians and Ficarans.

"They're sure it was Brian?" Colm asked.

"Of course it was him. That arrogant boy!" Victoria fiddled with her communicator, but only grew angrier. "He's not answering."

"Should I take a Flyer and follow him?" Colm asked.

"No, not yet. We know he's headed to the southern island to find his father, and I doubt the trip will be long. Once he finds the corpse, he'll return."

"I think he knew you weren't going to let him take a Flyer like you promised," Colm said.

Lithia smirked. She had been the one to tell Dione and Brian that Victoria wasn't going to lend him a Flyer. They'd taken one of the Flyers still being loaded with supplies at the Aratian settlement and zipped on over to look for his dad. That was the whole reason Brian had helped them when she and Dione crashed on this planet. He'd wanted a Flyer to go find his dad, and now he had one.

She felt Colm's eyes on her and looked back down at her manumed, scanning the words on the page but absorbing nothing. She tried to ignore him. She would wait a few hours before telling Bel and the others where Dione was. It was just a quick trip to the island, and it wasn't like the Vens were roaming the woods there. It was perfectly safe. Lithia heard the characteristic hum of a Flyer and looked up. It was approaching for a landing, coming in quite fast.

"Cutting it close, Sam," she muttered to herself. No one else seemed to notice or care, but why would they? They didn't have the flying experience that was setting off warning bells in her head.

She watched the shuttle, waiting for it to slow. It didn't.

She sprang into action. "Clear the pad," she screamed. "Out-of-control Flyer! Get inside!" The Ficarans reacted in what felt to Lithia like slow motion. Finally, they began to properly panic and hustle out of the way, some heading inside, others scrambling out of the way in what little time they had left to react.

Fortunately, as the shuttle crashed, its trajectory kept it toward the far edge of the landing pad, away from most of the other Flyers and people.

Unfortunately, it was right on course to crash into the *Calypso*.

Lithia retreated inside a Flyer and covered her ears at the moment of impact. The crunch of metal echoed through the mountains, and the vibrations of the impact resounded through the Mountain Base.

"Oberon," Lithia called over her manumed, "I hope you have good insurance."

"What was that?" he replied. "Are you okay?"

"You should come outside." She would let his own eyes break the news to him.

The Ficarans were pulling their last man from the crumpled shuttle, and somehow, everyone seemed mostly okay. They were all walking away. A few minutes later, Oberon, flanked by Bel and Zane, joined her on the landing pad.

The shuttle was a mess, though, and the *Calypso?* A monstrous hole revealed the crates of the cargo bay, though she was optimistic that the engine room was intact, based on the damage. Nevertheless, this wasn't the kind of damage that a ship recovered from. The *Calypso* needed to be rebuilt.

Oberon put both hands to his forehead and pushed back against his short, dark curls before linking his fingers behind his head. He took a few steps toward the wreckage and inhaled so deeply she could see his back move.

After another minute of mental processing, he turned around. "Was anyone injured?" he asked.

"I don't think so," Lithia replied.

"That's good," Oberon said, though Lithia thought his voice sounded strained.

"What happened?" Bel asked.

"I think I know," Zane said, looking at some readouts on his manumed. "The shuttles all have autopilot programs the Ficarans have been using, but Sam has been taking over the landing procedures when they get in close. She lost contact with the shuttle, and it crashed."

"How'd that happen?" Lithia asked.

"She's overtaxed. The Ficarans are asking too much from her, and so are we. Translating the datacore is going to take a lot of her. I wonder if this is a result of adding that additional task to her workload," Zane replied.

"You mean having her translate the datacore might have caused this?" Bel asked.

"Maybe."

"Then we can have her... stop the translation." Bel sighed.

"Aren't AIs supposed to be able to handle this kind of thing? Not to be rude," Lithia added to nobody in particular. She looked back to the base. Sam might be listening.

"Sam's not a regular AI," Zane said. "She's able to function at a higher level than true artificial intelligences, but she's starting to let things slip. The flame that burns twice as bright—"

"Burns half as long." It was Sam, speaking through Zane's manumed, who finished his thought. "I thought I would have more time. There's so much to prepare before I die, but I hope that you'll do me one final favor before you go."

"What do you need, Sam?" Oberon asked.

"It's a small task, but I'd rather not have the Ficarans handle it. And don't worry, it won't interfere with your journey home. I'll give you the details soon."

Oberon raised his eyebrows, but acquiesced. "We'll do our best."

"Thank you. Fortunately, there were no serious injuries, but I'll be scaling back the direct control I have over the Flyers. I am sorry about your ship. I hope the damage isn't too bad."

Oberon grimaced. "She's been through a lot. I'll see what we can do."

Lithia empathized. The *Calypso* was a beautiful ship, but the damage was more than they could repair. The nanotech could mend small breaches, but it couldn't manufacture entire bulkheads. She knew the *Calypso* wouldn't have been able to take them home, but it had at least been flight capable. Now even that wasn't true.

Lithia's mourning for the most beautiful ship she had ever flown was interrupted by Bel. "Where's Dione?"

"She's with Brian." She had hoped no one would ask for a few more hours, long enough for Brian to find his father. Maybe that vague answer would give her pause.

"Are they still with the Aratians?" Bel asked.

Lithia looked around to make sure that Victoria and Colm were out of ear shot. They were talking with the Flyer pilot. Lithia could easily lie, but she didn't see the point. After all, they were just going to find Brian's father. Bel knew that was why Brian had helped them in the first place. Plus, it wasn't like they were out in the woods fighting Vens or doing something dangerous.

"They went to find Brian's dad on the southern island."

Bel, Oberon, and even Zane tensed.

"What?" she said. "Victoria wasn't going to give him a shuttle, so they, uh, borrowed one on its way back from the Vale Temple. They'll be back tonight, I'm sure." The others still looked horrified, and Lithia got a sinking feeling in her stomach. "What's wrong?"

"The southern island isn't just another piece of land," Bel said. "It's apparently where Jameson released all of the 'unapproved' creatures he was working on. That's probably where that angler worm came from. Most things are contained on the island for now, but that place is extremely dangerous. We only have partial records of what he engineered."

Lithia bit her lip as Bel showed her a few highlights, including the percussor insect and the dragons. Lithia felt anxiety tighten in her chest as she thought about what was waiting for Dione and Brian on that island. "That's not good."

"I'll call her," Bel said. "They need to come back."

"No, let me tell her. I talked her into this."

Normally, Lithia didn't buy into the whole 'bad influence' thing, but this might be the exception that proved the rule. What had she gotten Dione into this time?

3. DIONE

Dione Quinn took a deep breath and stared through the viewing glass at the blue ocean sweeping beneath their shuttle. She couldn't smell or feel the ocean breeze, but she could imagine it. Every minute they got farther away from the mainland, the lighter she felt. No Vens to kill them, no Green Cloaks to betray them. There were a few crates of supplies in the back. They had stolen the Flyer while the Aratians were packing it. Victoria was probably mad at losing the supplies on top of the Flyer.

She looked at Brian out of the corner of her eye. Even her discomfort at being trapped with him in a shuttle was easing after a couple of hours of silence. She didn't find silence unsettling at all. She usually enjoyed being left to her own thoughts, though unfortunately her mind kept replaying her memories of kissing Brian, followed by the memory of finding out he had kissed Lithia, too. Despite the circumstances and explanations, she couldn't help feeling hurt. She glanced over at him once more, this time taking in his appearance. His brown hair was almost shoulder length, like hers, but darker and put up in a short ponytail. His biceps were visible under his short sleeves, and his expression showed that he, too, was lost in thought.

She sighed and resisted that part of herself that was still attracted to him. She tried to think of something else. Normally she daydreamed about experiments she wanted to run, though here on Kepos they always seemed to have bigger real-life problems to solve.

The buzzing of her manumed startled her.

"Is it Victoria?" Brian asked, frowning.

"No, it's Lithia." Dione answered the call. "Hey, we're getting close to the island. How's everything?"

"Umm, it could be better."

"Is Victoria—"

"Pissed? Oh yeah. But there are some other issues. Sam's having some problems and accidentally crashed a shuttle into the *Calypso*."

"What?"

"Yeah, no one got hurt. Except the *Calypso*."

"That's good," Dione replied. While she appreciated the update, she got the feeling that Lithia was holding something back. "Then what's wrong?"

"You can't go to the southern island. It's not safe."

Dione laughed. "Is anywhere on this planet safe? Are you serious right now?"

"Yes," Lithia said. "Put me on speaker. Brian needs to hear this, too."

Dione complied. "What is it?" she asked.

"Jameson was doing all kinds of off-the-books experiments, and he put the awful things he created on that island. Please come back. We'll find a way for you to get there safely." Lithia sounded uncharacteristically anxious.

"No. Victoria will never give Brian another chance, especially not now," Dione said. "I've got the stun rifle. We'll do a sweep from the air and stick close to the shuttle when we land. I think we can handle a maximute's evil cousin."

Bel cut in. Dione hadn't realized she was on the call, too. "You don't understand." She sounded angry. "This is nightmare island. He wasn't designing tamable machi and *pila* sword trees, he was stretching the bounds of genetic engineering by creating literal monsters, Dione. Look at the file I just sent you."

Dione swiped through the images. "Holy crap. Is that—"

"A freaking dragon, yes," Lithia replied.

"But it's so small," Dione said, noting the average size in the description, "and it doesn't have wings. I think we'll be okay. We won't take long, I promise. In fact, we're already here."

She looked at the camera feeds and saw the viridian paradise of an island untouched by man. Almost untouched. Something dark gleamed at its center, where the green canopy that covered most of the island was so sparse it was practically nonexistent.

"Please," Lithia begged. Dione could hear the desperation in her voice. "Come back. We'll figure out a way to check out the island safely. Once we know more about what's there."

It was Brian's turn to reply. "Victoria will never let me do this again. This is my only chance to find my father. And when I find him, I may just be able to save my mom, too. You saw her, Lithia. I don't have a choice."

There was a pause before Lithia spoke. "Do you think losing her son will do her any favors?"

The crease in Brian's forehead deepened. His voice was low as he turned and spoke directly to Dione. "I know I'm not your favorite person right now, but you know what this means to me."

He was pleading with her. She was the one flying the shuttle. She could lock him out of the controls, turn them around, and take them home. They could find another way. Once they had more information about the creatures on the island, they could come up with a plan. Wasn't it always better to have a plan?

"Hang on. Professor Oberon wants to say something," Lithia said.

Dione braced herself.

"Dione, listen to me." The professor's tone was uncharacteristically harsh. "It's not safe. Turn around and come back. We'll find another way." She said nothing, so he continued. "I hope that you trust me enough to know that I mean every word."

Dione felt like she would be sick. With his warning, every part of her screamed for her to listen. To obey. Ignoring Lithia was one thing, but the professor? He was a fair and reasonable man. A scientist she looked up to and admired like a father.

Like a father. That was the part that really mattered. If the professor were on that island, she would try to find him, just like she had saved him from the Vens when he had been trapped in that cave.

"I'm sorry," she said softly. "I have to do this." Dione ended the call and silenced her manumed. She wiped away a tear. She'd explain everything to Oberon later.

Brian looked Dione in the eyes for the first time the entire trip. "Thank you."

She gave him a nod while searching for the right reply, but something else caught her eye. A dark smudge marred the crystal blue of the sky. "Is that smoke?" Dione asked.

"I think so. It could be my father," he said, eyes wide with hope.

"Then let's check it out."

The sooner they found Brian's dad, the sooner she could get back to Lithia and the others. She checked her manumed. Missed calls and unread messages. She opened one with an attachment. "Nightmare island flora and fauna. You're an idiot. Be careful." Lithia ended her message with small image of a hand making a rude gesture. Dione smiled. Classic Lithia.

"Take over for a bit," she said, transferring control of the Flyer to Brian. She studied the first entry. It was a black and white sketch of a very creepy-looking spider with wings. There was no description. Maybe this one had never been brought to life. The next was some kind of bird. According to the notes, nodules at the bird's throat lit up to attract small insects to eat and to communicate availability to potential mates. It seemed harmless until Dione read the bit about its extreme territorial nature and fondness for eating the eyeballs of creatures both dead and alive. There was no information on how many of the creatures on this island were regular animals, and how many were Jameson's creations.

She paused on the next entry. It was the one Bel had already sent. The dragons. Honestly, they looked kind of cute. Dione wasn't really into reptiles, but she tried to imagine what these creatures would look like in action. The bifurcated tail looked sharp. Even if they couldn't fly, that tail and those teeth could do some serious damage. The hide looked tough. The description said it was fireproof, which made sense.

"Look at that!" Brian's eyes were fixed on a massive ship in the middle of the island. He flew them lower and closer, and soon Dione realized what it was. What had only been a dark gleam earlier was now clearly a ship.

"A colonizer," she muttered. This was the ship that had brought the colonists to Kepos. She looked it up and down. She didn't see any physical signs of damage, but the smoke blocked her view in some places.

"My dad must have found it!" Brian said.

"Yeah," she agreed, too lost in her own thoughts to process what he was saying. "Looks like it has three segments. I wonder if it still flies." Dione had barely asked herself the question when she figured out that something was wrong. She hadn't been able to see the last segment because of the smoke. In another moment, she pinpointed the problem. "There's more than one source of smoke. A lot of fires." *Fires.* She was an idiot. Such an idiot. "Brian, I don't think this is your father's camp. It's—" Dione broke off mid sentence when Brian flew them over to the other side of the massive vessel.

"There are hundreds of them," Brian said, flying low to get a better look.

On the opposite side of the colonizer was a sparse, blackened area dotted with small brown and pale green creatures. *Dragons.* The colonizer was being guarded by dragons.

"We're getting out of here," Dione said, taking back control of the shuttle.

Once she was flying, she realized how low they really were, just meters off the ground. She could make out the dragons' faces, as they stared at the shuttle. Unsurprisingly, they perceived it as a threat. The dragons thrashed their angry tails and began to attack as best they could from the ground, spitting a thin liquid into the air. A pair of dragons hit them head on, covering the viewing glass in light brown fluid. Accelerant. She was shocked at their range, but grateful that their thrashing tails would not get anywhere close enough to ignite the shuttle.

She heard accelerant hit other parts of the shuttle as she took them up, at last out of range.

"Can you believe how far those things can spit?" Brian asked.

"I guess it makes sense. Spitting cobras can spit two meters with incredible accuracy, and those were a lot bigger than a snake."

"I guess these have traded accuracy for distance. I hope my dad didn't run into the dragons."

"They're at the center of the island, and they may not venture far from that area," Dione said. "I don't see any other areas that are as open and burned down as that one. He came by boat, right? Maybe we're going about this the wrong way."

"Meaning?"

"If we can figure out the patterns of the currents, we'll have a better idea of where his boat landed. Maybe Sam can access the old researchers' data about—" Dione broke off mid sentence. A warning light was flashing among the controls. "The engine is overheating. There's a fire."

"How is that possible?" Brian asked. "They couldn't have ignited the accelerant from the ground."

"Hang on, I'm putting it out." Dione pressed a few flashing buttons, grateful that emergency symbols were universal. The temperature dropped sharply.

"Something's still wrong," Brian said. "The temperature is rising again."

She could see it on the display, indicator creeping back toward red.

"Another fire? I don't see any warning of that."

"No, it must be something else," he said.

"Like what?" Dione's heart was pounding.

"It doesn't matter. We need to land now! How about the beach there?"

Dione began to sweat. She thought the cabin temperature was rising, too, but it could have been her nerves. She directed the Flyer to the beach, landing close to the trees where the ground was a firm mixture of sand and dirt. There was no evidence the tide ever made it up this far.

"What now?" she asked.

"I don't know." Brian threw up his hands. "I'd never been in a Flyer until a few days ago."

She ran some diagnostics, but turned up nothing that would explain the problem.

Crap, she thought. *I need Lithia's help.* She swallowed her pride and gave her best friend a call.

Lithia answered, launching immediately into a tirade. "So now you're ready to talk? Or did you just happen to notice the bajillion missed calls—"

"Lithia, shut up. We've landed on the beach. The Flyer's engine overheated, and there was an internal fire. We put out the fire, and the temperature dropped at first, but then it started rising again. We can't figure out what's wrong. The engine and power cells are fine."

"Maybe it was the dragons," Brian said. "They did spit accelerant on us."

"Seriously?! Did you miss the part where we warned you to stay away from them?" Lithia exclaimed.

"Brian was flying. Got us a little too close."

"That's why the girl should always drive on a date. Overheating engine, you say? What about the cooling system?"

"Huh?"

"It's like when a dog is panting, or lying on a cool surface. The heat has to go somewhere. The dog needs to cool down."

"There's nothing on the display to indicate a problem."

"The display doesn't know anything. Did you check the shuttle? You can actually see the cooling vents. They're near the back on the sides and underneath," Lithia said.

Brian was already opening the back of the Flyer. Dione grabbed the stun rifle just to be safe. They ventured cautiously onto the sand and inspected the shuttle.

"Is it supposed to look like this?" Brian asked, pointing to the starboard cooling vents.

Dione examined them. They were clogged with something. Dione checked the other cooling vents, but they looked normal. She sent Lithia a picture of the damage.

"That's weird," Lithia said. "Hang on. The diagnostics turned up nothing? Not even minor errors?"

"Well, there were some, but none of them would have caused overheating. They were little things, like parts that were getting worn and should be replaced soon. None of them were important parts."

"Everything is an important part! You think I flew us down here in Nate without checking everything first?" Dione rolled her eyes. She'd forgotten that particular shuttle's designation, N8, which Lithia had turned into a nickname.

"Didn't stop you from crashing it," she replied.

"You want my help or not?"

Dione sighed. "I'm sorry. You're right. I'm an idiot about these things, which is why I need your help."

"Uh-huh. Send me the diagnostic results," Lithia said.

After a short wait, Lithia gave her the rundown. "Looks like there was an external crack."

"Why didn't the computer catch this?" Dione asked.

"It's a computer, not a god. Did you do a visual check before you took off?"

"No, we were a little busy stealing it," Dione replied.

"Hmm," Lithia replied, "I guess you were." She paused. "If it's a small enough crack, the computer doesn't always register it. These are old shuttles, Di. Your dad's car is higher tech than these. Anyway, that crack is how the accelerant got into places it shouldn't have been."

"How bad is that?" Dione said.

"It can muck things up. The real problem is that there's some old wiring in there. I'm betting it sparked and caught the accelerant on fire. That fire then melted something, and that something is now clogging the cooling vents," Lithia said. "Without serious repairs, you're not going anywhere."

Dione rubbed her temples. "Awesome."

"You've got terrible timing. The *Calypso* is grounded, too, but maybe we can borrow a Flyer. Cross your fingers Victoria's feeling generous."

"I won't waste my energy," Dione replied. She didn't think Victoria was capable of feeling generous. They were screwed.

Lithia ended the call, and Dione turned to stare out at the ocean. The midday sun reflected off the white sand, blinding her. They hadn't found even a trace of Brian's father and had ruined their shuttle almost immediately. It was so hot and humid, Dione found that even deep breaths were unpleasant. She returned to the shuttle and lay down, spread-eagle on the floor.

She was trapped on nightmare island in the sweltering heat with Brian.

"Damn."

4. LITHIA

Lithia sat on top of a crate in front of the hull breach, watching people scurrying to and from shuttles and the Mountain Base. She'd counted at least a dozen opportunities to slip inside an empty Flyer with no one the wiser. The temptation was so great, she almost forgot what was holding her back.

Oberon was asking Victoria, the Ficaran leader, to use a Flyer, but Lithia already knew that wouldn't work out. Victoria was stubborn and arrogant, but one hell of a marksman, as Lithia had learned during the Ven attacks. If she was being honest with herself, if she hadn't hated Victoria's guts, she might have admired her. When Lithia saw Oberon storming out of the Mountain Base, she knew what the woman's answer had been.

Her normally kind and thoughtful professor entered through the cargo bay doors, even though the gash in the hull was closer, and ripped a crate from a nearby stack. Its contents, dozens of packages containing lab supplies, scattered across the floor.

Lithia flinched. She had never seen Professor Oberon lose control before, but Victoria's refusal to lend him a shuttle, combined with the damage to the *Calypso*, had sent him over the edge.

"What can I do to help, professor?" She winced. She had been too polite. Too like Dione, and that was the last thing Oberon needed right now.

He didn't make eye contact. Instead, he began setting up the nanotech to make repairs. "Zane's going to help me with the nanotech," he said, "but I think the damage is too extensive. She won't be properly space-worthy again, not without undergoing real repairs."

Lithia already knew that. She'd watched the wreck, and there was no coming back from that. "I could... *borrow* another shuttle." Normally, Oberon wouldn't go for the underhanded route, but he seemed desperate.

"No, I'm sure she's on guard for that. We can't cross Victoria. We've finally built up some good will, even with Dione's part in taking that shuttle. Victoria blames Brian more, thankfully." He shook his head. "Push her too far, and I don't know how safe we'll be here. For now, she likes us enough to let us stay and do our own thing."

Lithia couldn't argue with his assessment. As Oberon worked, still avoiding her eye contact, she examined his face. He had to be close to fifty, but he didn't normally show it. Now she saw the bags under his eyes, the frown lines spanning his forehead.

Suddenly, inspiration struck. "What if we got more shuttles from the station?" Lithia asked. She had forgotten about the rather full shuttle bay on the space station that orbited Kepos.

He shook his head. "I already suggested it, but even the lure of supplies and shuttles didn't sway her. Things are too chaotic right now, and Sam told her the autopilot program she's been running for the shuttles wouldn't work in space."

"You and I could do it, though," Lithia replied. Oberon gave her a sad smile, and she understood at once. "And that's the problem. Even with Colm's supervision, she wouldn't let us?"

"No, though I'm hoping she changes her mind once she has a chance to think about how nice it would be to have even more Flyers. It's our best bet."

Lithia sighed. She hated this kind of red tape. It reminded her of being back home. Arbitrary rules, one size fits all. No exceptions, no matter how much sense they made.

"There's one other option," she said.

"I already told you, we're not stealing one." He stepped away from the screen where he had been programming the nanotech and looked her straight in the eye. "Lithia Min, promise me you won't steal a shuttle."

"I promise," she replied, not breaking his eye contact. "I want to ask Cora if I can borrow her shuttle."

"It's not hers. It's the Aratians' shuttle."

"But she's kind of in charge, right? It can't hurt."

When Lithia had first met Cora, she'd been surprised to see how alike they looked. Lithia's grandmother, Miranda Min, had abandoned her grandfather. Miranda had come to Kepos and started a new family once she settled in. Cora was her unexpected cousin, as she liked to think of it. Though Cora had rightfully grown to hate her, she seemed to be coming around. Before the battle against the Vens at the Vale Temple, Cora had asked for answers. Maybe she could exchange those answers for some time with their Flyer.

"How are you going to get over there?" Oberon was already thinking. "Victoria might lend us an ATV…"

"I have a better idea."

Lithia grinned. She had a feeling this would work.

Lithia was helping the volunteer nurses change bandages and check the nonfatal injuries when Victoria found her. She finished helping her current patient before excusing herself.

Lithia smiled and asked, "Is there something I can do for you?" Again, too polite. She didn't want Victoria to be suspicious.

"I've just heard from Moira, and she's requested your help. Says you have some more recent information on phytoremediation that could help her speed up the process." Lithia had met Moira when she'd first been kidnapped by the Aratians, and the scientist had agreed to help fix the Ficarans' poisoned farmland using a weird plant technique called phytoremediation. Lithia had contacted Moira, offering to bring her, in person, all the data her little group had about the technique.

Lithia nodded at Victoria. "I do have some knowledge about the techniques, as well as information in our database that would probably help." That first part was technically true, but that second part, the newer data, was the real reason Moira had agreed to help Lithia get over to the Vale Temple.

"And it really works?" Victoria said. "A few plants can remove the poison from the ground?"

"It's a bit more complicated than that, but yes," Lithia replied. "The plants suck the contaminants out of the ground, and then you dispose of the plants, contaminants and all." She didn't blame Victoria for being skeptical. It sounded ridiculous, like something out of a fantasy holo. Magic plants. But there was a lot more to this process than Lithia truly understood. That's why Bel was preparing everything the *Calypso* had on phytoremediation for her to give to Moira.

"Fine. We're opening up trade again. Slowly. The first exchange is happening this evening. This place," Victoria gestured to the base around her, "is full of Artifacts and spare parts. I'll let you join them, but the earliest you'll be able to return is tomorrow evening."

"No problem. I understand. I'll get ready," Lithia said. Did she sound too eager?

Victoria raised an eyebrow. "Don't try anything stupid," she said. "I know that will be hard for you."

Lithia took a breath, preparing to launch into a tirade about how she had saved a lot of Ficaran lives with her so-called stupidity. Victoria put a hand on her hip, as if waiting for it, so Lithia simply exhaled. It felt like an act of defiance.

What is this woman's problem? she wondered. Hadn't Lithia done enough to earn some good will by this point? Or was Victoria just doubling down on being an abrasive dictator since that was all she'd ever known? Maybe this was her way of being nice.

"Thanks for letting me know," Lithia said.

"Be outside and ready in an hour. No weapons."

Lithia nodded, and Victoria left. Time to check in with Bel.

***

Lithia found her on the *Calypso*, compiling the phytoremediation data and adding in notes where appropriate.

"It's been a while since I looked at this stuff," Bel said, "but there's really a lot that's been done with phytoremediation in recent years. I think this information could help Moira speed up the process. I know you offered it as an excuse to get to the Vale Temple, but it's actually a good idea."

"I have those from time to time," Lithia said, folding her arms across her chest. *God, does everyone think I'm an idiot?*

"I didn't mean it like that," Bel backpedaled.

Apologetic Bel reminded her of Dione in that moment, and she felt a pang for her missing friend. "I know. The biology stuff isn't my forte. Thanks for organizing it all."

"No problem," Bel said.

Oberon and Zane joined them then. Lithia held up her wrist, displaying her manumed. "Freshly loaded with all the data Moira could want."

Oberon smiled, and even though it was a tired smile, Lithia was glad for it.

"I'm happy it worked," he said, "but be careful over there. We don't know when the Vens will attack again. With small numbers, they might rely on biting as many as they can to create Berserkers."

Lithia understood his point. With a bite, Vens could turn regular people into adrenaline-fueled Berserkers who couldn't recognize friend from foe. They had done so at the Field Temple when they attacked the Ficarans.

"This also isn't the most stable time to be among the Aratians," Oberon continued. "It sounds like there might be some anger and tension within the settlement itself. I heard Victoria complaining about some guns that went missing after the battle."

"I'll be careful," Lithia said, rolling her eyes.

Her stomach did a flip. This was just the first step. Getting to the Aratian settlement was only half the battle. Convincing Cora to lend her the shuttle? That would be tough. Cora had been in bad shape emotionally the last time she had seen her. Losing her father and the guy she wanted to marry in the same day? Lithia couldn't imagine her pain. She didn't want to imagine it. She could still see the look on Roy's face when she left him to die during the invasion of the Ficaran settlement. He had only been a kid, and the Vens had killed him because she hadn't been able to save him. She pushed the thought away. It was too painful to dwell on loss. She had to focus on something she could fix.

She was going to rescue Dione.

5. DIONE

Brian sat next to Dione, who leaned back against the bulkhead inside the shuttle. It kept them out of the scorching sun, at least. She waited for him to speak, but he didn't say anything. She was fine with that.

The last time Brian had suggested they land at the beach felt like a lifetime ago, even though it had only been a week. She had even kissed him then, though at the time she'd thought it was more of a kiss goodbye than anything. She still felt a connection to Brian, but the feeling grated on her because she wasn't in control of it. She didn't want to feel that connection. She'd thought Brian really liked her, then he'd gone and kissed Lithia. He hadn't technically done anything wrong. He hadn't cheated since they weren't together, but it made her feel small.

Her manumed buzzed with an update from Lithia. Apparently, Victoria had refused to help, but Lithia was going to ask Cora to borrow the Aratian Flyer. Dione sighed. They might be here a while.

She got up and looked through the contents of the supply crates. They'd taken the Flyer before it was fully loaded, but there were still several crates in the back. She was getting hungry, and depending on how long they were stuck here, they'd need food and water.

"There's some water here, and I think this is juice," she said, holding up a bottle of pinkish liquid. After refilling her water bottle, she opened the next few crates and called out their contents to Brian. "Some canned vegetables, and a good amount of grains, nuts, and dried fruit. We should be fine to stay here while Lithia finds a way to get us." Dione grabbed a handful of nuts and dried fruit, along with a bottle of juice and sat back down.

When she'd been focused on taking inventory, she'd been able to ignore the fact that she was alone with him. Now that she was stuck waiting for rescue, no other objective to occupy her mind, her idle thoughts turned toward Brian. His presence felt like an intrusion.

At last he spoke. "I want to go looking for my dad."

"Blocked cooling vents aren't something we can fix," Dione said.

"We could go on foot," he suggested.

She removed her manumed and tossed it to him. "Look through what's on this island. Do you want to get strangled by death vines, torched by dragons, or poisoned by murder bugs?"

"Are those their scientific names?"

"Funny. They were right when they said this place was nightmare island. I never should have come with you." She barely recognized her own voice, it was so harsh.

Dione watched him skim through the creatures Jameson had put here. Brian was just looking at the pictures, not reading into the very real threat each one posed. "These guys look kind of cute," he said, flashing her the image of the bioluminescent birds.

"They do, until they peck your eyeballs straight out of your skull. Then they don't look like anything because you don't have any freaking eyes."

"So you think it's impossible to survive here even for a few days?" Brian's voice was soft.

She knew he wasn't asking about whether they'd make it. He wanted to know if his father could still be alive after all this time.

"Impossible? No," she replied. His shoulders relaxed. She could have stopped there, but something inside her, something still angry, added, "But it's not very likely. Without a way out of here, we won't last long. No one could." She got up off the floor of the shuttle, but didn't look at him. She was getting hot, and she could see the leaves of the tree line trembling in a light breeze. The air inside the shuttle was stagnant.

"So we're supposed to wait here until someone finds the time to rescue us?" Brian asked, all softness gone from his voice.

"They need a Flyer. Maybe you should call Victoria and apologize. She might send someone to get us just so she could punish you herself."

"Excellent plan, but she'd never waste the resources when this place will do the job for her. If there's one thing Ficarans are good at, it's making the most of what we're given."

Dione didn't reply. She took a step outside the shuttle, trying to catch a hint of the breeze, but the sun was too strong.

"Face it, Dione," he said, "we're stuck here. My people aren't coming, and neither are yours."

"Lithia's going to ask the Aratians—"

"They'll say no."

"Professor Oberon will—"

"He doesn't have any options, not with his ship damaged." Brian raised his voice. "No one is coming."

"So what's your plan then? Build a boat, start rowing, and hope for the best? The trees here are as likely to kill us as we are to kill them." They might be able to avoid dragons, but when the entire environment was rigged against them? Dione wished she had read a few more entries before writing off Bel's warnings.

"What if that giant ship still flies?" Brian said.

Dione looked him in the eyes, just to be sure he was serious. He was. "You mean the colonizer?"

"Yep."

"The one guarded by dragons?"

"I bet the fabricator's on board, too," Brian said. "The stories say he would fly back to the Vale Temple with fresh supplies. I asked Sam if there was anything like the fabricator at the Mountain Base. She said no, so the fabricator must be on the colonizer. Two problems, one ship. Solved."

Dione sighed. She wished she had never told Brian that fabricators, machines that used raw materials to create nearly anything they had a template for, were real. Now he was set on finding a fabricator to produce more Artifacts and improve trade between the Ficarans and Aratians.

"Even if it does fly and has the fabricator on board, that still leaves one huge problem. The dragons."

"If this place is as bad as you say, there must be something out there that eats dragons."

"If there is, I hope we don't find it. Our best bet is to stay here and wait for Lithia and the others to come up with something."

Brian's gaze darkened as he approached her. He towered over her, his brown eyes intense. "You didn't strike me as the damsel-in-distress type, sitting around waiting for rescue. I guess I was wrong."

Dione didn't back away. "Well, I *did* think you were the rush-in, guns-blazing type of idiot, but I'm used to being right. So, if that's really what you want to do, don't let me stop you." She pointed to the woods.

Without another word, he grabbed a bag, filled it with supplies the Aratians had intended to send to the Ficarans, and left, stomping off into jungle.

Dione definitely didn't care. She never should have come here with him. If only she had listened to the professor! She always did as she was told back at StellAcademy, and now, the one time she decided to go off on her own, she'd made a complete mess out of things. All because she felt some sense of obligation to a guy she barely knew. A guy who clearly didn't live by the same rules she did, and who was incredibly stupid, on top of that. He knew what was out there, and yet off he went, blazing into a nightmare jungle.

After fifteen minutes, her anger faded gradually into worry, like a sunset turning from flaming orange to cool lavender. Worry came naturally to her. Where was he going? Did he really want to find the colonizer, or was he just hoping to find evidence of his dad? Should she follow him? Stupid as it was to enter the jungle, it was still a good idea to stick together. She should give him a few more minutes. He might come back.

Dione fanned herself as she cooked in the heat. She stared at the tree line, debating sitting under one of the trees at the edge of the jungle. The breeze would be better able to reach her there.

A scream pierced her thoughts. Her body reacted with a rush of adrenaline before her mind could process it. Predator? No. Bird? No. It was Brian. She was sure of it, even though it was distant. She stood up and grabbed the stun rifle, heart pounding in her ears. She called his communicator, but there was no answer.

In the shade of the first row of trees, she hesitated for just a moment. She didn't know what she might run into. It wasn't just the birds and bugs and... dragons. She knew enough about plants to know that trees, not angler worms, but actual trees, could kill, as well.

She only knew a few of the threats in the world she was about to walk into, but she didn't have a choice. She stocked up on supplies. She still had her utility knife in her bag along with a standard water bottle. She kicked herself for not replacing the fancy, self-purifying bottle she had given to Victoria. She added in a few jars from the crates of Aratian supplies, hoping that their contents would taste better than they looked. Finally she strapped the machete to her body and put the rifle strap over her shoulder. She felt heavy, but with some luck, she and Brian would be back at the shuttle before dark.

She inhaled deeply, tasting the salty air, then began reciting to herself: "Three point one four one five nine..."

6. CORA

Cora was tired. She was tired of listening to her Uncle Benjamin argue with Victoria via communicator about the missing guns. She was tired of watching her aunt coordinate the funeral feast. She was tired of enduring her cousin Evy's uncharacteristic attention.

"I'm not hungry," she said for the fifth time.

"Are you sure? I can get you some food." The ten-year-old made the offer every fifteen minutes.

"No, thanks." Cora sat in her room inside the Vale Temple. *Temple.* The word she had used all of her life to describe this building suddenly seemed wrong. This wasn't a temple. Her grandfather, the Farmer—no, call him Jameson—hadn't been a god. This building and all the others, Field and Forest Temple included, were nothing more than abandoned research bases, not actual temples.

She stared out the window of her lofty room, exhausted from her recent cleanup shift, yet unable to tear her eyes away. The town seemed smaller. The funeral pyres seemed brighter in the cool afternoon light. They called to her, drawing her in like she was one of Evy's bugs. "I'm going to tend the pyres," she said.

"I'll come with you."

"No, go help your mom," Cora replied. Amelia should get to take advantage of Evy while she was stuck in help mode. It was such a rare occurrence.

Cora stepped outside the Temple into the evening air. The town was unrecognizable to her eyes. Debris littered the ground in places, and the market in the distance was in shambles. Everything looked wrong. She just wanted to be alone for a while.

Alone. The word struck her. Without her father, without Will, she was alone. Will had died in the battle against the Vens, saving her. Her father Michael, the Regnator and leader of the Aratians, had been betrayed. A Green Cloak had murdered him. The Green Cloaks had betrayed all Aratians when they let the Vens inside the walls. Benjamin and Amelia couldn't replace her father. And Will? He had been her best friend. He had been her future. Without them she was lost.

Cora bowed her head when she reached the pyres. A fresh bundle of sweet-burning wood had just been added to the central fire. The fruity smoke pluming into the air was a strong contrast to the smell of burning bodies. There had been too many bodies to cremate in the traditional way, so they were being cremated in a cold, efficient machine in the lower levels of the Temple. The pyres would stay lit, however, until every dead Aratian was turned to ash.

In front of the pyre was a boy with tear-stained cheeks. His mother stood behind him, hands on his shoulders.

It was a cold reminder that grief did not belong to her. Grief was the collective burden of her people. She was alone, yet surrounded by others who felt just as alone as she did. She longed to reach out, to offer some comfort to this family. Or perhaps to take comfort. She wasn't sure.

Cora closed her eyes and took several calming breaths. When she opened them again, she caught sight of Lithia, standing back at a respectful distance.

What is she doing here? It didn't matter. Cora was glad to see her newfound cousin, even if she wasn't sure why. She approached her with purpose.

"Tell me the truth about Kepos," she said. She felt the tears sting her weary eyes. "Please."

Lithia furrowed her brows and hesitated before pulling Cora into an embrace.

"I'm not good at this emotional stuff," Lithia began, "but I'm so sorry for what you're going through."

She barely heard Lithia's condolences. "Tell me everything. I need to understand," Cora pleaded. She had asked Lithia before, but there had been no time to get answers. Before, it had been about the Matching. Now, she just needed to hear the truth. She needed to understand what had happened here, and she wasn't the only one. So many people had questions. She saw it on their faces and heard it in their whispers: "Is it true? The demons are aliens? The Farmer isn't a god?" *We all deserve the truth.*

Lithia took a seat in the last row of mourning benches that had been assembled in front of the pyres. "Where should I start?"

"Who are we?" Cora asked. The question had been bothering her since the moment she began to believe Lithia—after the Matching, when she had been paired with Jai, rather than Will, where she had seen other girls unwillingly paired with their Matches. From that moment, she had been plagued by doubts about the Farmer and his legacy. Lithia had planted those seeds of doubt when she revealed that the Farmer had been a man, not a god, but it wasn't until Cora watched Will die that she had truly believed it.

"What do you mean?" Lithia asked.

"If we're not the Farmer's chosen, then who are we? Is there anything special about us?"

"Jameson recruited people who wanted a new life, packed them on a ship, and brought them here," Lithia said. "It doesn't mean you're not special—"

"Yes, it does. What about my—our grandmother? Why did he choose her?" Cora wasn't sure why this was so pressing in her mind, but it was. She had spent so long believing, *knowing*, that she was special, only to find out she was just like everyone else.

"I'm not sure. I never knew her. She left when my dad was just a baby. She abandoned them. All I can tell you is that there must have been something about her because my grandfather never stopped loving her despite what she did."

Lithia took a breath and looked up at the pyre. Cora watched as a row of benches in the front filled with a new family, and the pyre attendants offered up another few pieces of wood.

"What about the Vens?" Cora asked, still watching the flames dance around the fresh logs. "Why did they come here? What did they want?" Maybe the answer would help her understand the Green Cloaks.

"We were being honest when we told you. The Vens wanted to kill everyone," Lithia said.

"But why?"

"We don't know. We think it's a cultural thing. It doesn't seem to be about resources, and they don't take over colonies they defeat. They even attack space ships. It's about battle for them. We just found those recording devices in their heads, like they're training. They spare no one."

"Then why," Cora began, her voice catching in her throat, "why did the Green Cloaks help them?" She blinked hard a few times.

"Maybe they didn't understand what the Vens were really like," Lithia replied.

Cora frowned. "Lithia, can I tell you something? I think you're the only one who would understand. Aside from Will…"

"Sure," Lithia said softly.

"I can't tell my uncle, or anyone else, but… I don't want to rule. I don't want to become the Regnator. It's all fake. My grandfather wasn't a god. He was a liar."

Her cousin smiled. "Then don't. Is there any reason you have to? Let Benjamin do it."

"There's more," Cora said. "I want to stop the Matching. When I was on that stage, I saw up close how people really felt. They do it because it's their responsibility. But if it's true what you say, that there are lots of other worlds…"

"Hundreds. Full of people."

"Then there's no need," Cora said. "We'll invite them here. Otherwise, I'm afraid we'll go back to the days of triple Matches."

"What's a triple Match?" Lithia asked uneasily.

"In the past, a woman could be matched with three men over the course of her life," Cora explained. "The first remained her husband, but she was expected to bear children of the other two as well."

Lithia frowned, and Cora mirrored her expression. "What's wrong?"

"Aside from that sounding awful, I'm not sure your plan will work. We have something called the Bubble," she began. "It's an area of space that the Vens don't usually enter. Inside that Bubble, it's safe. Not many people choose to live outside it."

After a moment of confusion, Cora pieced together what Lithia was trying to say. "Kepos is outside this Bubble, isn't it?" Lithia nodded. "Well, what if there were no Vens?"

Lithia gazed off into the distance, as if she were trying to imagine that scenario. "There are tens of thousands of them. I think if the Alliance could have found a way to eradicate them all, it would have by now."

"Do you think people would try to come here, if it was safe?" Cora wasn't sure if the thought excited her or scared her. She didn't especially want outsiders, but she'd grown up hearing stories about the dangers of genetic drift and too-small gene pools.

"I have no idea."

Cora sighed. "Either way, the Matching can't go on. It's no longer necessary." She paused. That revelation would have meant so much more if things were different. If Will were alive. "But my uncle will never allow me to stop it," she said. "It's his life's work."

"Then you might have to become Regnator," Lithia said.

"I know." Cora had circled through these thoughts a dozen times, always ending in the same place. She'd hoped that Lithia would be able to offer her an alternative. "But I don't have the right. In order to claim leadership, I'd have to use my birthright, but my support for eliminating the Matching comes from establishing the Farmer as a liar. If the Farmer is a liar, I have no birthright."

Lithia bit her lower lip. "I see your dilemma, but I'm sure we can find a work around."

Cora stood and smoothed the creases from her shirt. "There's a funeral feast tonight, to honor the dead, if you'd like to join us."

"I'd be honored," Lithia said, but her face fell.

"What is it?"

"I actually came to ask you a favor," Lithia said.

Before she could finish her request, there was a commotion at the gate. The guards were shouting, and those nearby were hustling to safety.

"Vens?" Lithia asked.

"I don't know." The guards had not given the agreed upon signal for a Ven sighting, but Cora rushed to the gate all the same, with Lithia following close behind.

A few men on machi had come through the gate, and Cora caught sight of a man draped across the front of one of the beasts. The rider dismounted and called for a stretcher. The body draped across the machi moaned, and Cora gave it another glance.

"Who is he?" she asked.

"A Green Cloak," the rider replied. "He keeps mumbling apologies and excuses."

Her concern shifted immediately to anger. The Green Cloaks had opened up a secret entrance into their town, allowing the Vens to easily make their way inside and murder her people. They might have once been Aratians, but they'd become traitors once they showed their true colors. "Where did you find him?" she asked the rider.

"In the woods. He was attacked."

"The Vens?"

"I don't know, but his wounds are severe."

"Can he speak?" Cora asked. She barely recognized her own voice it was so low.

"Yes, but—"

"Lay him on the ground." Cora would be able to ask the questions that had haunted her for days. "While we wait for the stretcher."

Lithia stepped up alongside her. "If he doesn't survive, you won't be able to get any answers," she said, as if she had read Cora's thoughts.

"That will be one death I won't lose sleep over." Cora pushed aside the tightness in her chest and knelt over the injured man. He moaned.

"Why did you join the Green Cloaks?" she asked.

"I was trying... to leave," he panted. "They wouldn't let me."

"Why did you join?" Cora repeated.

"The Farmer. All his lies. All for con—" he gasped, "—control. I never meant—"

"Where are the others? How many are left?"

"Raynor Farm. But things are changing."

"What do you mean they're changing? What are they planning?" Cora leaned in closer, but the stretcher had arrived along with a small crowd. Her time was up. She would get more information in the morning, but she had the most important piece. She knew where the Green Cloaks' base of operations was.

She turned to Lithia. "I'm going to the Green Cloak hideout."

"But what if he was lying? What if it's a trap?" Lithia replied.

"I have nothing to lose," Cora said. "Plus, I don't plan on going alone."

7. DIONE

Dione had been searching for Brian for nearly half an hour. She had asked Sam for help tracking his communicator, but the AI told her she was at capacity and unable to help until later. She supposed this was what Zane had warned them about. At least in the shade of the trees it was cooler, if more ominous.

She'd gone on plenty of hikes in wild areas back home, but she had never felt anxious like she did now. Every now and then, her fingers began to ache, and she'd realize she was clutching the stun rifle again.

She couldn't find Brian. He couldn't have gotten that far in, but she didn't know which direction he'd taken. She'd heard him yell, after all. Maybe she had imagined it, or it hadn't been a big deal after all, like a stubbed toe.

Or maybe something got him. She wished that particular voice in her head would shut up. It was the voice that kept telling her that there had been movement in the shadows to her left, or that the giant red welt on her arm had come from a deadly insect and that her hours were already numbered. She risked calling out his name again.

"Brian!" she shouted into the trees.

She waited, trying to discern any hint of a human sound mixed in with the background noise of bugs and birds. She heard a groan.

It's just a frog. Probably venomous.

No, definitely a human groan. She headed toward the sound, afraid of what she might find.

A minute later, she discovered him, face up on the ground, covered in moss and dirt. A large tree loomed above him. "Brian!" she called. No response. Dione grappled with the instinct that urged her forward to check on him and took time to survey the scene.

He wasn't bleeding, at least not that she could see. She inhaled the damp air, noting the scent of salt and rotting leaves. Maybe even a rotting animal? She looked around and saw a few dead rodents decaying in the leaves. She looked up at the tree. A variety of birds perched among the branches, which were covered in beautiful nets of hanging moss that glistened with moisture. Was this the kind of tree whose sap was so toxic it could kill? Were those birds immune? It seemed unlikely that so many different species would have adapted to it, but these were not normal circumstances. Who knew what Jameson had done?

She had to get Brian away from the tree. She reached out to grab a handful of moss that covered Brian's neck, but the second her finger tips brushed against it, she realized she had made a mistake.

She screamed in pain, as did Brian, eyes suddenly wide awake in agony. Nothing had hurt this much before. No bug bite, no broken bone, not even the Ven's scratch on her back. She felt dizzy and realized that she was panting. She was barely aware of the birds flapping away, startled by their screams. Brian twitched, but seemed to be unconscious again. It seemed like moving the moss had caused him more pain.

She stared at her hand, afraid to touch anything. Swollen red lines appeared on her fingers. Were oils from the moss causing this reaction, like poison ivy?

She pulled out her water bottle, but without soap to bind to the oil, it wouldn't do much good. She didn't care. A few seconds of cool relief might help her think.

Pouring water across her fingers was like fuel to a fire. She yelped as the pain intensified. What the hell was causing this reaction? With trembling hands, she searched the files of nightmares that Lithia had sent with no luck. In a moment of clarity, she called Sam. Maybe she would answer this time.

"Sam, I really need your help."

"I can assist you briefly. What's wrong?"

"There's some kind of moss here," Dione said. "It stings and burns when you touch it. The reaction is almost instantaneous. Water makes it worse. It doesn't match anything in the files Lithia sent me. Any ideas?"

"Let me check," Sam replied.

In the intervening silence, Dione did her best not to think about the throbbing pain in her fingers. She glanced down at Brian. His chest was rising and falling, too fast for someone unconscious. His hands were marred by the same welts as hers. He must have tried to remove the moss as well. What had happened? Had he been making his way through the forest, only to run headfirst into its snare? She couldn't imagine how excruciating it must feel on the sensitive skin of his neck and face. She hadn't been able to see it before, but she could make out a jumble of thin red lines, so concentrated in places that they raised into one solid welt. Her attempt to remove it must have aggravated a renewed reaction.

"I've found something in his personal records," Sam said. "Nematocysts. He was working on a way to incorporate them into amphibious insects or aquatic plants. He may have changed his mind later. I don't have all of his records."

"Thanks, Sam. Nematocysts, aside from making no sense on land, may explain why water made it worse."

Nematocysts were what made jellyfish sting. Prey came into contact with them, and the pressure triggered the nematocysts to launch like tiny harpoons. These became lodged into prey with little barbs, pumping the victim with poison.

Poison. Only a few species of jellyfish could kill a human. If the timing of his scream was any indication, Brian had been lying like this for half an hour, and he was still breathing. But it could just be a matter of time. Either way, Dione knew she needed to remove the moss without disturbing it and causing more nematocysts to fire. Not all nematocysts would have fired at the same time, and if she triggered more, she didn't know how much more poison Brian's body could handle.

Dione didn't know how nematocysts could work in a dry environment, but a washed-up jellyfish could still sting an unwitting beachgoer. She looked back up at the glistening moss. It was wet. The fresh water she had poured on her hand had affected the pressure differential, triggering more nematocysts to fire, so more of the poison could be released.

What did she know about stings like this? Water was bad, though it was unfortunately too late for that realization. She closed her eyes and tried to remember what she had read years ago before her first beach trip. She'd been Type A even then, researching what to do in case something went wrong. Riptides, heatstroke, jellyfish—think!

Vinegar, then heat. The beach was warm, so heat would be no problem, but vinegar? Was there any in the supplies on the shuttle? She had stuffed some bottles and jars in her bag before venturing into the jungle.

She had brought water and a bottle of juice, but everything else was food. Granola, dried fruit, and nuts.

Dammit! There had been some sort of pickled cucurbits back in the shuttle, but she hated pickles. Now, she needed the vinegar in the pickling solution. Would it take too long to go back to the shuttle? Should she remove the moss then drag Brian back anyway?

A meter away, she saw Brian's bag. He'd stuffed some supplies inside before slinging it over his shoulder and walking into the jungle. Maybe he'd packed some pickles.

Bingo! She wrinkled her nose as she opened the jar, then cracked a relieved smile. Pickling might ruin perfectly good vegetables, but the juice should contain enough acetic acid to neutralize the tiny stingers. There was one way to check.

She braced the jar between her legs, opened it with her good hand, and dipped her fingers inside. She braced herself, but the pain didn't come. Her fingers felt a little better, though they still throbbed. Now to help Brian.

Moving the moss had activated more nematocysts, but she only had enough pickle juice to neutralize the stingers on his skin. She would have to find a way to remove the moss first. The strands were all clumped together like a tangle of thread, which was good. If she could remove that central mass, that would be it. No need to pick off individual strands of moss.

Using a stick would be too imprecise. She needed a glove or… a sock. She removed her boot, then sock, careful to put the boot back on immediately. While she didn't have the precision of a glove, this was a lot better than trying to use sticks like tweezers or a giant leaf from some other poisonous tree.

She reached out for the moss with her sock-covered hand, but pulled back. Would it work? It didn't matter. She had wasted enough time already. Once again, she extended her hands toward the clump of moss. She had to be quick. The less disturbance, the fewer stings. The fewer stings, the less Brian would squirm.

Dione hesitated for one more second over Brian's neck before rapidly scooping up the moss and chucking it far away toward the base of the tree. She peeled off the sock like a contaminated glove and tossed it, too, toward the tree trunk. Brian tensed and yelled out in pain before passing out again. Dione picked up the bottle of pickle juice and poured it generously over his neck. With what was left, she treated his hands from where he had grabbed at the moss at some point.

Dione sat back on her heels. The stingers were neutralized, but she couldn't leave Brian here. He didn't wake to her touch. She certainly couldn't carry him.

Could she? Dione stared at his muscular frame. It wasn't that far to the beach, but she knew her limits. She thought about dragging him, but the undergrowth would make it difficult.

Dione began breathing faster, and she could feel a telltale prickle at the corners of her eyes. She was going to cry. Ever since landing on Kepos, she had never felt this alone. Or this afraid. Even on the Ven ship, there had been a clear course of action and someone to share the burden of failure. What had she gotten herself into? She couldn't survive this place alone. The tears were flowing freely, but she suppressed her sobs to keep them silent.

She looked at the death trap around her, blurred by her tears, when she saw a familiar plant. Aloe. She couldn't pinpoint the exact species, but there was a good chance it might come in handy.

She wiped her eyes and took a deep breath, regaining some of her composure before making a call. "Sam, I think I see an aloe plant. Is that possible, here, on this island?" Dione waited for a reply. "Sam?"

"The Aratians cultivate an aloe variety that Jameson improved. It's possible he seeded some on the island as well. He would have included ways to help him control and counter what he set loose there. I doubt he would have given his monsters free reign. He had to be king."

"Thanks," Dione said. "I'll be in touch."

She ended the call and moved cautiously toward the aloe. Its gel could be used as a salve to reduce inflammation. Had Jameson put these two organisms together for this very reason, in case he brushed against some moss?

Dione recalled her first encounter with the plant. Once as a child, she'd tumbled into a formiceps nest. Her legs had been covered in welts, and her father hadn't been home, so she'd torn a few leaves off the potted aloe plant on the patio, mashed them up with a rock, and smeared the slimy gel all over her legs. The immediate relief was like magic. That moment had sparked Dione's love of plants.

She plucked a few leaves off the plant on the forest floor and, with the help of her knife and a couple of rocks, quickly turned them into a gel. The familiar medicinal scent calmed her as she smeared the salve on Brian's neck and hands.

Then she waited. It felt like forever, but soon she heard a low groan. Brian was waking up.

"Hey, don't move yet. Take it easy," she said, leaning over him. "You ran into some moss that stung you, but I removed it. I put some aloe on the welts on your neck and hands, too. Does it hurt anywhere else?"

Brian heaved a sigh and looked at her, but his eyes were unfocused, his pupils unnaturally dilated. He managed a shake of his head and started to sit up. She helped him. He reached for his neck, but she intercepted his hand.

"Don't touch it." At the sound of her voice, he gripped her hand tightly, eyes wide and darting around.

"I won't let them." His eyes focused on a spot behind her.

"Huh?" She turned around, but nothing was there, save the forest. "Brian, it's me, Dione. What's going on?"

Finally his eyes focused on her, and a confused smile lit his features. "Dione? What happened?"

She explained again what was going on, relieved that he seemed to be himself again. "Do you think you can walk back to the shuttle? I don't like being in the jungle."

"Yeah, I think so."

Dione helped him to his feet, and the two headed back toward the sound of waves breaking on the shore. She left his bag on the ground. It was too much for him to carry right now, and they could get it in the morning. She didn't want to get caught out here in the dark.

Brian had already fallen asleep in the shuttle, so Dione watched the sunset light the ocean on fire by herself. She'd been so excited to explore this place, but now she was too afraid to even move a muscle, lest something hear her and find them. She tried to relax and let the rhythmic ocean waves soothe her. After a while, it seemed to work. Her muscles loosened, and when she opened her eyes, she gasped.

She had never seen a sunset like this. A perfect halo of orange, so bright she could almost smell the citrus, had settled on the horizon. Beyond that warm center extended a corona of thick pink, rich and glossy, and rough purple, textured by wisps of cloud. Dione stared in awe. The colors were so unnaturally bright and beautiful she couldn't focus on anything else.

She blinked, and the colors faded rapidly, shaking her loose from the hold the view had on her. It was time to get some rest. She hoped that if she locked herself and Brian in the shuttle while they slept, they would be safe.

Dione trudged across the sand, which was already cool, and entered the shuttle. She grabbed two blankets from a supply crate. Brian might need an extra. Blankets in hand, it took her brain a long moment to realize the problem.

Brian was gone. A new set of tracks in the sand led into the jungle. There was no evidence of a struggle.

"You have got to be kidding me," Dione muttered to herself. She put her palm to her face for a moment and shook her head. Why had he gone back into the woods? He knew it wasn't safe, especially in the dark. It didn't make sense. If he'd seen something, he would have told her.

Unless there was something wrong with him. He'd seemed out of it after his encounter with the moss, but she'd chalked it up to pain and exhaustion.

Dione peered into the now dark and still foreboding trees. Could she really go back out? The jungle made her uneasy in the daytime, but in the dark, it petrified her. On top of the other supplies she had packed early, she added the two tightly rolled blankets and some more pickled cucurbits, just in case.

She took a deep breath and clutched the stun rifle, hoping she wouldn't need it. After enabling the flashlight on her manumed, she forged ahead once again into unknown and dangerous territory with the aim of saving Brian.

He's gonna owe me big time, Dione thought, but a tiny voice in the back of her head whispered an unsettling rejoinder: *If you survive.*

8. LITHIA

The Aratians moved busily all around the square. Long, rectangular tables draped in rich navy cloths had been set up parallel to one another. A head table stood perpendicular to the rest at the front, with half its seats already filled. Lithia recognized Benjamin and Moira, who were already seated there. Glowglobes, all pure white, had been hung around the area, though enough daylight remained to light the meal. The pyres flickered nearby, and the sweet-burning wood nearly overpowered the warm scent of the soups and breads that were set out along the tables.

Lithia had dreaded the funeral feast, but she knew she belonged here. She had fought, and nearly died, alongside these people, but she did not have anywhere close to an equal share in the Aratians' grief. It was hard to be surrounded by others in pain. What comfort could she offer? A few glared at her, an outsider, but many remembered her from the battle and smiled as she took a seat near Cora at the head table. Jai, Cora's betrothed from the Matching, sat on Lithia's other side. She had the feeling that Cora had placed her between them to make it easier to ignore him. Lithia wondered if she was here simply to act as a physical barrier.

Her manumed buzzed. It was Dione: *Heading into jungle. No choice.*

"Don't you dare," Lithia muttered under her breath. She swiftly crafted her reply: *Don't. I'll be there by morning.*

That was a lie, but maybe it would be enough to stop her. Cora leaned back in her seat, poking at the roasted vegetables on her plate while everyone around them ate. "What's wrong?"

"Huh?" Lithia said.

"You said earlier you had a favor to ask. Is something wrong?"

"It can wait until after this," Lithia said. "Probably." She shoved half a potato into her mouth to keep it busy. This was not the time. Truthfully, Lithia didn't know how bad things were on the island or why Dione was doing something as stupid as walking into a mad scientist's smorgasbord of deadly flora and fauna, but she wasn't about to cause a scene in the middle of a funeral feast.

Dione's reply settled like lead in the pit of her stomach: *Sorry. Hope we are back at shuttle by then. Don't tell Oberon.*

Oberon? That's what she was worried about? And since when did she call him Oberon? It was always *professor* this and *professor* that.

"You look upset," Cora insisted. "If there's something I can do to help, tell me. Is it the Vens?"

Lithia finished chewing and swallowed, then took a deep breath. "For once, it's not. Dione and Brian went to the southern island, but they can't get back. We have no way of getting them back, and Victoria won't send anyone. I was hoping I could borrow your Flyer."

Cora's reply was calm. "They will probably be fine for a few days. The Flyer they took had some of the food we were sending to the Ficarans. I doubt my uncle will lend you the Flyer, though. Victoria will send someone. Brian is a Ficaran."

"That woman can hold a grudge for longer than a few days, but the problem is more than just being stranded." Lithia locked eyes with her cousin. "Before Jameson brought everyone here, he was a scientist. He genetically engineered plants and animals to enhance colonial life. He shared that aspect of his work with you all to some extent, but he made other creatures, too, things he never intended for this colony to encounter. He put them on the southern island. That's why he and Sam both tried to keep people away from it."

"Why would he do that?" Cora asked.

"To see if he could. To challenge himself. I don't know." Lithia shrugged.

"It can't be that bad, can it?" Jai asked. He had apparently been listening in to their quiet conversation.

"Actually, Jai, it's very bad. Lots of nasty, violent creatures. A couple of those creatures have started to make their way to the mainland. For example, I almost got eaten by this thing that looks like a flower, that grabs you and tries to pull you underground before it devours you."

The woman on the other side of Jai was giving her a look, so she lowered her voice. "I'm not going to bet my best friend's life on the hope that the creatures over there 'aren't that bad.'"

Cora knitted her eyebrows. "I don't think that I can help you. Things are really tense with the Ficarans still. Victoria thinks we found some of their guns on the battlefield and that we're keeping them. My uncle won't lend out the only Flyer we have."

"Why is it his decision?" Lithia asked. "Why aren't you in charge?"

Cora glanced over at Jai, who was sipping from his cup. "It's complicated. And like I said, I don't know if—"

She stopped abruptly, and Lithia followed her stare. A man was bending over and whispering into Benjamin's ear. They were too far away for Lithia to make out the words.

"That's the doctor," Cora whispered to Lithia before raising her voice enough to reach her uncle. "The Green Cloak is dead, isn't he?"

Benjamin nodded. He didn't seem interested in discussing this news, but Cora pressed him further. "Did he say anything else? About their plans?"

"No, child." His response was firm. "Now is not the time."

Lithia saw Cora's jaw clench. "I understand. Can I at least announce my plans for the memorial?"

"Very well."

The meal was winding down, and some people were already getting up to leave when Cora stood and raised her hand to get everyone's attention.

"Not one of us has escaped this disaster untouched by grief," she said. "Our own people betrayed us because they forgot the stories passed down about the Demons. They ignored these stories. Now, we know the truth, that these Demons are an alien race called Vens. To ensure we will never again underestimate them, we will build a memorial at the entrance to the market, including all the names of those who fell in defense of the Vale Temple. I look forward to beginning construction soon."

Benjamin and the others applauded, but Cora did not sit down. "However, we cannot begin to build the memorial and rebuild our town until the threats to its safety have been neutralized. There are still Vens out there and, what's worse, Green Cloaks. I've learned where the Green Cloak traitors are hiding, and in the morning, I plan to lead a team of volunteers to root them out. Who will join me?"

The tables erupted in whispers. Lithia saw fear in the eyes of many, but she could tell others were prepared to volunteer. Benjamin, on the other hand looked furious. Cora had definitely not cleared this with him.

A man dressed in dark gray harem pants and a white shirt stood first. Lithia disliked him on sight. His greasy hair stuck to his sweaty forehead, and he breathed heavily, as if standing was an act of extreme exertion. Cora smiled at him. "Are you volunteering, Elijah?"

His frown heralded his reply. "What right do you have to organize such a venture? Are you the Regnator now? Benjamin, are all of the pairs from the Matching allowed to confirm, since your own niece has apparently confirmed her match?"

Lithia glanced at Cora, who was blushing. *I guess that explains why Benjamin is still in charge.* Jai took a long drink from his cup, though it was only water. Lithia was pretty sure she knew what "confirming a match" meant. She was also pretty sure that Cora had confirmed nothing with Jai. She could barely look at him, which was a pity. He seemed really nice, not to mention attractive.

"The moratorium on the matches stands," Benjamin replied. "With all of our losses, we need time to process our grief, as well as to examine what this means for the genetic strength of our people."

Lithia's lip curled. A delay to reassess the Matches and probably make adjustments, shuffling people around like emotionless pawns on an old game board.

"If Cora has not confirmed her Match, then she is not yet the Regnator," the man said. "She doesn't have the authority to lead a force like this and call for volunteers."

"No, she doesn't." Benjamin gave her a pointed look. "But I do. I've stepped in for my brother, as tradition allows."

"You permitted this? A mere girl leading this sort of expedition?" Elijah asked, eyebrows raised.

Jai stood and slammed his cup down on the table. "This *girl* fought with us on the front lines during the attack. Where were you?" He paused briefly, glaring at the greasy old man. "I'll join you, Cora. You've more than proven yourself to me."

Cora gave him a grateful smile, and Lithia nodded. Jai wasn't as bad as Cora made him out to be.

Elijah's upper lip curled, but rather than reply to Jai, he turned to Benjamin. "So it's decided? You approve this expedition?"

Benjamin looked hard at his niece for a moment, but that was all it took. Lithia saw his predicament. He had not permitted her call to arms, nor did he condone it, but this public confrontation was forcing his hand. To admit that Cora was acting on her own might be a breach of tradition. These people were already weird about women doing anything, and if Cora didn't have the special rights of the Regnator, whatever those were, it might look bad.

"Yes," Benjamin said. "We have the opportunity to bring the Green Cloaks to justice, and Cora, as Michael's daughter, is an appropriate choice for this task."

Elijah furrowed his brow. "Such a dangerous mission for such an important individual." He turned to Cora and bowed his head slightly. "I hope you are well protected. Gavin, would you consider accompanying Cora on her expedition?"

A short, muscular man with a shaved head stood and nodded. Elijah was sending this man to be his spy, Lithia was sure.

Lithia felt a presence behind her and jumped, caught off guard by the tension of the moment. She turned to see a dark-skinned man who appeared to be in his mid-thirties looking down at her. He bent over to speak quietly to Cora. "If you have need of a man who can follow orders, I'd like to volunteer."

Cora smiled, and her shoulders relaxed. "Yes, thank you. We met in the stables when you returned with the machi. Theo, right?" The man nodded.

"I fought alongside Michael," Theo said, loud enough for the crowd to hear him. "He was a good man, but no Demon took him from us. I, for one, would like to bring these Green Cloak traitors to justice."

This is really happening, Lithia thought. Though most stayed quiet and looked down at their plates, several men stood and offered their assistance. Theo nodded at them, and she recognized them as members of the cavalry. They had worked with Cora's father, Michael, when he had led the cavalry. Some of them might have even witnessed his murder.

Lithia hesitated, uncertain of what she should do. Images from the battle flashed through her mind. The blood. The bodies. The giant, black Ven. She wanted to join Cora. She, too, wanted vengeance, but as much as the Green Cloaks disgusted her, it was the Vens she truly despised.

But what good would it do to hang around the Vale Temple, trying to convince Benjamin to lend her the Flyer? He wouldn't budge, not unless she gave him a compelling reason. If she could help Cora and the others, maybe that would earn her enough credit to borrow the Flyer once she got back. In the meantime, the others could keep pestering Victoria. It was the best scenario, right? Roy's bloody face and lifeless eyes, the image of her nightmares, flashed through her mind. She wasn't sure if she was doing this to put her own heart at ease or to help Dione, but she didn't care. She had to act, had to stay in motion.

Two young women stood, and the taller one spoke. "We will join you." Her voice trembled a bit, but her eyes were determined. Murmurs swept through the crowd.

Many Aratian women had joined the battle against the Vens to save the Vale Temple. Lithia didn't see what the big deal was.

Benjamin spoke up. "I know we made exceptions during the attack, but—"

Another woman who must have been in her forties stood, cutting Benjamin off. "We don't have as many able-bodied men as we once did, Benjamin, and this job still needs doing." She turned to Cora. "I will join you. I will not stand by while my family is threatened."

After her, a few more volunteers stood, including a couple. When it seemed as if no one else would join, Lithia seized the opportunity. She stood and put a hand on Cora's shoulder. "I'm coming, too. Someone's got to watch your back."

Cora smiled. "We'll meet at the stables at dawn."

Cora returned to her seat, as did the other volunteers, and soon the conversations picked back up. Lithia sat and stared at the food remaining on her plate. What had she gotten herself into?

9. BEL

Bel read Lithia's message from her own cabin on the *Calypso*, with Zane reading over her shoulder. Though the damage from the crash was extensive, only the cargo bay had been affected. The cabin beds were too small to share, but that didn't stop them. After the chaos of the past few days, having a few hours to relax together, to be close to Zane, meant more than Bel could put into words.

Bel had always thought she would end up alone. She'd kept Zane at a distance for so long, afraid that her version of intimacy wouldn't be enough for him. Her fears had been unfounded. Zane liked her just the way she was, and said that they'd figure out her boundaries together. It felt unfamiliar yet peaceful to be in a couple. Even Lithia's news that she was running off with Cora to find the Green Cloaks couldn't take that peace away from her.

Bel: *You're losing sight of why you went there.*

Lithia: *I'll be in a better position to bargain after this. Cora all but told me Benjamin would say no.*

Bel: *Your emotions are getting the better of you.*

They waited for a response from Lithia, but she never replied.

"That makes two," Zane said. "Dione's off in the jungle, now Lithia's going after the Green Cloaks?" He pulled Bel closer, which filled her body with warmth. She closed her eyes.

"And the Vens," she replied. "She plays it off, but I could feel the anger radiating off her after the battle. I get where she's coming from. They pose a risk."

She felt Zane go rigid. He pulled away and propped himself up on his good elbow. His other arm had been injured in the battle, and he wasn't responding as quickly to the Aratian tea as Lithia and Oberon had.

"You want to join her." It was an accusation. Bel felt her cheeks grow red in the dim light of the cabin. "I thought this drive for revenge was over. You got the datacore. You destroyed the Invader."

His tone had shifted from accusatory to helpless. How could she explain it to him? There was a fire inside Bel that would never go out. When she had been at StellAcademy, it was glowing coals. When she had been downloading the datacore, it burned white-hot. Her hatred would always be there, and there was nothing she could do to stop it. The best she could do was manage it and not let it overtake her like it had on the Ven Invader. She couldn't let it take over Lithia like that either. The guilt from her stunt of downloading the datacore was fresh, and she knew it would temper her actions.

"So what are you going to do?" Zane asked.

"I'm going to find Colm and tell him what the Aratians are planning. Maybe some Ficarans want to join." Though Colm was a large, imposing man, he had shown that he had more compassion than his sister, Victoria.

"And what am I supposed to do?" Zane said. "Stay behind while you go fight the Vens? Again?"

"Do what you do best. Keep everything from falling apart. Sam needs you. Oberon needs you. Dione will need you, too."

"But you don't need me?"

Bel placed a hand on the back of his head and pulled him closer until their foreheads were touching. "Of course I do. You understand me like no one else ever has. That's why you know that I need to do this. You're too level-headed to come with me. You know that you'll be more helpful here. I can see the wheels turning. You'll be figuring out how to get a shuttle to rescue Dione because you know you can use it to help me, too."

Zane pulled her in close and kissed her forehead. She found his lips and gave him a lingering kiss. The sensation was still strange to her, but mostly pleasant.

With that, she left Zane in her cabin and went to find Colm. The Ficarans, she hoped, would have an interest in stopping the Vens and remaining Green Cloaks, too.

***

In the dewy darkness before dawn, she could make out Colm and three Ficarans preparing a Flyer. Bel yawned in the fresh air. Victoria's brother hadn't needed much convincing to join her. In fact, she suspected that before she asked, he had been planning to hunt down the Vens, maybe even the Green Cloaks, on his own.

"You ready to go?" She thought about asking him how Victoria had reacted to his decision, if she even knew about it, but Bel couldn't pretend to care anymore.

"Our pilot's just arrived," Colm replied, gesturing to a man approaching from the direction of the base. Behind the pilot came another figure, racing toward them. The shoulders were too broad to be Victoria's.

Oberon.

"This will only take a minute," Bel told the others. The quiet of the early hour filled her with an unshakable calm. Dione and Lithia might have wanted to hide their dangerous situations from the professor, but Bel would try to make him understand.

"Bel, what are you doing?" Oberon demanded as he reached the shuttle. "You can't just leave."

"Zane told you?" She couldn't blame him. She probably would have done the same.

"Yes, but only after I asked him what you were up to. I heard you leave in the middle of the night."

Oberon needed a dose of reality. A gentle one. "I know you're worried about us, and you should be. Your instinct is to keep us together, to shelter us, to protect us. But the rules are different here. We all have to do our part. If I do this"—she corrected herself—"*when* I do this, no one will blame you."

"Blame me? Do you really think this is about the repercussions I might face? It's about losing students I love. If anything happens to any one of you—" His voice broke.

Bel peered at him. He thought he was still fighting the battle. He didn't realize he'd lost long ago. "So much has already happened to us, Oberon. We'll never be the same. None of that is your fault. We are stuck here for the time being, and that authority you once had over us? It's gone. You have to trust us."

"You have to see this is a struggle for me. The risks Dione is taking, that you and Lithia are taking... How can I trust you after you nearly sacrificed yourself for a datacore?"

"Then don't trust me," Bel said. "Add another tally to my future detentions. Fill out my expulsion paperwork. None of it matters. I plan to do everything in my power to watch Lithia's back and make sure she doesn't do anything stupid. I know what it's like for anger at the Vens to consume you. I just had a refresher of that feeling, and I'm not anxious to repeat it. Lithia needs someone to help her right now, and I'm the only one who can."

Oberon watched her in silence, chest heaving, before offering two final words. "Be careful."

Bel felt for the professor. They weren't making his life easy, but they were all doing what they thought was right, a principle that Oberon himself had taught them. Dione was helping Brian find his father. Lithia was helping her cousin Cora. Bel was going to keep an eye on Lithia. If anything, Oberon should be proud. Maybe if they all returned safe and sound, he would be.

Without another word, Bel joined Colm and the others on the shuttle. Soon, with luck and preparation, Kepos would be completely free of Vens and Green Cloaks.

10. DIONE

The farther into the jungle Dione moved, the smaller the beams of moonlight that slipped through the canopy, and the more she relied on her manumed's flashlight. She felt something smooth brush against her ankle and jumped.

It's not a snake, she told herself for the tenth time. *Just a leaf.*

But that thought was troubling, too. For all she knew, Jameson had engineered some cross between a poison dart frog and an unassuming leafy plant, and she had just been poisoned.

Dione took a deep breath and pushed those thoughts away. There was no good in worrying about it now.

"Sam, do you have anything?"

She'd immediately lost Brian's trail when she entered the jungle, but she realized Sam might be able to track his communicator and give her directions this time. After all, it was the middle of the night. With many of the Ficarans asleep, the AI had more opportunities to guide Dione.

"He's stopped moving," Sam replied. "You're close. Keep walking north for about two kilometers."

Dione's pulse quickened. If Brian wasn't moving—no, she wouldn't let her thoughts go there. Nevertheless, she stepped up her pace.

After a while, she heard his voice, but couldn't make out the words. Who was he talking to? Had he found his father?

In another minute, Dione entered a small clearing. Dew glistened in the trees on the opposite side, illuminated by the moonlight. The sweet fragrance of some tropical flower hung heavily in the stagnant air. She could make out Brian on his knees in front of a rock, still talking. He was crying, too, and didn't seem aware of her presence. The scene was eerie, and it made her pause long enough to hear what he was saying.

"I thought I'd never find you. You've been gone so long that I didn't think you were even in there anymore." With that, he hugged the rock, confirming Dione's suspicions.

Brian was hallucinating. The moss's venom must have been more than agonizing. It had shown her the sunset of her life, and it had caused Brian to see or hear something that had drawn him away from the shuttle into the jungle. Now he was lovingly embracing a rock that he thought was a person, his long-lost father from the sound of it.

She didn't want to startle him into flight, so she approached slowly, pausing a few meters away until he caught sight of her. His eyes went wide with confusion, and he looked around.

"Where—? Dione? Where did she go?"

She? Who had Brian been talking to, if not his father? "Brian, it's okay. I'm right here." Dione took another step toward him, her arms outstretched. "You were hallucinating. You might still be seeing things."

"No, she was here. Everything was fine. Until you showed up." Brian abruptly got to his feet and backed away from her across the clearing. Behind him, dewy branches glowing in the moonlight began to move strangely in the breeze.

"Brian," she began, turning her focus back to him. "Wait. Listen to me. The moss—" Dione glanced back to the trees. There was no breeze. They shouldn't have been swaying like that. The higher branches were curling in.

"*Drosera,*" she whispered. A sundew. The recognition was immediate, though she had never seen, or imagined, one this huge before. The branches were wide and flat like tentacles, covered not in dew, but sticky balls of digestive enzymes, ready to trap and wrap their prey. The plant must have caught some bird or bat, and as Dione glanced back to Brian, she realized it was about to snag something much bigger. "Brian, don't move."

He ignored her and continued to back away. He was shouting at her, but she wasn't listening. He was getting closer and closer to the trap the massive sundew had laid. She charged toward him, hoping she could catch him in time, but it was too late. He stepped on one of the tentacles, feet sticking enough to trip him. He landed right on another tentacle, and with a thick, wet smack, it curled around Brian's torso, pinning his arms to his body in seconds.

"Argh! No! Let go!" Brian's shouts did nothing to deter the organism. The *Drosera* could not be startled into dropping its prey like some creatures could. Its leaves curled in response to physical stimulus, and a plant, even a monstrous one like this, did not have free will.

Brian's weight seemed to hinder the sundew's motion, but it steadily rolled him inward, activating a third sticky tendril as his legs and feet dragged across them. With the added support, the terrible plant lifted Brian off the ground as its leaves curled inward.

Dione stopped her advance only long enough to draw her machete. There was no time to think. She maneuvered her way toward the base of the tentacle that had trapped Brian's feet and began hacking. She had to time every movement perfectly in order to hit the moving target in the same place each time, but after a few thwacks, she severed the tentacle. Brian dipped half a meter lower toward the ground, the remaining tendrils struggling under his weight. One down, two to go.

But no, Brian's change in altitude had dropped his neck right onto another small tendril. Dione wasn't sure if it could crush his windpipe outright, but she was certain it would apply enough pressure to suffocate him. The shouting she had been ignoring turned to coughing and sputtering. She needed to be quick.

As she repositioned her body to get a better angle on the neck tentacle, she narrowly avoided stepping on one herself. The dodge sent her off-balance and she fell, the bulk of her body missing the tendril. However, her arm—the one wielding the machete—landed on something sticky.

Immediately, the tendril closed around her wrist. *How is it so fast?* She knew that the sundew was simply responding to stimuli, curling around whatever touched its sticky triggers, but she found herself imagining a dark, hungry intelligence at the center of the outstretched leaves. She fought the tendril, fought to keep her grip on her only weapon, but her wrist began to ache. She would not be able to pull it free. Fortunately with only one point of contact, the sundew was not strong enough to wrap her up like Brian.

Brian. He was running out of time. She had to free herself. Pulling against the sundew with all her might, she reached with her left arm and took the machete from her right.

Using her off hand was challenging. She couldn't aim properly, and the harder she came down with the blade, the more difficult it was to line up her strike.

Many smaller blows eventually freed her good hand, though the tendril still stuck to it like a slimy bracelet. Her skin felt warm beneath it, and she realized with horror that it was probably the digestive enzyme in the goo getting to work.

There was no time to remove it, though, because Brian was still trapped. She switched the machete back to her dominant hand and cut the tentacle around Brian's neck. She couldn't tell if he was still breathing, so she hacked away at the two tentacles holding his body off the ground.

With a slash through the remaining tendrils and a quiet thump, Brian was back on the ground. Dione dragged him out of range of the giant sundew, careful not to trigger any more leaves.

He wasn't moving. *Please don't be dead. Please.* Another prayer to a deaf universe. She didn't think she could bear it if he were dead. She tried to feel for a pulse, but her hands were shaking. Instead, she stared helplessly at his chest in the darkness, willing it to visibly rise and fall. She couldn't tell. Tears welled up in her eyes. She cared about him more than she wanted to admit, and now that he was lying before her unconscious, she thought back to their last exchange. It had been awful. She couldn't leave it like that.

At last, his chest rose with a deep, unmistakable breath, and she sighed in relief. She carefully removed the sticky leaves from his neck, torso, and legs. Once she removed the leaf from her own wrist, she could see, even in the moonlight, that her wrist was red. She quickly grabbed one of the blankets from her pack and wiped the abrasive goo from her wrist and Brian's neck and legs.

His clothes were a mess. Brian's shorts were fine, but his shirt was covered in *Drosera* slime. She lifted his shirt to check his abdomen, and sure enough, a light pink mark marred his chest where the sundew had gripped him.

Careful to keep the caustic slime contained, she clumsily cut off his shirt with her knife and tossed it aside. Once she had washed all affected areas, she covered Brian up with the second blanket.

Throughout her ministrations, he had stayed unconscious. Dione hoped it was just another side effect of the nematocyst poison, because she hated being out here alone.

Once the task was complete, she sat a moment and thought. They were too far from the shuttle to go back in the dark. She looked over at the monstrous sundew, its unharmed tendrils still glistening in the moonlight.

This might be the safest place for them tonight. The sundew had a good chance of catching anything that approached from that side, and if something did attack, she might be able to use the sundew just like she had used that angler worm to trap a Ven a couple of days ago. Of course, that was assuming whatever was coming didn't kill them both in their sleep.

Her fears struggled to keep her awake, but they were no match for the post-adrenaline fatigue that weighed her down. *If I'm going to die on this island*, she thought drowsily, *in my sleep might be the best way to go.*

11. LITHIA

"I don't know why you think I can help you," Lithia said. "I barely know her." Even in the gray light of early morning, Jai's features were still handsome. The dark eyes, smooth skin, and warm smile momentarily distracted her from the broken buildings behind him.

"She trusts you," he replied, snapping her back into the conversation.

Lithia suppressed a snort. "Yeah, she shot me a few days ago because I lied to her. I don't think trust is the right word." She stepped out of the way as Theo led a pair of machi, creatures that looked like large tapirs, to the group of waiting riders, who wore loose white shirts and brown harem pants in typical Aratian style.

"Well, I do. She listens to you now. She looks up to you. You have to see that."

Lithia's playful smile slipped away. He was right. Ever since the battle—no, the Matching—Cora had looked at her with new eyes. "Even if you're right, why should I help you? Cora doesn't want to marry you."

"I know. That's not why I want your help. Cora just lost her father and Will. She needs a friend."

"She's got me."

"And having another couldn't hurt. You're new here. You don't know how isolated she was, growing up as the Regnator's daughter."

Lithia bit her lip. That almost reminded her of Dione, growing up as the child of a powerful man, protected to the point of isolation until StellAcademy. Cora didn't have anything like that here. Maybe Jai had a point.

"So what do you want me to do about it?"

"If she sees that you treat me as an equal, I think it would go a long way."

That was easy enough. "You promise this isn't some ploy to seduce her or something and become Regnator?"

Jai looked at her quizzically and laughed. "I promise. Cora's not really my type." He glanced past her, and Lithia heard someone coming.

She turned to see her cousin approaching. "We're almost ready," Cora said. "Theo is getting the last of the machi ready."

Cora spoke as if Jai wasn't there. She refused to acknowledge his existence with even a glance.

"Good," Lithia replied. "I was just asking Jai if he had any ideas—" She broke off and looked up. Her ears were attuned to catch the hum of the Flyers, and for a moment, she was back at the Ficaran settlement, death and destruction creeping in on all sides. Suddenly the hum of the Flyer sounded more like screams and growls and gunshots.

She felt a hand on her shoulder. Both her shoulders. "Lithia?" Jai gave her a little shake, and she snapped out of it. He and Cora were looking at her, brows furrowed in concern. *That was one way to bring them together.*

"Are you okay?" Cora asked.

"Yeah, I'm fine. Just zoned out for a sec."

Before Cora could ask her any more questions, Lithia's manumed buzzed. It was Bel.

"Hey, what's up?" she asked, eager for a distraction.

"Colm and I are here with a few other Ficarans. We want to help you find the Green Cloaks, and thought you might want some company, especially if you run into the Vens."

"We're at the gate," Lithia said. "Why didn't you warn me?"

"Better to beg forgiveness than ask permission," Bel replied. "We already cleared it with Benjamin. See you in a few."

Lithia turned to Cora, but she was already on it. "Theo," she called, "prepare a few more machi. We've got more volunteers on the way."

Benjamin appeared and beckoned to Cora. It seemed he wanted a few words with his niece before she left. She walked off, leaving Lithia and Jai alone again.

"I see what you mean," Lithia said. "I'm sure she'll come around eventually. Why do you care so much, anyway?"

"I know the whispers about the Vens," he said, "and how some are saying the Farmer wasn't really a god, but I was matched with Cora for a reason. If not to marry her, then to help her in some way, I can't explain. It's just this feeling I have."

That sort of plea might not have swayed Dione, the queen of needing proof, but Jai's intuition struck a chord with Lithia. She had felt almost the same thing last night before volunteering to join Cora. It was decided then. She would help him.

Dione kept popping up in Lithia's thoughts. She saw her friend's shadow in every situation. She was worried about her friend. *Best friend.* It had been a while since Lithia had sent her a simple, one-word message: *Update?*

Dione had not replied yet, but she would. That nerd had figured out how to save her from the angler worm without an instruction manual. She would be fine, even on a nightmare island.

Lithia's thoughts were interrupted by soft chatter. The Ficarans had arrived. Colm's bulky form dwarfed Bel's thin frame as she walked closer. Bel's long hair was pulled back into her typical braid, and something in her expression reminded Lithia of an ancient warrior goddess whose name she had forgotten, but that Dione would have remembered.

Colm headed straight for Benjamin and Cora. Lithia saw Bel scanning the area for her, so she waved her friend over.

"Have you met Jai?" she asked after they got the initial pleasantries out of the way.

"Not officially," she replied. "I'm Bel." She extended a hand, which he shook.

"He got matched with Cora," Lithia explained.

"Oh," Bel said. "Umm... it's nice to meet you."

Time to change the subject, Lithia thought. "What inspired you to join us?" she asked.

"The Vens are still out there, and I have a feeling we'll cross their path," Bel said. She held up a hand. "And before you ask, I'm good now. No more crazy risks."

Lithia nodded. "Got it." She'd heard about Bel's refusal to leave the Ven ship while she was downloading the datacore. It had nearly cost Bel her life. Dione had been horrified, but Lithia? She understood. She finally got it. Something had happened during that final battle, and any hint of mercy she might have felt for the Vens had been snuffed out. No, replaced. Something inside her felt clenched and hot, and not even her flippant jokes could provide any relief. The only time she felt any reprieve was when she was focusing on something else, like helping Cora.

All three were silent for a moment, which allowed them to overhear the loud—and growing louder—conversation between Cora and Benjamin nearby.

"Now is not a good time for this," Benjamin was saying. "People are uneasy, the Matching is on hold, and now the presence of Ficarans on your team? It's unbecoming."

"You approved it," Cora said.

"Because I thought it would help keep you all safe! You can still step down and leave this expedition to Theo. People are whispering."

"People will never stop whispering, uncle. Never. And I'm sick of this. The only way you can get me to stop is by forbidding me to go, as the Regnator." Cora lowered her voice again, but Lithia was still close enough to hear. "And you won't do that, because it weakens your position."

"Cora, you can't just do whatever you feel like. There are rules. Traditions." Benjamin lowered his voice so that Lithia could barely hear him. "Our claim to rule is weak at the moment. You don't understand—"

"I *do* understand your objections. I just don't care. If our claim is weak, then maybe we should step aside."

"So you want the chaos of a power vacuum? Have you forgotten your studies?"

"I want revenge. Nothing more, nothing less. Power, interregnum, the Matching, all of it is an indistinct blur. The only thing that looks clear when I imagine the future is this: hunting down the Green Cloaks and avenging my father. Saving our people from internal rot. That's what a ruler does, right? Protects her people?" Lithia could see the fire in her cousin's eyes.

Benjamin sighed. "Don't let your anger consume you, child," he said. "I can't stop you. You've forced my hand. At least listen to Theo. Your father trusted him."

Cora turned her back on her uncle and beckoned to Lithia, Jai, and Bel. "Let's join the others. I need to speak to everyone before we leave."

Lithia smiled at Cora. The change in her cousin probably seemed incredible to some, but Lithia knew the truth. Cora the Leader had always been in there. She had looked up to her father's example for years, and she had Miranda's blood in her veins. She was strong and stubborn, just like Lithia. All she had needed was a catalyst, though Lithia would have preferred something other than the deaths of her father and boyfriend to spur her forward.

Cora mounted a beautiful, solid black maximute, a giant dog that the researchers had programmed to respond to musical commands. Theo was perched atop a brown one by her side. Theo's men from the cavalry were also on maximutes. All the others, including Lithia and Bel, sat atop machi.

"We're heading to Raynor Farm," Cora said. "If the Green Cloak we recovered is telling the truth, that's where the remains of their group are hiding. We should arrive tomorrow by late morning if we keep a good pace. You all volunteered, and if you've changed your mind since last night, I won't hold it against you if you back out now. Our mission is dangerous."

Cora paused, and Lithia glanced behind her. No one budged. The two young women who had seemed uncertain last night now looked resolved. One reached out and squeezed the other's hand quickly before dropping it. *Reassurance.* The kind she had given Dione a number of times.

That sign of friendship stirred up the fear she felt for Dione in the back of her mind, but that fear was soon replaced with a sardonic smile. As worried as she was that her best friend had gone off into the jungle on nightmare island, she didn't have room to talk. She had spontaneously joined this crusade, and as much as she told herself it was to earn enough clout to borrow the Aratian Flyer, she knew deep down that it was to satisfy her thirst for revenge. She hoped they would come across a few Vens she could kill with her borrowed *pila* blade. They were sharp, thin, and flexible. Perfect for slipping between Ven carapace plating.

"The outsiders Lithia and Bel have decided to help us, as well as Colm and a few Ficarans," Cora said.

Lithia was glad Colm had come. Bel had a machete, but Colm and the Ficarans all had guns. They had scavenged enough ammo from the Field Temple to feel comfortable sending it along with Colm. *Bullets should go a lot further against the Green Cloaks than the Vens.*

The thought caught Lithia off guard. She hadn't asked Cora whether this was a kill or capture mission. She dearly missed the stun rifle. She didn't think she could kill a human being, but if she could, there was no likelier target than a Green Cloak. She decided not to put Cora on the spot in front of all these people. No need to make her feel locked in to whatever choice she made spur of the moment.

From the corner of her eye, Lithia saw Elijah standing apart from their group, flanked by an enforcer type and with a few others. They were listening, too, and Lithia guessed they didn't have good intentions. Everything about Elijah set off her sixth sense. He was bad news, and Lithia didn't like the smug smile on his face.

12. BRIAN

When Brian woke, the haze of sleep lifted slowly from his mind. Too slowly, like he had spent the previous night drinking. Dione was staring at him. He was shirtless and didn't remember how he got that way, which made him uncomfortable.

"Checking me out?" he asked. His attempt to lighten the mood failed. She frowned at him.

"Yep, just making sure your injuries aren't getting worse," she replied. "I want to put some more of the aloe gel on your neck. Just finishing a message to Lithia and letting her know we survived the night."

Her message sent, Dione pulled some leaves from her bag and worked them into a gel.

He pushed himself into a sitting position and groaned. Now that he was awake, his perception of pain was heightened. He put a hand to his neck, which was hot to the touch.

"In all seriousness, Brian, how much do you remember?" Dione asked.

"It's a blur, really. We were arguing at the shuttle, then I left. I remember running into some hanging moss. That had to be the most painful thing I've experienced." He reached up to touch his neck again, wincing as he did. "I think I passed out. After that, things are really hazy."

"So you don't remember running off into the jungle after I saved you from the moss and brought you back to the shuttle?"

Brian's eyes went wide. No wonder she was so pissed. This was about more than his mistake with Lithia.

"And you don't remember talking to that rock last night before stumbling into the giant sundew over there and getting trapped?" She motioned to the red and green plant across the clearing that was obviously missing a few leaves.

He remembered it now. In the late morning light, he got a good look at the sundew. Its vibrant green leaves, speckled with long, red feelers, looked festive. In the dark, its muted tones, all appearing gray, had seemed more ominous.

"In case you didn't know, sundews are carnivorous plants," Dione said. "Those tentacle-like leaves curl around their prey. The gooey balls that look like dew? They stick to struggling prey and also contain digestive enzymes. That's where these faint pink lines came from." Brian followed her gestures and touched the line across his chest, as well as the one on his legs.

"That's why I cut off your shirt. It was soaked in digestive juices." She pointed to a heap of fabric several meters away. It still looked damp, but more than that, it was now unusable.

"Damn. That was my favorite shirt."

When he looked back to Dione, she wasn't laughing. Last night must have been rough on her.

She moved closer until she was sitting right across from him. "Here, let me put this on your neck," she said. "It will soothe any residual pain. Jameson must have engineered his aloe plant to be extra potent."

Brian obediently leaned forward, allowing her to smear the cool gel on his back. "You're hurt, too," he said, catching sight of her wrist.

"It's nothing."

"The sundew got you when you charged in and saved me?"

"Just barely. I'll put some of this gel on it when I'm done with you. Your body has taken a lot of punishment in the past twenty-four hours."

When she touched his neck, he flinched, even though she applied the ointment gently. Dione took some of the gel for her own wrist, then leaned back and offered him the rest. "You can coat wherever still hurts."

"Thanks," he said, taking the ointment. A few moments of silence hung in the air before he spoke again. After everything Dione had done to save him from the moss and the sundew, he knew his next words wouldn't go over well.

"He's here, you know. My dad."

Dione sighed. "You were hallucinating last night. I think you just imagined it."

"I remember now. I didn't see my dad. I wasn't talking to him." Brian paid close attention to the administration of the salve, avoiding eye contact.

"Then who did you see?"

"My mom."

Dione had never met his mom, who had been sleeping every time Brian had checked on her at the Mountain Base.

"Okay," she said.

"I saw my mom the way she's supposed to be. The way she was, before he left."

"What do you mean?"

"After my dad left, my mom just… stopped being herself. She doesn't eat. She spends most of her time sleeping. I take care of her the best I can, but…" He trailed off. It was hard, and only getting harder. Melanie helped, but some days his mother ate next to nothing. Other days, she wouldn't get out of bed.

"What did she say?"

"Nothing really. We just talked. We haven't done that in years, and I miss it. I have to find my father. Seeing her was a reminder of why I'm here. It was a sign."

Dione blinked at him. "It was an hallucination," she said. "I'm really sorry about your mom, but finding your dad isn't going to magically fix whatever's wrong with her. She needs a doctor."

Brian said nothing. For the first time in years, he felt hopeful. He had been carrying this burden for so long that the chance of finding his father and bringing his mom back to life had become like a dream. He was finally here on the island, and he wasn't going back until he found his father, dead or alive. He had to know.

Dione's voice cut into his thoughts. "Look, we're almost out of water. I used a lot last night to clean off the sundew's residue. We need to go back to the Flyer. There's more water on board, and that's where we should wait for the others to find us."

"You can go wherever you want. I'm going to find my dad."

Dione stiffened at his words. She pointed emphatically across the clearing. "Normally, sundews catch and eat insects. Some of the largest ones I've seen could catch small mammals, like a squirrel, maybe even a cat. That monster over there almost got its first taste of human last night. That is the island we are trapped on. Why don't you get this?"

"No, I don't think you get it," he said, raising his voice. "I'm grateful for all of your help, but I'm used to every move I make putting me in danger. Whether it was pissing off Victoria or getting captured by the Aratians, my world has never been safe. *Your* world was safe. You're the one who's nervous, not me." He paused and looked her up and down. "Maybe it was unfair to ask for your help. I'm sorry for that."

He watched Dione's shoulders slump.

"Look, we'll come up with another way to search for your dad," she said softly. "This doesn't mean you're giving up. It means you're being smart about it."

"If we need water, there's a stream nearby," he said.

"You're changing the subject."

"You said we need water. Well, there's water in that direction." He pointed northeast.

"How do you know that?"

"I can hear it. Can't you hear that?" It was faint, but he was certain it was running water.

She cocked her head to one side, as if straining to make out the sound. "I don't hear it. How do I know you're not lying to avoid going back to the shuttle?"

"Because I'm telling the truth to avoid going back to the shuttle," he said. He got up and took a few steps in the direction he had pointed. "Victoria will never give me another chance. If I don't find my father now, no matter what's happened to him, I never will. If I can't bring him back, at least my mom and I will have closure. I'm going to look for my father, then fly out of here in the colonizer. Are you with me?"

Dione closed her eyes. Brian balled his fists. He didn't want to do this alone, but he wouldn't force Dione to head deeper into the jungle with him. It was dangerous, but to him it was worth the risk.

Finally, she opened her eyes and looked at him. "We should stick together," Dione said. "Who knows what else is out there."

"So you're coming with me?" he asked, surprised.

"With your track record, you'll be dead in a few hours without someone watching over you."

Brian grinned at the insult. "Let's go find that creek," he said.

As he led the way, he couldn't help feeling something warm billowing up inside him. Gratitude? Maybe. He looked back at Dione. No, it was more than gratitude. It was the same thing he had felt before. He wanted to be close to her. He wanted her to forgive him.

13. ZANE

After the Vens were taken care of, Zane thought he'd be able to spend some time with Bel. Instead, he was alone in the basement of the Mountain Base, running another diagnostic on Sam. She hadn't noticed yet. She was overtaxed.

Zane visualized it as a rope bridge. Before the Ven arrival, Sam had been doing very minor tasks on rare occasions, like one person crossing the bridge every now and then. When she had been helping Dione and Lithia, that had been like regular foot traffic. In time, it would take its toll. After the Ficaran escape to the Mountain Base, it was like a crowd was jumping on the bridge all the time.

He checked the progress of the translation on his manumed. About halfway there. He was surprised that she'd made so much progress, then grimaced, wondering what this was costing her.

Zane sighed. He wished Bel had stayed with him, but he knew her too well to try to hold her back. Everyone was doing their part. It was time he stepped up and did his. Somehow, one of them would gain access to a ship that could rescue Dione. Sure, she was stubborn and arrogant, but that island was no place for anyone.

When Sam finally noticed what he was doing, her response didn't surprise him.

"I'm dying, Zane," she said.

At these words, he felt a pang of loss. He felt like he had found a friend in the human-AI hybrid that was running things on Kepos. He'd always found machines better companions than people, at least until getting to know Bel. There hadn't been a lot of other kids on the freighters growing up, and the ones he did meet were the children of the wealthier officers who could afford the additional cost. That is to say, they were spoiled brats.

"I think I can extend things a bit, if I slow the Ven datacore processing. It's not like we're in a rush."

"No, don't bother. I've known for a long time that I would die," she said. "I knew, back when I was Dr. Samantha Myers. After a while, my consciousness would degrade, and I'd slowly go crazy."

Zane nodded. It's why so few tried to extend their lives by uploading their consciousness. Human minds could not maintain themselves inside man-made machines. After time, memories and personality faded into something unrecognizable. Sam had managed to delay this fate by spending much of her time dormant, but with all of the new activity brought on by their arrival, and then the Vens', Sam's borrowed time was running out.

"Long ago," she said, "I put some measures into place that will stop me before I slip too far and become dangerous. It's almost better this way. I thought I'd go to sleep one day and never wake up. I never thought there would be anyone to say goodbye to."

"Let me finish this diagnostic first," he said.

Twenty minutes later, Zane got the preliminary results. They were bad.

"I thought we had weeks, but it looks like we're talking days."

"That's why I need your help," Sam said. "Someone needs to look after this place when I'm gone. The old AI I took over can't do the job. It's not sophisticated enough."

Jameson had installed an AI to power the Icon, the planet's defensive weapon, but it hadn't worked properly. Sam had sacrificed her body and uploaded her consciousness into the Mountain Base to merge with the old AI and control the Icon.

The young man shifted uncomfortably. "What exactly are you asking?"

"I've scanned the *Calypso*. She doesn't have an AI, but her hardware is a lot newer than the old AI that ran this place before me. I can leave behind instructions for the humans and programs for the old AI, but it won't be able to use them as is. If you use parts of the *Calypso*'s computer to upgrade the hardware here, the system will be able to support the old AI and necessary functions, like using the Icon."

"That's a tall order," Zane replied. "Oberon's not ready to abandon ship. He's still trying to fix her."

"You need to convince him."

"How?"

"I'll get you a Flyer once it's done," Sam said. "Victoria doesn't control everything."

"I think I can work with that. I'll see what I can do."

"Thank you. Fail safes I set up will ensure that once I degrade to a certain point, I'll be completely erased from the system. I don't want to lose myself and hurt someone."

Zane bit his lower lip. She sounded sad, maybe worried. He couldn't imagine what she was going through, what it was like to feel the end coming as parts of her slipped away. Maybe that was why she had been getting quieter and quieter. She was losing herself.

"Zane, I have another favor," she said, sounding more human than ever. "When I'm gone, will you bury me? My real body, I mean."

"Yes," he said, without hesitation. Dione had been the one who found Sam's body in one of the basement labs, still hooked up to the machines she had used to transfer her consciousness. Sam had asked them to seal that room off at the time, but now her desires had apparently changed. That was one last kindness he could give her, one final homage to her humanity.

Zane figured it was time to check on the professor. He found the man in the cargo bay, sitting on a crate and tapping away at the tablet in his lap.

"Still no luck convincing Victoria?" Zane asked.

"She wouldn't even see me this time," Oberon said. "She's busy coordinating recovery teams at the Field Temple." The professor looked up from his tablet. "I'm glad you're here." Oberon had decided he would fix the *Calypso,* since Victoria kept denying his requests for a Flyer. "Take a look at this," he said, passing over the tablet. "I haven't finished the program, but I think it might work."

Zane skimmed the program. He recognized an exercise in futility when he saw one, but he would help anyway. It bothered him to see the professor, usually so calm and rational, acting like this. Oberon was a brilliant biologist, and he knew a lot about maintaining the *Calypso,* but this damage was above his pay grade. They both knew it.

"This is for the nanotech?" Zane asked.

Oberon nodded. Zane looked the program over again. The gaping hole in the cargo bay was too large for the nanotech to repair, but Oberon was proposing a graft. Not just a sheet of metal clumsily welded on to close the gap, but a metal web so that the nanotech could integrate it smoothly.

"She'll never be space-worthy like this," Zane said, "but this could work. It will take the nanotech some time."

"I know."

Zane's stomach was in knots as he handed back the tablet. Had the professor come up with a plan for the other issues? "This fixes the hull, but you know better than I do that there was more than just hull damage. Most of the wiring has been destroyed, and we can't fix that. It's beyond patching, by hand or by nanotech."

"I think I can repair the vital systems," Oberon said. "It won't be pretty, and this area wouldn't have certain… amenities."

"Like lights?"

"And life support. Like you said, not space-worthy, but it might be enough to fly to the island and get Dione."

"Oberon, I don't think it's going to work. The damage is just too much for the supplies we have and our skill sets." It felt strange to be the voice of reason.

Oberon lowered his head and clenched his fists for several long moments before sighing. "You're right, but I'm still going to try. I've exhausted every avenue of reasoning and bargaining with Victoria. She won't even let me go up to the space station where there are other Flyers."

Zane looked hard at Oberon. Had the wrinkles on his forehead always been that pronounced? "I've got a suggestion," he said.

Oberon looked at Zane without raising his head. "I'm open to any and all ideas at this point."

"You're not going to like it."

"That seems to be the pattern with things my students have told me today," he said, putting down the tablet.

"Sam is degrading more quickly than anticipated, and without her, the old AI that Jameson installed can't operate the Icon or support the colonists in any meaningful way."

"Let me guess, you want to plug your brain into the system and become the new Sam," Oberon said wryly.

Zane resisted the urge to roll his eyes. "Yep. I mean, when you convinced me to come on this trip, you told me I'd have the chance to experience new things. After running over Vens with farming equipment and landing the *Calypso* by myself, I figured becoming a computer doomed to eventual insanity sounded like a good time."

Oberon sighed. "What is it, then?"

"Sam wants us to upgrade the base with parts from the *Calypso*. Without her consciousness overlaid with the base's AI, things around her will work with a fraction of her efficiency. The old AI couldn't even use the Icon. She's written programs for when she's gone, but without the upgrades, she doesn't think the old AI has any hope of running them."

"I have doubts about Sam's ability to deliver on that promise in her current condition. She's the one who wrecked the *Calypso* in the first place." Oberon thought a moment before adding, "What if it was on purpose?"

Zane cocked his head to one side. He hadn't thought of that. He didn't think Sam would do something like that, but the timing was convenient. "I don't think so. She would have asked, just like last time with the charging matrix. Even if she did do it on purpose, it doesn't matter now. The damage is done, and by refusing, the only people we'd be hurting are the colonists. I don't think it's much of a choice."

"No," Oberon said. "I still think I can fix the *Calypso*. She's been with me for so long. I'm sure there's something I haven't thought of yet. I just need a little more time."

"If there was a way, you'd have figured it out by now," Zane said. "Sam said she'd be able to get us a Flyer if we help her."

"There's a way back for the *Calypso*," Oberon insisted. "I won't give up on her any more than I'd give up on you or one of the girls."

"Let me see," Zane said, holding out his hand. Oberon once again handed over the tablet. Zane exhaled and studied the simulation carefully, checking all of the parameters Oberon had entered, but nothing seemed amiss. He might be able to do a physical hull repair, but the damage to the internal systems was beyond the capability of the nanotech. Zane handed back the tablet. "I have another question."

"What now?"

"Why bother fixing her? Her jump drive is useless. We're never getting that charging matrix back. We're never going to leave this planet in the *Calypso*. Fixing her is a waste of time and resources."

"She's my ship!" Oberon protested. "When we do leave, whatever ship takes us can dock her."

"But she can do good here. Integrating some of her components will allow this base and the Icon to continue to function. What if the Vens come back?"

Oberon frowned.

"Think of it like organ donation. Without Sam, this base has a brain with no real processing power. Grafting the *Calypso* onto the old AI will save both of their lives."

The silence that hung between them was heavy. Finally, Oberon bowed his head. "Do you know what I went through to get this ship? The amount of paperwork and grant applications? Have you ever filled out a grant application, Zane?"

Oberon cracked a sad smile. Zane could tell that deep down, the professor knew the *Calypso* was dead, but his emotional connection kept him hanging on to a hope that wasn't there. Zane needed to find a way to help him say goodbye.

"Don't think of it as a goodbye," he tried. "Think of it as her new legacy."

Zane left the professor in the cargo bay staring at his tablet. Whatever was on his mind, for the moment, it wasn't the *Calypso*'s repairs. Bel was right when she said that none of them would be the same after Kepos, but she hadn't really included Oberon in her assessment. Zane was coming to realize that she should have.

14. BEL

The day passed slowly. Bel's legs ached, and her backside was sore from uneven gait of the machi. She hadn't ridden an animal since she was a child back on the Dappled Rim, before the colony had been destroyed. Back then she'd shared with her brother Halen, and she didn't remember it being so uncomfortable. She enjoyed the machi's damp, earthy smell. Its speed also impressed her, even though a maximute could easily outpace one.

Lithia rode in silence next to her, a frown wrinkling her face. Normally, Lithia didn't stop talking. Bel and Dione could work in silence without a problem, but Lithia? Any time they got paired up at school, Bel had struggled to focus under the constant barrage of questions and snarky comments.

Bel enjoyed the silence, though, and soaked in the breeze that rustled the tree branches. The buzz of insects was musical, beating throughout the forest like a pulse—easy to tune out, but omnipresent, a reassuring vital sign. She basked in the warmth of the day and the arboreal melody, relaxing so much she didn't realize her hunger until Theo called for a lunch break.

She and Lithia ate quickly. The food filled her, and she found herself lost in her thoughts again until Lithia finally said something.

"Are you going to eat that?" She pointed to the heel of bread in Bel's hand.

"Here." Bel handed it over and stood, more restless now than hungry. "I'm just going to stretch my legs a bit."

Lithia's response was muffled by a mouthful of bread, but Bel was already off. Careful to stay within earshot of the caravan, she began to explore the forest. This was her first time really examining her surroundings. Before, withthe Vens in full force, she'd only had eyes for research and revenge.

Looking around her now, she saw the imperfect beauty of the native trees, scarred by insects and birds. Not everything on this planet had been engineered by Jameson and the other scientists, and those organisms deserved just as much of her appreciation.

Shouts abruptly broke the serenity of the wilderness. Bel crunched through the bushes back to the caravan.

A man two or three years younger than Cora struggled against Theo in vain. He had dark hair and a large nose. He had not been a part of their group, and it didn't take long for Bel to put the pieces together.

They thought he was a Green Cloak.

The boy shook his head as he replied to a question Bel had not heard. "I'm not with them."

"Then why are you out here?" Cora said. "I recognize you. What's your name?"

"Asher. I had to get out of the town. I was going to check on the farms, see if they were all right." His voice shook when he spoke.

"Everyone was supposed to stay put," she said. "Why are you really out here? Going to warn your Green Cloak friends?"

"I already told you, I couldn't stand being in the town anymore. I can't be the only one. Doesn't your cousin Evy run off all the time? What if you found her out here?"

Cora's voice was stone. "She's ten, and she didn't open the gates for the Ven army. Did you?"

"No, I didn't."

"Are you a Green Cloak?"

"No, I'm not." His eyebrows knitted together in a frown.

Cora looked the young man up and down. "I don't believe you." When he protested, she drew her *pila* blade and held its tip to his chest.

Cora was going to kill this boy, and Bel had doubts about his guilt. He was tall and lanky, barely old enough to be involved. If he were a Green Cloak, he had probably been manipulated or dragged along by a trusted adult. She could see in Cora's eyes that she wouldn't care about this distinction.

Bel made her way to Lithia. "Do something," she urged.

"Like what?" Lithia replied. "Stop her?"

"Exactly that, yes," Bel said. "Or she's going to kill him in front of us."

Lithia clenched her hands at her sides, but did not turn to look at Bel. " If he's a Green Cloak scumbag, maybe he deserves it."

"And if he's not?" Bel was afraid of the answer. She felt the anger radiating off of her friend. Lithia didn't have the chance to respond before one of their group spoke up.

"He's just a boy." Heads turned toward the voice. It was Gavin, the man Elijah had volunteered. "Just think, he's somebody's child."

"He's Elijah's son," Theo replied. "As you well know, since you're close to him."

"Elijah's not the enemy. Just because he asked a few questions at the dinner last night, you're going to kill his son?" Gavin shook his head in disgust.

"This has nothing to do with last night," Cora said, lowering her blade.

Theo stepped toward her, then whispered into her ear. Her brow remained wrinkled in anger, but she nodded in acquiescence to his request.

With a gesture, Theo signaled for the boy to be tied up. "Break's over. We leave in five minutes," he said.

Uneaten food found its way into bellies or bags, and every one returned to their mounts. The presumed Green Cloak was loaded onto a maximute with one of Theo's men.

Bel paid closer attention to Lithia as their caravan returned to the trail. Her silence, which had been welcome in the morning, seemed sinister now. Bel knew better than anyone what hatred for the Vens could do, the depths to which it could pull you down.

The more she thought about the Vens, the more she began to doubt what the Alliance said about them. Why hadn't the Vens regrouped and attacked? Or fought to the last man? That was what she'd expected based on the Alliance literature. She wondered if shutting down the Vens' communication had anything to do with their behavior. Next time she spoke to Zane, she'd ask him to look into it.

15. DIONE

When she got the message that Lithia and Bel were pursuing the Green Cloaks, Dione immediately composed a reply about how dangerous it was and how they should have stayed with the professor. Once she read it over, she deleted it. Her message had been so hypocritical even she had noticed. She had a better idea.

Dione: *Since we're both doing stupid, dangerous things, let's just do check-ins. I'm alive. You?*
Lithia: *Alive. Sounds good.*

Whenever they were worried, one could just ping the other. No need for explanations or apologies, just reassurance.

Dione pulled up the read and ignored messages from Oberon. She sent him a reassurance, too. His response was almost immediate.

Dione: *Alive.*
Oberon: *Thank you.*

Just those two words. Dione felt a wave of guilt wash over her. She should have replied sooner. Underneath all of the scolding, he was just worried.

"Dione?" Brian called. She had stopped in her tracks, allowing him to take the lead.

"Coming." They were nearly at the stream. She could hear it gurgling loudly. "We need to be careful. Everything needs water to survive. We don't know if we'll be sharing the stream with anything."

"Oh, is that how streams work?" Brian smiled, but Dione didn't, leading to an awkward silence that lasted until they could see the water flowing in front of them.

Poison. That's all Dione could think when she looked at the water.

"We need to boil it, but what if it contains some type of toxic compound from the nearby vegetation? We can't trust anything on this island."

"I think we don't have to worry about that at least," Brian replied, pointing to a small, furry creature drinking upstream.

In a moment, Dione had her stun rifle pointed at the beast, her whole body on alert.

"Relax," Brian said. "It's just a rabbit."

"More like death rabbit. Remember that innocent-looking moss that nearly killed you?" Dione fired at the rabbit, but missed, scaring it away.

"You've saved us," Brian said, rolling eyes.

"I'll add it to the tally," she replied, looking pointedly at him. "Let's just get this water safe to drink so we can be on our way. Here." She handed him the machete. "Get some larger pieces of firewood."

Dione herself searched for smaller kindling. This part of the woods was full of tough little shrubs that seemed to shed dry leaves and twigs.

Once they'd accumulated enough fuel, Brian lit the fire. She had to admit when it came to things like that, Brian was an expert. She cleared a patch of ground nearby and took a seat. They'd have to boil the water in batches, as they only had one large metal container.

When they had filled all of their containers with water, Brian doused their small fire. "Thank you," he said.

Dione raised her eyebrows at him, so he continued. "Thank you for saving me from the sundew. And the moss. And for coming here with me, even when you didn't want to."

She hesitated a moment before replying. "You're welcome."

"But more than that, I'm sorry. I know I really hurt your feelings, and you didn't deserve that. I don't like Lithia like that, so I didn't see it as a big deal. It wasn't like when I kissed you. That felt like something. I know it probably doesn't make a difference to you, and that you're mad at me for more than one good reason, but I meant it when I said you were special. I don't expect another chance, but I want you to know that I care about you, Dione. More than I've cared about any girl before."

Dione looked away, formulating her response. Several possibilities flew through her mind, some angry, some forgiving, but she still didn't know where on the spectrum she had settled. Her heart and her head were not in agreement.

As she was searching for her reply, something on the tree she had been staring at caught her attention. She stood up. "It's an arrow."

"What?" Confused, Brian followed her gaze.

"An arrow, come on." Dione was already off the ground and at the tree where the shape of an arrow had been carved into the trunk.

"My dad," Brian said, reaching out and tracing the arrow. All of the gravity of his recent speech was replaced with something beyond excitement.

"Or the Farmer."

"No, it's my father. It has to be."

Dione stumbled over one of the large roots and took a moment to try and identify the tree. The three deeply cut lobes of the leaf gave it the appearance of large, thick bird tracks. "It's some kind of fig, I think."

"Here's another." Brian approached the next fig tree a few meters away. "Pointing in the same direction."

He was already on his way to the next tree when Dione said, "Hang on. We don't know where they came from."

"I know you have doubts," he said, "but my father carved these arrows. I can't give you any evidence, but looking at them, I can just tell they're his."

Intuition was something Lithia relied on with an uncanny amount of success. After a certain point, Dione had done some research into it. "Sometimes our intuition is just our brain putting together clues we've noticed subconsciously to reach a conclusion our conscious mind can't," Dione said.

She studied the arrow again. "Maybe there's something about the type of tree he chose or the way the shape was cut that makes you recognize your father," she conceded. "Or maybe it's just wishful thinking. Either way, whoever carved these arrows was human, and even if it was Jameson, I think we should follow them. Maybe your father found them and followed them, too. Any direction is better than no direction at this point."

Dione was not interested in wandering aimlessly in the wilderness. Even if it was the wrong direction, having an objective, a path to follow, comforted her. Her curiosity about the arrows outweighed her caution, though she didn't think she was ready to face the dragons guarding the colonizer at the center of the island yet.

Only the fig trees had arrows, which made the next one easy to find. It was a clever way for the carver to make sure that their directions could be followed. They talked pleasantly as they walked, mostly about what StellAcademy was like, and in the conversational lulls, Dione thought back to what Brian had said next to the fire. She was glad to have more time to replay his words and dissect them. *I care about you.* Sometimes people really did make mistakes and deserve second chances, but Dione wasn't sure if this was one of them.

Not too long after they'd begun their journey, the fresh, clean forest smell gained a dusty quality. It wasn't a bad odor, but it wasn't good either. The air smelled pungent and a little stale. After a few more minutes of walking, she barely noticed it anymore and figured they had walked past something decaying, or maybe some creature's lair.

When Brian spoke next, though, his tone had changed. "Do you feel that?"

"Feel what?"

"Like we're being watched."

They continued along their path for several more minutes before a sense of foreboding grew in Dione. "Yes, I feel it." The dense undergrowth on her left seemed to shift, but when she turned, she didn't see anything. Another few minutes went by before she again noticed the shifting of the bushes on her left. "Did you see that?"

"I can't tell what it is, but something is definitely following us," Brian replied.

This happened a few more times until a thin patch in the undergrowth gave her eyes enough information for her brain to put it together. "It looks a bit like a dog."

"I saw it, too. Not a maximute—too small—but it's stalking us."

The undergrowth shifted again. *"They* are stalking us." She was certain there was more than one, based on the movements she had seen.

"Any ideas?" Brian asked, slowing his pace. "What are they waiting for?"

That was a good question. She thought back to her biology classes at StellAcademy. If these animals were doglike pack hunters, they might behave like wolves. "Don't run," she said. "We need to maintain our pace. Some animals that hunt in packs wait for their prey to run before attacking. Or to display a sign of weakness. If these things don't think they can take one of us down, they might give up and leave us alone."

"Do you think that's likely?"

"We're in Jameson's twisted playground. I assume everything will try to kill us."

"Right. Like the death rabbit."

Dione readjusted the stun rifle so she'd be able to respond more quickly to a threat. Despite his jokes, Brian took her cue and kept his hand on the machete's handle.

"I think we'll just have to hope that we look too difficult to kill, and they move on to easier prey," Dione said.

"Right." They spent another few minutes in silence, following the trail.

Brian broke the silence. "There's another fig tree up ahead."

"Try not to stop as you check the direction."

"I can see it from here. Keep going straight."

Dione glanced at the tree herself, no longer carefully picking her way through the thick undergrowth. She tripped over one of the roots, coming down hard on her knees and bracing herself with one hand. She cried out as pain shot through her wrist. This was the moment the creatures had been waiting for. One lunged from the undergrowth, and the only thing Dione noticed was its teeth, long and sharp.

She would not be able to reposition the rifle in time, so she raised her free arm to shield her face and neck from the attack. Instead of feeling pain, she heard a thud, followed by a yelp. Brian must have struck it.

"Back," he commanded, brandishing the machete. Dione watched the creature back away. It had a short, rounded snout to match its short, rounded ears, and it was the size of a large dog. *Not a wolf. Hyena?* Dione thought. But what caught her attention more than its squat features was its fur, if it could be called that. Along its back were leaves, or a facsimile so close to the real thing she could hardly believe her eyes. These hyenas were masters of disguise.

"On your feet." Brian was spinning from one direction to the next, trying to look menacing as other hyenas approached, but he couldn't look in all directions at once.

Dione stood and shook off the pain in her wrist, readying the stun rifle just in time to shoot down the hyena that was running toward Brian's turned back.

An eerie, almost-human laugh rose up from the undergrowth in front of Dione. It caught like wildfire as more of the hidden hunters joined in. Instinctively, she and Brian stood back to back as they realized the horrifying truth. They were surrounded.

16. DIONE

"How many?" Dione asked.

"Maybe five or six. I can't tell."

Before she could come up with a plan, the hyenas began attacking, one after the other. They made quick charges, offering little more than nips at her arms and legs. She fired a couple of shots but missed. It was hard to aim at close-range targets while dodging wildly in the onslaught.

They weren't going for the kill, but Dione didn't have time to wonder why as she fended off another attack, this time stunning one of the hyenas.

"They're trying to separate us. Hang on," Brian said, swinging his machete again. Another yelp as his target limped away.

The beasts had determined that she was the weaker one and were trying to isolate her so they could more easily kill her. *Not gonna happen*, she thought.

She managed to stun another, though her overall accuracy wasn't very good. In order to track the creatures, she had to rotate her whole body, which reduced her reaction time. With two of their number stunned and two more injured, the hyenas halted their attack, disappearing back into the undergrowth.

Brian paused, as though ensuring there would be no second wave, and then turned to her. "You okay?"

"A few bites, but I'm fine." Blood was dripping down her left arm from the deeper puncture marks, and her hands trembled. She didn't think she was seriously injured, but seeing that much of her blood made her momentarily lightheaded.

"We need to get out of here," Brian said.

Dione took a few deep breaths to steady herself. She didn't know if the hyenas would attack again once they started moving, but it was a chance they had to take. "Lead the way."

They moved at a light jog through the trees, slowed at times by patches of thick undergrowth. She felt droplets of blood roll down her arms and legs, staining her remaining sock. Her right calf began to ache where one of the creatures had bitten her, but it wasn't bad. The heat, on the other hand, was starting to get to her. When she dared take her eyes from the path in front of her, she caught glimpses of the hyenas still stalking her, waiting for their chance.

She turned and fired a few shots into the bushes where the creatures with their leafy fur blended in so well. She missed and was met by the hyenas' mocking laughter.

When they approached the next tree, Brian adjusted his course. Where were they going? What was the point of all this?

"We need to find a defensible position," she said. "Maybe then we can pick off these last ones." There were at least two in pursuit, maybe a third that was injured. "Like an outcropping of rock we could keep at our backs?"

"I haven't seen anything like that. Plenty of trees to climb, though."

Before Dione could respond, the eerie laughter rose up again, sending chills through her body. She nearly ran into Brian as he halted abruptly. Glancing ahead, she realized why. Two of the hyenas blocked their path, laughing as they slowly approached.

"Oh no," she said, her stomach sinking. "We only saw the ones they wanted us to see. There were more out there this whole time. They let us escape while the others got into position." She looked at the blood drying on her arm. *They were hoping my injuries would weaken me*, she thought.

"Watch out!" Brian shouted. The warning was too late. A hyena leapt toward Dione's neck, catching her shirt in its mouth. It might have missed its mark, but snagged the fabric with its teeth. The garment pulled tight against her throat, and she fell backward onto the ground.

Immediately, the other hyenas joined in, making quick attacks as they tried to avoid Brian's machete. This only slowed their onslaught. Dione tried to protect her neck and other vital areas, flailing her legs, kicking anything that came too close, but there were too many of them.

True panic set in, and Dione fought with everything she had, ignoring the pain of the fresh wounds. Some were deeper than those from the previous attack, but Dione didn't care. She was struggling to stay alive.

Somewhere in the back of her mind, she knew there was no hope. Brian couldn't fend off so many, nor could she from her prone position, but the will to survive was not something she could turn off even in the face of certain death. She screamed, but that only made the attacks come more quickly.

She couldn't stop screaming. She stopped only to take a breath, and in that gap she heard a strange sound. Music. Was Brian singing? The assault stopped as quickly as it had started.

Dione didn't waste time getting up, now that her attackers had backed off. It didn't make any sense. She could still hear the melody. She looked at Brian, but his mouth was closed. He appeared as confused as she felt, looking around for the source of the music.

The hyenas were backing away. She let her guard relax, just a bit, but that was enough. By the time she saw the hyena in her periphery, Brian was already reacting. He didn't have time to position his weapon, so he tackled the beast to the ground before it could sink its jaws into her neck.

The source of the music was getting closer, the melody stronger.

Brian struggled against the creature, but he was at a disadvantage. Dione raised the stun rifle that was still strapped across her shoulder. They were too close together for her to get a clean shot, but it didn't matter. She could stun them both. She could drag Brian through the woods if need be. She fired and got lucky, hitting the hyena.

Then, the source of the music came into view. A tall, bearded man rushed into the fray the next instant, knife raised. Still singing, he dispatched the hyena, managing to do so with less blood spatter than Dione would have imagined possible. Brian had a few bite marks, but seemed mostly unharmed.

Dione wondered who the man was, but her question was answered before she even had the chance to voice it.

"Dad?" Brian asked. The look on his face, one of pure joy and relief, filled her weary body with energy. They had done it. They had found his father. Well, technically he had found them, but that didn't matter. Brian's dad was alive and standing right in front of them.

17. BRIAN

Brian gazed up at his father's face. There were more wrinkles there beneath his beard and at the corners of his eyes, and his hair, once jet black, was almost completely gray.

"I thought I'd never see you again," the man said, pulling his son to his feet and clapping him in a full embrace, unfazed by the hyena blood on his chest. "We need to get moving. I'm sure you have questions, as do I, but they'll have to wait."

Brian burned with questions, but he had waited this long. He could manage a little longer.

His dad looked at Dione and smiled. "I'm Oliver."

"Dione."

"You're bleeding quite a bit, but we can't stay here."

Brian frowned as he looked Dione over, but she seemed okay.

"Most are shallow bites," she said. "I'm more worried about the risk of infection. Puncture wounds are notorious for that."

"We'll make sure to clean the bite wounds thoroughly," Brian said.

His dad looked around, corners of his mouth dipping into a frown. "Can you walk?"

She nodded. "I can walk."

"Good. This way," he said, beckoning for them to follow. He began singing again, and Brian recognized it as the song he had heard just before the hyenas backed off. Now that he was listening closely, it was less a song than repeated series of notes. Things clicked into place.

"The tune!" Dione exclaimed to Brian. She had pieced it together, too. He wasn't surprised. "Jameson must have genetically programmed them to flee when they hear this sequence."

His dad stopped singing and gave her a wink, then glanced to Brian.

"This one's got a head on her shoulders," he said. Addressing Dione directly, he asked, "A recent Aratian deserter? I don't remember you."

"Umm," Dione looked to Brian for help.

"Not exactly," Brian said. "Dad, there's so much to explain."

"Save it for dinner. We'll be home soon, and we need to get you both cleaned up."

Brian looked at the blood coating Dione's clothes and arms. He would let her go first.

"Home?" Brian asked.

"What passes for home out here, anyway. It's a little place I built and fortified once I realized I was stuck here."

Home turned out to be a tree house with layers of protection. A sad-looking fence surrounded the tree, but Brian recognized the filamentous tangles placed at short intervals along it as the stinging moss. He reflexively touched his neck, which was still sore despite the aloe.

"Don't touch that moss," his dad said.

"We know," Dione replied, casting a meaningful glance in Brian's direction.

His dad grimaced. "Once you know what to look for, it gets easier to survive out here. Hope it didn't get you too bad."

"Brian got the worst of it."

"I can see that. On the neck, huh? What's that mark on your torso from? It doesn't look like the moss."

"A giant sundew," Dione replied.

"Never heard of it, so you'll have to tell me all about it later. First, let's get you checked out," Oliver said. "You both look a mess." His voice had returned to a regular volume, but still caught in his throat with emotion. "There's water out back. I'll be there in a minute." He climbed up the ladder into the tree house. Brian recognized the flooring. It had been made with pieces of his father's boat. The walls and roof, however, had been woven from local materials.

Dione and Brian walked to the back of the tree and were amazed to find not just barrels of water, but a transport system that was channeling water from what Dione presumed was a nearby stream.

"Incredible," she said.

Brian smiled. "He always liked to tinker."

"This is more than tinkering."

"I guess you're right."

Oliver reappeared, holding some spare clothes and a small drawstring bag that fit neatly in the palm of his hand. "Here are some clothes, though you're welcome to wash your own and leave them out to dry since they probably fit you better than these. I've also got a spare shirt for you, Brian, but it's a little more worn."

"No problem," Brian replied.

"What's in the bag?" Dione asked.

"Soap! Not as refined as the stuff we made back home, but it's better than nothing," Oliver said. He was grinning. Brian had never seen his dad so happy about soap before, but then again, he had a feeling it wasn't the soap.

"I saw a rabbit in one of my traps on the way back, a close one, that I want to clean for dinner," his dad said.

"I'll help." Brian looked at Dione, whose arms were covered in dried blood. "You can wash up first."

"You sure?" she asked.

"Yeah," he replied, grinning. "You look terrible."

She rolled her eyes, but returned his smile. "Thanks. I feel gross."

Brian left Dione to her shower, glad to finally have a chance to talk with his dad. The only problem was that he didn't know where to start.

"How far out is this rabbit?" Brian asked.

"Shouting distance of the tree house," his dad said, stepping outside the fence and leading the way into a copse of trees.

"I get why you did it. You came out here because you thought the Farmer was lying about creating us," Brian said. "You were right, you know."

"Yes, but I was wrong about what he was hiding. I expected to find a thriving civilization on this island that could provide me with answers. Instead, I found poison and venom and fangs. The most important thing I've discovered out here is that family is more important than asking questions and getting answers. I got so wrapped up in my own theories I lost sight of what really mattered," Oliver said. "I regret coming out here. All of the answers and all of the new questions weren't worth this. I'm sorry I ever left you. You and Bethany deserved better."

Brian, who had been following, stopped. In the moments it took his father to notice, tears had begun streaming down Brian's cheeks. Once he saw his son's tears, Oliver's own resolve broke, and he embraced Brian once again.

"I've missed you every day. I think about you and your mother every morning when I wake up and every night when I go to sleep. It's what kept me sane out here."

"We've missed you so much," Brian said, pulling back from his embrace to wipe his eyes with a dirty hand.

"After everything I did to try to get back to you, I'd given up hope of leaving this island. Instead, I dreamed of rescue. I never thought it would happen, but here you are. You found me."

Brian closed his eyes, and a few more tears rolled down his cheeks. He hadn't realized it until that moment, but he was no longer alone. He was no longer the sole caregiver for his mother, the one making all of the decisions, carrying all of the guilt and worry. His father was alive, and they would figure everything out together. He might even have some ideas for getting through to Victoria.

"We don't have a way off the island yet, but we'll find one," Brian said. "Others will come for us. There's so much to explain. I don't even know where to start."

"On a full stomach," his father replied, offering him a sleeve to dry his eyes. "Let's go get that rabbit."

They might still be trapped on this island, but they were stuck here together. And if there was a way home, they would find it.

18. DIONE

They left Dione to the tepid water, which she used to rinse the blood off her body. A few of the deeper puncture wounds started bleeding again. They made her uneasy. Puncture wounds, because of their shape, were more prone to infection because they were difficult to clean well.

They would be rescued soon, though, and she'd have access to the *Calypso*'s supplies again. Now that they had found Brian's dad, they had a safe place to rest and wait. Surely Victoria would spare a Flyer to come get them now.

She stepped into the Ficaran-style clothes. They were too loose, and Dione took Oliver's advice about washing her own. Even with a few holes, they'd be much more comfortable. She bandaged her worst injuries and went to find Brian and Oliver.

They were butchering the rabbit in the dying light, and Dione noticed the soft light of glowglobes lighting the area, though all but one were unlike any she had seen before. They were varying degrees of translucent.

Oliver followed her gaze. "I only brought one with me. Propagated the rest myself. Again, I couldn't refine the resin like the Aratians do, but I manage to get good enough light out of them."

"Do you ever eat hyena?"

"It tastes terrible and the texture's bad, but it's protein. Once it's dried with the right herbs it's not so bad. Normally, I would've brought that hyena carcass back with me." He turned to his son. "I'll finish up here, Brian. You should go rinse off."

Still shirtless and covered in hyena blood, Brian made no argument. He headed in the direction Dione had come from. She stood off to the side, watching Oliver work.

"How did you survive out here?" she asked. "We've been here a day, and it's been one thing after another."

"There was a bit of an adjustment period, some close calls, and a lot of luck."

"You'll have to tell us about them," Dione said.

Oliver stopped his work for a moment and looked at her. "You don't sound Aratian, and I know you're not Ficaran. I've been gone a while, but not that long. Who are you really?"

Dione opened and closed her mouth to speak several times before finding the words. "I think Brian should be here for that."

Oliver peered at her, but returned to his work. "If my son trusts you, then I suppose that's good enough for me."

An uncomfortable silence hung in the air as Dione watched Oliver butcher the creature. Her mind wandered back to the attack in the woods, how one hyena hadn't fled with the others.

"What about the hyena that didn't flee?" she asked. "That tune you were singing. It repelled them, didn't it?"

"Yes, all except that one. Usually the song repels all of the hyenas, but every so often, one is completely unaffected. I make sure to kill any like that so they don't spread their genes. If this response to music is anything like what I've seen in maximutes and machi, which I suspect it is, then it's genetic. I've seen it before with machi. Every now and then we'd get one born that didn't know the songs."

"What happened to those machi?"

"They weren't much use as mounts, but I promise we didn't let them go to waste."

Dione didn't need clarification. "How'd you learn the song?" she asked.

Oliver gave a short laugh. "It was complete luck. After I got here, I explored a bit. At first, I was curious. Soon, I was just trying to find somewhere safe. Unfortunately for me, I stumbled into hyena territory. They chased me. They'd gotten me pretty good in the leg and were just waiting for me to tire out."

He rotated his leg to reveal chunky, white scars on the back of his calf. "I ended up collapsing at the foot of a sitac tree, you know, the ones with all those twisting branches and the yellow fruit? Completely filled with parrots. When the hyenas came close to finish me off, the parrots all started singing. It was like the hyenas had been shocked. They jumped and ran away faster than I could blink. I think it's because the parrots were so loud, because they don't flee my song that fast."

"That's incredible," Dione said. "Jameson must have built fail safes into these creatures. Protection for whenever he visited the island."

Oliver nodded. "I had enough time to stop the bleeding and recover. You know, finding that hyena song was one of the reasons I set up camp here. I had a way to protect myself from the hyenas, who, in turn, unwittingly protect me from other things."

Dione's mind immediately shifted to the images Bel had sent her. "Like the dragons?"

"You've seen one?" Oliver's tone had changed. "They shouldn't come this far south."

"When we were in the Flyer we got too close," she reassured him. "We haven't met any since we landed, though."

His shoulders relaxed. Dione didn't press him, but it was clear that he had encountered one of these dragons, and the occasion had left a lasting impression.

"Dione, come up here. I'm in the tree house," Brian called. "I've got something for you."

"Go on, I'm nearly finished." Oliver said.

"Thanks for the story," she said.

"My stories have to be enjoyable to make up for the food."

Dione climbed into the tree house. Once inside, she studied her surroundings in wonder. More glowglobes lit the interior. The floor was sturdy, but the walls were different. They looked to be made out of some sort of woven husks, meaning they were strong yet flexible. In one corner, there was a pile of dead leaves that Dione realized was actually a blanket made from hyena pelts. The bright green of the facsimile leaves had faded to a dull brown.

"Can you believe your dad built this place on his own?"

Brian smiled, pulling out a small jar from his pocket before looking at her. "Of course I can. This," he gestured to their surroundings, "is his thing. He can always cobble something together. Come here, I have something for you."

Dione inspected the jar in his hand. "What's that?"

"Antibiotic ointment."

"How'd you get that?" There hadn't been any in the cargo on their stolen Flyer; she'd checked when doing inventory.

"I swiped it from one of the crates they were loading back at the Vale Temple."

Dione wrinkled her forehead. "But why? It was already going to your people, so what was the point?"

"Because I couldn't be sure that Victoria wouldn't horde and ration it out only to those she deemed worthy."

That made sense. She remembered how Brian had hidden all of those meal bars they'd found in the Forest Temple. He'd been saving them for people in need instead of handing them over to Victoria. Dione smiled at the memory. Brian's desire to help others was one of the reasons she'd liked him in the first place.

Brian patted the floor next to him, and she sat. Without another word, he inspected her wounds and smeared the deepest punctures with the ointment. Her heart raced at his touch, and in the silence, she was sure he could hear it. She had to say something, anything to cover up the sound.

"How are you feeling?" she asked. "I mean, your neck." She gingerly touched the bright pink skin at his throat, feeling its unnatural heat.

"Everything's still tender. I washed off most of the aloe, so it's starting to sting a bit."

"Oh, I can go look for some more. We passed a few on the way here, and there's still some daylight left."

"No," he said softly, looking into her eyes, "stay here. I can bear the ache for a night. One more." He had finished with her arms and legs, leaving only the bite at her collar bone. It had been dangerously close to her neck, and now he leaned in close to tend to it.

Dione closed her eyes and willed the pounding in her chest to quiet. She had spent all day thinking about what he had said to her, replaying his words over and over: *I care about you, Dione. More than I've cared about any girl before.* It wasn't a big romantic gesture. He hadn't declared his undying love for her. He had been honest, and that meant his confession about Lithia had probably been honest, too.

That realization had been liberating. Brian had almost died yesterday, and she had come close today. Tomorrow would present the same dangers. Was it her fear pushing her to open up to Brian? Or did she really like him? She heard Lithia's voice in her head telling her to take a chance and live. She had nothing to lose.

With that realization, she allowed herself to feel what she'd been fighting. Brian's touch sent a pleasant fire through her whole body.

"Does it hurt?" He put down the jar, suddenly concerned.

Dione opened her eyes to find Brian was still close. "No, but I care about you, too."

She watched as surprise shifted into understanding. Dione didn't know who started the kiss, but it didn't matter. It felt like taking a drink of water on a hot day, longed for and invigorating.

Dione wasn't sure how long had passed when they finally broke apart. "Just to be clear, I'm not sharing."

Brian smiled and pulled her into an embrace. "Understood."

The sound of steps on the ladder announced Oliver's arrival. He laid out some fresh fruit. "Rabbit's almost ready, too."

"I'll get it," Brian said.

Dione took a bite of the fruit, and in another few minutes Brian returned and the meal began in earnest.

For a few minutes, there was only the sound of chewing. Dione hadn't realized how hungry she was until she found herself thinking about how amazing the rabbit tasted. Brian seemed just as hungry, and Oliver held his questions until they were finished.

He peered at his son, and the joy that had dominated his demeanor since their reunion faded away. Dione thought she

123

knew the source of his apprehension, but she waited for him to ask.

"You said that Dione is neither Aratian nor Ficaran," he said to Brian. Though phrased as a statement, it was clearly a question.

"She and a few others came here on a ship from another world," Brian said. "You were on the right track about our origins, but not about this island. The Farmer and Architect had a different reason for warning us away from it, but there's a whole empire of other worlds out there, from what Dione tells me."

Oliver laughed bitterly, the first sign of negativity she had seen from him. "I've been staring my mistake in the face every day for years now. But tell me more about these other worlds." He was looking at Dione now.

"There are hundreds, but I mostly know about my own home."

"Then tell me of yours."

Dione hesitated. No one else had asked her about her home. They'd been curious to find out the truth about their own origins, but even Brian hadn't asked her about home.

"I live on Lavinian, one of the core planets. It's a cluster where most of our Alliance—the government—works."

"Lavinian," Brian repeated.

"Is it beautiful?" Oliver asked.

Dione felt a pang in her heart and nodded. "Yes. I live outside the capital city, Haisukia, near one of the parks. It's a protected area of wilderness. The city itself…" She trailed off a moment as she visualized home in painful detail. "The city center was built all at once, so all of the buildings are uniform, but each one has its own architectural flourishes." She felt tears sting in her eyes, and she remembered the tour she had taken of the city with her father and uncle for her twelfth birthday. She had been a tourist in her own city, seeing everything through fresh eyes.

"Here, let me show you." She pulled up some pictures on her manumed, wishing she had a holo interface so she could really share them.

Brian and Oliver went through the pictures in awe. They had never seen a city so large. While the Temples were imposing, most of their houses were small. Even the Ficaran apartments could not compare to the towering buildings of home.

"I always knew there was more out there, just not so far away." Oliver returned the manumed to Dione. "I came to this island because I thought the truth was here. Maybe a city. The way that both the Farmer and the Architect wanted to keep us away from it, I knew I had to come here."

"But you never came back," Brian said. It wasn't an accusation.

Oliver put a hand on his shoulder. "It was never my plan to stay. The currents make it impossible to leave by boat, and after several attempts—different times of year, different launch points—my little boat was wrecked, and I nearly died."

"So you built a home for yourself here?" Dione asked.

"Not right away. Between attempts, I did some exploring. Shortly after my arrival, I realized that there was no one living here. Still, I was convinced this place was hiding something. That's how I found the giant ship."

"You saw the colonizer?" Dione asked.

"The ship in the middle of the island? Yes, but I couldn't get close. I nearly got burnt to a crisp just going to look at it."

"Dragons," Brian muttered.

Oliver rubbed a conspicuous burn scar on his arm. "They're vicious."

Dione and Brian exchanged a look. She knew what he was thinking.

"Dione got the Flyers working again, but we crashed here. Victoria won't send anyone to get us."

"My friends are working on a way to come get us, but it will take days, at least," Dione said. "Are you sure she won't change her mind now that we've found your dad?"

"I think we'll need a bigger bargaining chip than my father. She hates him. No offense, Dad."

Oliver shrugged. "She's not exactly my favorite person either. I've waited this long. I thought I'd never see another person again. Another few days won't matter."

"Dad, you remember the stories about the fabricator? How the Farmer used to leave and come back with supplies? Dione says it's real, and I think it's on the colonizer."

"I see where you're going with this, but it's impossible to get anywhere near it. I nearly died for a glimpse."

Brian wasn't deterred. The tenor of his voice changed, and instinctively Dione grabbed his hand. "A few days ago, the demons found us. At least, Jameson called them that. Dione and her friends explained that they're actually aliens called Vens. They attacked the Field Temple."

Dione saw the color drain from Oliver's face. "Bethany?"

"Mom made it, but we had to abandon the Field Temple once it was overrun. Those of us who survived escaped in the Flyers to the Mountain Base," he said. "It's like an undiscovered Temple. We teamed up with the Aratians against the Vens and killed most of them."

Oliver and Brian fell into quick conversation—more details, followed by a flurry of questions and responses about individuals whom Dione had never met, and some that she never would. She noticed a few tears well up in Oliver's eyes.

"Dad, there's more." Brian frowned. "Things got bad after you left. The rationing got stricter. Right now, we have a temporary alliance with the Aratians, but that's because of the Vens, and all of the Artifacts and supplies we found in the Mountain Base. Without a way to manufacture the things we need, rather than scavenge them, we're going to end up back in the same place. Starving. If you could see mom right now…" He trailed off.

Pain swept across Oliver's wrinkled face. "What's happened to her?"

"She won't work. She barely eats. She's weak," Brian replied.

"But there's more food now. She'll get her strength back." Oliver seemed to be assuring himself just as much as his son.

"Mom's sick. Lack of food is only one aspect of it. Plenty of others have been affected, too. So many lost children. I don't want that for our future. Finding the fabricator would be insurance for our people. A way to guarantee trade and cooperation."

"We need to get back," Oliver said. "We can head to the beach in the morning. A Flyer would be able to find us there easily. You say you've got a way to contact her? I'll speak to Victoria myself."

"She hates you," Brian repeated.

"I'll find a way to convince her."

"What about the fabricator? We need it."

"We'll stand a better chance with more people. The dragons are too much for us to take on alone."

Brian stopped arguing in order to yawn. The yawn was contagious, and a moment later Dione and Oliver followed his lead.

"I think it's time to get some rest. Take some pelts and get as comfortable as you can. We can talk again in the morning." Oliver took Brian's head in his hands and kissed his forehead. A tender display of affection. It made Dione ache for her own lost family, though it was her uncle rather than her father who first came to mind.

19. LITHIA

Lithia watched Cora from a distance. She looked fine, helping two young women with their tent. It was a far cry from what she had witnessed hours earlier.

"I'm worried about Cora," she said. "I thought she was going to kill that guy today."

"Took you long enough." Bel rolled her eyes. "At the time, you seemed pretty on board with killing a potentially innocent boy."

"You're exaggerating," Lithia said, returning the eye roll.

"Am I?" Bel replied. "I'm worried about *you*. You can talk to me. I've been through the same things."

No, you really haven't. Lithia swallowed her retort. Bel had been through something terrible, but something very different. Bel had lived because she had avoided the battle at her colony. Lithia had lived because she had fought through it.

"I'm fine," Lithia said. "Looks like Theo is putting dinner on. I'm going to investigate." She smelled something sweet and earthy, accented with garlic and some other scent she couldn't place. *Definitely worth investigating.*

Bel was wrong. She was fine. No matter what had happened during the battles, she was still Lithia. Underneath these thoughts, a nagging voice whispered back, *Are you, though?*

Cora was still finishing up with the tent, so Lithia took a seat by Jai, the only other person she kind of knew.

"What's for dinner?" she asked.

"Squash with herbs," he replied. "Hot food has a way of bringing people together, don't you think?"

She nodded. Others, lured by the scent and promise of food, were finding seats nearby.

Cora arrived and placed herself between the young couple and the middle-aged woman who had volunteered. She was speaking animatedly with them, almost as if she had forgotten the coldness she had displayed earlier. Lithia listened to their stories.

The couple, Taylor and Lena, had not been matched in the previous year. Her husband had not been bad to her, but he hadn't been good, either. He had died in the battle. They'd joined Cora because they'd heard about Will.

The woman, Amber, told her story in a few sentences. "They're gone. My husband and my oldest son. I just wanted to do something."

Cora squeezed Amber's hand. "I'm sorry for your loss."

"Maybe I shouldn't have left my daughters with their grandmother to join you, but I couldn't sit idle. I just couldn't." Lithia watched Amber trying to convince herself, but before she could offer any consolation, Cora spoke.

"You have given them the best possible example. They'll grow up knowing that you sought justice, even when others cowered. They'll see your example and realize that bravery is in their blood."

Lithia nodded in agreement. Jai leaned over and whispered, "See? I think she'd make a great Regnator."

"Yep," she replied. "Wait, this isn't some ploy to convince me you should marry her, right?"

Jai chuckled. "No, not at all."

"You promise?"

"I promise. It still feels strange—and wrong—to think that she needs me to become Regnator," he said.

"That's because it is wrong," Lithia replied.

The squash was ready, and silence fell around the fire as people passed around bowls of food. When she finished, Lithia made a show of yawning and stretching her arms. "The squash was delicious, Theo. Thanks. I'm off to get some sleep," she said.

"Good night," Jai said, when she stood to head to her tent.

"Thanks. Good night," she replied, smiling. As soon as her back was turned, the smile slipped from her face.

It won't be, she thought grimly, bracing herself for more nightmares.

***

"Lithia! Lithia, wake up!"

Lithia recognized the voice but couldn't place it. She was in a fog. She felt hot and fought the urge to obey. In another moment she was torn out of the hellscape of her dream, but she still couldn't breathe. She sat bolt upright and looked around at the unfamiliar canvas that sheltered her from the wilderness.

Bel's brown eyes were large with concern despite the fact that it must have been the middle of the night.

"What is it? Why did you scream?" Bel asked, sitting up and fumbling for her *pila* blade.

The memories rushed back to Lithia, the darkness, the bodies, the metallic stench of blood. It had been a dream.

Only it hadn't, not really. Those images hadn't come from the vids or holos. They'd come from the battle for the Field Temple. Or was it the Vale Temple?

"Just a nightmare," Lithia said. "I'm fine."

"You're sweating," Bel said.

A worried voice called through the tent canvas. "Lithia? Bel? Are you both okay?"

"Jai?" Lithia asked.

"Yes." She could see the outline of his shadow on the canvas.

"We're fine," she said. It was nice of him to check, though she wondered how many she had woken with her apparent scream.

"What happened?"

"Nightmare," she said again, feeling even more foolish now.

"Oh, I'll tell the others. We thought maybe it was the Vens or the Green Cloaks."

In a way, it was, she thought. "Okay. Sorry if I woke people."

"Don't worry about it." His shadow moved and disappeared, leaving her alone with Bel.

"Do you want to talk about it?" Bel asked.

Lithia settled back down and pulled the blanket over her arms. "Not really. Just your classic Vens-killing-everyone nightmare."

"I've had my share of those," Bel replied quietly. "It helps to talk about it. At least, it did for me."

Lithia was silent for a long time.

"Bel? You still awake?"

"Mm-hmm."

"You were dead. Dione, Zane, Oberon, too. Cora and Evy. Not peaceful dead, either, like at a funeral. The Vens had killed everyone and left you, bloody and broken, where you fell. I was too late."

"I've had that dream before," Bel said, "where I'm too late to save my family."

Lithia shook her head. "No, it wasn't like I was too late to save you. I was…" She hesitated. In her dream, it had been so clear. "I was too late to die with you."

They were silent a moment before Bel spoke softly. "I've had that one, too. It was just a dream, though."

"But it wasn't a dream. The bodies were ones I saw during the battle, but they had your faces." Lithia shivered as she vividly remembered the fatal injuries she had seen.

Lithia felt Bel's small hand wrap around hers and squeeze. She was trying to comfort her, but she wasn't very good at it. Lithia missed Dione. She put her free hand into her pocket and wrapped her fingers around the stone that Dione had given her, rubbing its polished surface with her thumb so hard that she was sure by morning she wouldn't have a fingerprint anymore. She heard Dione's voice echo in her head. *The flow of the river is like the flow of time. It smooths the rough edges of your pain.*

When she heard Bel's breathing slow and her hand grew limp around her own, she slipped out of the tent.

One of Theo's men was keeping watch. She thought his name was Felix. She saw him take a drink out of a bottle and went to join him.

"Should you be drinking while on watch?" Lithia asked. He was a good twenty years older than her, with rough hands and broad shoulders. He smiled, which emphasized the crow's feet at the corners of his eyes.

"Ever had *vigo*?"

"No, what's that?" she asked.

"It's a stimulant. Keeps away the drowsiness on a watch like this."

"Can I try it?"

"Not if you plan on going back to sleep. There's a few hours left before dawn."

"I'm definitely not going back to sleep." She shuddered at the thought of returning to the battlefield in her dreams. The man misinterpreted it as a shiver and handed her his blanket. She accepted it, along with the bottle. She tilted her head back and drank deeply.

"Go easy on it, if you've never tried it before."

She righted the bottle and heard the liquid slosh around inside. It tasted bitter but not unpleasant, and after a few minutes, she felt it working. Her mind lit up like Alliance Day fireworks.

She started composing a message to Dione. A long one. There were even paragraphs. She just needed to tell Dione. At the end, she read through it all one last time. Her vision blurred as she stared at it, and on impulse, she deleted the entire thing. Dione had enough to worry about. She was on her own island of nightmares and didn't have time for Lithia's whining. It was just a bad dream.

Lithia typed out and sent a new message: *Alive?*

"Lithia?" She recognized Jai's voice.

"What are you doing awake?" she asked.

"I couldn't get to back sleep. You either, huh?"

She shook her head. Everything she had tried to write to Dione was still on her mind, and she couldn't bear it. She just needed to talk to someone. "How am I the only one having nightmares? How can anyone sleep?"

"You're not the only one, trust me," he replied.

"Are you?"

Jai nodded. "They chase me, but I can't run properly, so they catch me. Luckily, that's where I wake up. I imagine that as things calm down and people begin to process everything that's happened, there will be more fallout."

"I'm sorry."

"What are yours like?" he asked.

She repeated what she had told Bel, and he just listened. Somehow, repeating it now that she was awake and had some time to process it, made her feel better. Just a little bit. She shivered. Jai hesitated, but then put an arm around her, drawing her in close.

Their closeness reminded her that he was technically engaged to her cousin. "Do you want to marry Cora?" Lithia asked.

"I would be lucky to marry Cora," he replied.

She read between the lines. "I'm not trying to trap you into saying something bad about her. I'm just curious."

Jai relaxed a little, but didn't answer for a long time. "I don't know. I don't have someone else in mind, and she seems nice enough, but it's strange. My sister gets along with her husband, but their match is functional, not loving. My brother hasn't been matched yet, and it's hard on him. You should see him with our nieces. He loves them to pieces and just wants a family of his own."

"So refusing Cora would mean you couldn't have a family?"

"Yes, but refusing isn't an option. It is our duty as Aratians to accept the results of the Matching. What's going on now, with the Match confirmations getting delayed, is completely unprecedented." He released Lithia from his embrace, and all the warmth from his touch dissipated into the cool night air.

Lithia bit her lip. She probably shouldn't say anything, but she couldn't help it. "Cora wants to end the Matching."

A crease formed between Jai's brows. "Really?" He looked a little hurt.

"I don't think it's personal," she said, realizing where his mind had gone. "She loved Will, and seeing the Matching up close shook her. Now with all of the new information she has, she doesn't think the Matching is necessary."

"There's a fine line for her to walk between tradition and pride, and this new information," he said. "I don't know where popular opinion will land on this one. My sister may not love her husband, but she's proud of her commitment to our traditions. My brother, on the other hand, would gladly give up the Matching if it meant he could find a wife on his own terms instead of waiting for his name to be picked out of a hat."

"I don't know if she can pull it off," Lithia offered.

"Neither do I," he said. "It would mean a new kind of freedom for a lot of us, one we never expected."

They sat in silence for a while longer until the dark blue of the night sky began to fade. Soon Bel would wake up.

"I'd better get back to my tent before Bel wonders where I am."

"In that case, good morning," he said.

Lithia took one more drink from the watchman's bottle and returned to her tent. She lay down and closed her eyes, but her mind raced. She didn't need to fear the nightmares if she didn't fall asleep.

20. DIONE

There had been a message from Lithia waiting for her when she woke up that morning. Dione replied with the expected response.

Lithia: *Alive?*
Dione: *Yep. You?*
Lithia: *I think so.*

The words were only somewhat reassuring. She decided to press for more information.

Dione: *What's on fire?*

It was their way of asking what was wrong.

Lithia: *Small dumpster at most. Nothing compared to the past few days.*
Dione: *Be careful.*

There were no more responses. Lithia was laughing it off, but Dione wasn't so sure. She had a bad feeling about her friend. She was more convinced than ever that they had to get off this planet before something finally happened to one of them.

Despite the unsettling messages from Lithia, Dione felt strangely at peace as she ate her breakfast. She'd opted to leave the tree house and sit on a nearby rock. Everything was green and vibrant, with splashes of color here and there. The air had that cool, dewy quality, untouched by the heat of the day, that only early mornings could offer. She felt like she was on an immersive vacation, the kind that rich people took where they stayed completely in nature. Except for the running water and electricity in their bungalows, of course.

She threw the pit of whatever fruit she'd been eating into the woods and licked the juice off her fingers, wiping the rest on her borrowed clothes. Her own were dry, and she slipped behind a large tree to change back into them.

Up in the tree house, Brian and his dad were chatting away. Upon seeing her, Brian gave her a smile that made her stomach do somersaults. She returned the smile and sat down next to him.

"Brian's filled me in on the communicators. We're about to call Victoria," Oliver said. Brian's smile evaporated at the sound of her name.

"Let's get this over with, then," Dione said.

The first two calls went unanswered. The third Brian placed to Melanie, who sounded like she'd been asleep. His news woke her up fast.

"Oliver? Is that really you?" Melanie asked.

"Yes, it's really me," he said.

"I have so many questions! How are you?"

"Ready to come home," he replied.

"Melanie," Brian cut in. "Can you find Victoria? She's ignoring my calls."

"Shocking." Melanie did not sound shocked.

"I know. But now that we've found my dad, she might be willing to come get us."

"I'll see if I can find her." They could hear Melanie walking, opening doors, and greeting people as she asked Oliver a few more questions about what he'd been up to on the island. After several minutes, she interrupted their conversation. "Found her," she finally said.

"What do you want now?" Victoria's voice sounded distant, but already annoyed. "If you're here to ask about borrowing a Flyer for the thousandth time, the answer is still no."

"Brian found Oliver. He's alive."

"I guess that explains the calls." Dione could imagine her scowl.

"They called me, too. They want to talk to you."

"I don't want to talk to them. They both made a choice. I'm not going to waste resources on headstrong fools who get into messes they can't get out of."

"What if he's found useful information?" Melanie asked.

"Like what?" Victoria was speaking to Melanie, but Oliver was the one who answered.

"The fabricator," he said. "It's here. There's a whole ship full of Artifacts."

"A whole ship, huh? I'll send someone to check that out when I'm ready, and they'll have orders not to pick you up. That's enough, Melanie. I've got to meet with the others." They heard a door slam.

"Sorry, guys, she's gone. That's the best I can do. Is there really a fabricator, Brian?"

"I think so."

"Stay safe. We haven't forgotten you, but it might take some time. So glad you're okay, Oliver! Dione, keep an eye on Brian. Someone has to stop him from being an idiot."

"You have no idea," Dione replied.

The call had barely ended before Oliver spoke. "We should wait. There are others working on a way to come get us. One that doesn't involve heading to the ship."

Brian opened his mouth to speak, but Dione cut him off. "It's the logical plan. At least wait few more days, just to see if Lithia or Zane can pull something off."

Brian nodded. She thought he was coming around.

"Do you think it still runs?" he asked.

"I've been wondering about that," Dione said. "See, normally, all parts of a colonizer are broken down and used to create and fortify the settlement. Jameson didn't do that. He parked it over here on this dangerous island, so that even if someone did use a Flyer to get here, the local wildlife would probably kill them. We can guess why he hid the fabricator here. He wanted to preserve that power of 'creation' for himself. But why leave all of these materials unused? Why keep the ship intact, unless he planned to fly it again? I think it still flies, or at least, it did when Jameson used to come here."

"Then we take it home, along with the fabricator."

"In a few days—"

Brian cut her off this time. "What if it can get you home, too?" He was looking directly into her eyes, but it was his words that gave her goose bumps.

The ache that she had been ignoring flared up, like fire exposed to a new source of oxygen. She had resigned herself to living on Kepos, at least for a while. She thought that maybe in time they could finagle something, either from the *Calypso* or the

Ven Marauder, or even go back up to the space station and look for something they missed. Something Jameson had hidden.

Was this how Brian felt, hope expanding like dust kicked up from a shockwave? Was this why he was so set on going to the colonizer now? She was beginning to understand. She knew it was stupid, that they should still wait, that her risk-taking adolescent brain was clouding her judgment, but biology didn't care about logic.

Oliver looked concerned. "Those dragons are vicious. We won't be able to get anywhere close to that ship. They've staked out that area as their territory. I live here because it's the area where I have the most control over the threats against me. Once we leave hyena territory, my knowledge is limited. I have no way to protect us against the dragons."

Something in those words set the gears of Dione's mind into motion. She closed her eyes to remove all distractions while she thought, trying to gather the wisps of information in her mind and fashion them into a cohesive idea.

Her eyes opened wide. "There's a dragon song!"

Brian looked confused. "What are you talking about?"

Oliver, on the other hand, understood her immediately. "How do you know that?"

She answered Brian first. "There has to be a dragon song. Think about it. The hyenas respond to musical commands just like the maximutes and machi. Jameson bred a song into the hyenas. It only makes sense he did the same for the dragons. He liked being in control, and he never would have left the colonizer here unless he was sure he could return to it unharmed."

Brian was beaming at her, but Oliver was skeptical.

"And what about when the song doesn't work? What if it's got a high failure rate? I've been killing off the unaffected hyenas for years. I encounter immune ones less and less often because of that."

"How did you even learn about the hyena song?" Brian asked. Oliver repeated the story he had told Dione about the parrots and his near-death experience.

"Oliver, why don't we try? If things get too dangerous, we can come back and wait." Dione tried to sound as calm and reasonable as possible. It felt strange to act as a bridge between father and son, between their cautious experience and reckless hope.

"All right. We'll go out tomorrow morning to visit nearby sitac trees and look for the song, but before we go anywhere near the dragons, we have to test it. Assuming it even exists." Oliver, despite his objections, looked eager. He was an explorer, Dione reminded herself. He had risked everything to come to this island and search for the truth that had been denied him. Nevertheless, he was still hesitant, which she again assumed was the result of his journey here. He had learned firsthand that risks had consequences, and expeditions didn't always turn out the way one planned.

Oliver left the two of them in the tree house to start making preparations. Brian was quiet, but moved toward her, hugging her.

"Thank you," he said.

"Don't thank me. I still think this is a bad idea, but I'm just as desperate as you now."

Home. Dione had tried not to think about it too much. An avalanche of what-ifs cascaded through her thoughts. What if the colonizer was beyond repair? What if Jameson had booby-trapped it? What if the dragons had damaged it? Despite her doubts, she couldn't pass up the chance to return home.

Before going to help Oliver with his pre-departure checklist, she sent a quick message to Lithia.

Dionc: *Heading out to find dragon song and see the colonizer. Cross your fingers.*

Lithia: *Crossed x2. And let Brian do the singing. He's better at it.*

21. DIONE

Brian had convinced his father to prepare for a longer trip than originally discussed. Just in case. The trio would trek toward the center of the island where the ship and dragons were, stopping at all of the sitac trees that the parrots loved so much.

Dione noticed something different about Brian as they left the treehouse. Even though they were headed toward danger, he seemed more relaxed than she'd seen him before. His father's absence had weighed heavily on him, she realized. Or maybe now that he had been reunited with his father, the burden of care for his mother and colony could finally be shared.

Dione liked Oliver. As they made their way toward the dragon-infested heart of the island, he asked her questions, not only about the worlds outside Kepos, but about her own education and research. She couldn't imagine how it felt to be as curious as she was about the world around her, but find herself faced with disapproval and false information at every turn. Even among the Ficarans, this island had been considered cursed, forbidden by the Farmer and the Architect alike.

In the middle of their conversation, Oliver held up a hand. "Can you hear that?"

Dione nodded, but it was Brian who spoke. "Parrots."

"We're getting close."

They followed the chattering birdsong for several minutes, but before she even saw the sitac tree, she could smell it, a fragrance so thick she could taste it. Fruity and sweet, with just enough tang to make her mouth water. Less than a minute later, she caught sight of bright pink blossoms standing out against a background of dark, leafy fronds, with yellow fruits perfectly sized to fit in her hand.

Dione eagerly strode forward, curious to get a closer look at the marvel before her, when a bright blue blur collided with her collarbone, knocking her off balance. She shielded her face with her arms and closed her eyes, but the angry fluttering of wings grew louder until she felt something brush against her arms.

She felt a hand on her shoulder, guiding her backwards, but she didn't open her eyes and lower her arms until the fluttering stopped.

"They're singing. Listen," Brian said.

Sure enough, Dione recognized the melody. Even though the three of them were humans, the hyena song had the parrots' desired effect. Within the minute, Oliver was leading them away again.

The song had been eerie, and after a few minutes, Dione realized why. "They synchronized their song. All of the parrots sang as one."

"Pretty cool, huh?" Oliver smiled. "The next tree I know of is a bit of a hike, but we may get lucky and pass a few parrots on the way."

They did not get lucky. Dione was getting tired, but Brian looked rough, too. She had little scabs all over her arms and legs from the hyenas, and the deeper bites on her legs felt sore as she walked. Between the moss and sundew, Brian's neck seemed to bother him. Everything ached, and Dione wished she had argued harder for a longer rest period before going back out.

They reached the next tree around midday, shortly after taking a lunch break. This time Dione approached slowly, searching for that sweet spot that would make her a threat to be sung away but not dive-bombed.

Again, the parrots sang in unison, and Dione's heart sank a little.

"Wait. Do you hear that?" It was Brian. He stepped forward to stand by her, which only made the parrots get louder. Then she heard it. Like that one kid in primary chorus who was always a measure behind, there was a single parrot singing a different tune.

"Can you make it out?" she asked.

He closed his eyes a moment, and she could tell from the creases at their corners that he was straining hard to pick out the errant melody.

After a moment, he replied. "No."

"Me neither," she said. She could see him hesitating. "What is it?"

"What about your stun rifle? We could stun birds until we isolated the one we need."

Dione looked at the branches of the sitac tree. "I think the others would attack or fly away before we could get them all."

"What if we stunned the one with the different song?" Brian asked.

Dione visualized what might happen if they went that route. "Even if we could figure out which one that is, the fall might kill it. I didn't think about that before. I don't want to kill these parrots."

Dione had learned that there was a time and place for killing, and that had been a hard lesson. She didn't want to kill anything she didn't have to.

"What if we eat it afterward?" Brian said. She turned with eyebrows raised to see him trying to hold back a smile. "I'm sorry. I know what you mean. There's no need. There are more sitac trees, right, Dad?"

Oliver nodded. "I don't know their locations, but the noise of the parrots and fragrance of the fruit make them a little easier to find."

Dione took a deep breath. She wanted to remember what these trees smelled like when she made it home.

22. DIONE

The third sitac tree they found was huge, its branches more full of parrots than fruit. The parrots puffed up at their arrival, and a few attacked, flapping and squawking. They seemed more aggressive than the previous two flocks, perhaps as a result of increased threats. She was certain there was a second, maybe even third, melody under the hyena song, but again the familiar tune dominated the area.

"We ought to head back. We're too close to dragon territory to stay out here unprotected."

"One more," Brian said.

Oliver sighed and acquiesced. "Lead the way."

Brian closed his eyes a moment, considering their next moves.

In the moment of stillness, the ache of exhaustion settled into Dione's limbs. She hoped the next tree wasn't far. "Maybe we should head back and rest," she suggested, "then come out tomorrow, refreshed."

"We're close to one. I know it. This way."

"How do you know?" Dione asked.

"I can't explain how, but there's—it's like a template," he said. "There's a place where these trees like to grow. I can't describe it, but now that we've seen a few, I'll know it when I see it."

"All right," she said. She believed him. When they had been on the Ven Marauder, trying to shut down the transmissions array, he had noticed a pattern in the Ven symbols that clued them in to the backups that were preparing to send a transmission. "I'm right behind you."

Brian led them toward the center of the island. When Oliver had been guiding them, he had kept them from going too far in. They passed a few burnt patches on the ground before Oliver spoke up. "We're too far in. We need to turn around."

"If we want the dragon song, we have to find parrots who are in a position to repel the dragons," Brian said.

"I get what you're saying, but we can't defend ourselves right now," Oliver said. "It might take longer, but we can find the song outside of dragon territory. These parrots clearly travel from tree to tree."

"We're close. Just another minute."

Dione and Oliver exchanged a look. They had to turn back, but how to convince Brian?

Oliver opened his mouth again, probably to reason with his son, but Brian spoke first. "Hear that?"

The parrots. He'd done it, found another tree. Relieved, Dione turned to smile at Oliver, but the smile disappeared from her face when she saw that he'd gone pale. His terrified eyes stared back at her. No, beyond her.

That's when she heard something else, closer than the parrots. A clicking noise, followed by a loud thump. Dione was already turning when Oliver whispered to Brian. "Dragon."

When Dione turned all the way around, she caught sight of her very first—and hopefully last—dragon. The first thing that caught her eye was its tail, clicking and thumping, creating sparks, but not lighting anything on fire yet. Its green-brown scaly body was only as large as a medium-sized dog. She guessed it weighed ten to fifteen kilos, but its fat, rounded snout and bright yellow eyes looked mean.

"To the tree," Oliver said. "Run!" As if it had been waiting for a reason, the dragon opened its mouth and spit, but Dione had already turned to run. She heard something wet smack across the ground. Accelerant. The fumes were unpleasant, but in another moment they were behind her. After another click-thump of its tail, Dione felt the warmth of fire at her back.

In the noise and chaos of their escape, Dione had lost the direction of the tree. Oliver and Brian had, too, judging by their hesitation. All three stopped for just a few seconds, their heavy breathing the only sound they made.

She heard it again, the frantic squawks and chirps of the parrots, their only hope of escaping the dragon that was bounding after them. She looked back to gauge its pursuit and cursed.

Dragons. Plural.

"There are two of them," she said. "Let's—"

She turned, expecting to sprint away toward safety, but collided with Brian's outstretched arm. Good thing, too, because three more dragons had headed them off. The other two dragons arrived a moment later. Brian pulled her close to him, and they put a large tree to their backs.

Before Dione could process even the need to form a plan, all five were spitting accelerant, but not at her. At the ground. Odd.

The acrid fumes set her stomach churning, and she felt a little light-headed.

The moment she heard the click-thump of their tails, her heart pounded as she understood. A circle of flames sprang up from the ground around them. The flames were low, but with the dragons just on the other side, there was no escape.

One of the beasts spit again, this time aiming directly at Brian. A spout of flames erupted as the accelerant passed through the ring of fire. Brian dodged, and the flames left a dark scorch mark on the tree trunk.

"Climb!" he said.

"What if the tree catches fire?" Dione asked. The fact that it wasn't already on fire amazed her, but Jameson had apparently created a few resilient tree species to ensure the dragons couldn't burn everything on this island. They'd been fortunate to get backed up against one.

"We're not going to be up there long," Brian replied. "But we're toast if we stay on the ground."

He boosted Dione into the tree like she weighed nothing. She gripped a thick branch overhead and pulled herself out of the way so they could follow. Another jet of flame singed the grass at the base of the tree, catching Oliver's pant leg on fire. He quickly put it out and climbed into the tree. He was nimble for an older man, but his foot slipped on some loose bark and he toppled backward onto Brian.

She could see another dragon readying its shot. Wrapping her legs around the sturdy branch she was straddling, she leaned back against the thick trunk and aimed the stun rifle. She doubted it could penetrate the hide of the beast, but maybe...

She fired, hitting the ground at its feet, startling it and thwarting its attack. The stun rifle didn't have much kickback, but holding herself in the tree without using her arms was no easy task. She lowered her weapon and steadied herself with one hand on the branch above her. She relaxed her muscles a moment before again clenching the branch between her thighs in order to fire again.

Her shots kept missing—her aim was mediocre even under the best conditions—but they were enough to agitate the dragons. Brian and his dad made it into the tree. Maybe if she kept it up, she could scare them off. She braced herself with her legs, freeing her hands once again.

Without warning, something struck her right thigh. One of the dragons had climbed up behind her and whacked her with its tail. She screamed, pain radiating through her leg. Her grip on the thick branch loosened, and she began to slip out of the tree. She let go of the rifle in order to try and grab another branch, but the tiny twig she managed to pull against snapped off in her hands. As she slipped around the branch, her left foot caught against the small stub left by a broken-off branch. Her right thigh throbbed with pain, and she was holding almost all of her weight with her left foot.

She was now upside down, the rifle's shoulder strap digging uncomfortably into her neck. All of her focus should have been on righting herself, but she caught a glimpse of movement above her. In the chaos, she had failed to keep count of the dragons on the ground. *That sneaky little beast.* She was going to kill it and wear its hide for boots.

"Hang on," Brian said. "Dad, get Dione. I'll get the dragon."

Dione didn't know how Brian was going to beat the tenacious little beast, but the broken-off stump she was bracing all of her weight against was starting to dig painfully into her foot. She needed to right herself before anything else.

"I'm taking the rifle now," Oliver said, removing the strap from her neck. It was an immediate, albeit small, relief to have the discomfort and weight removed.

"I'm going to support some of your weight. Try to grab that branch above you and right yourself." He pushed against her back, and she reached up to grab it. She tried to ignore the sounds of battle up above as she wrapped her fingers around the branch.

"Now see if you can get a foot on this branch down here."

She saw what Oliver wanted her to do, but now that the blood wasn't rushing to her head anymore, she could see Brian and the dragon battling. If she could pull herself up, she could help him.

Ignoring the pain in her leg, she climbed back up to her former perch. Brian and the dragon were one level of branches above her, both knocking down bits of loose bark and dead twigs. She moved around to the other side of tree. She knew she wouldn't be able to sneak up on the dragon as effectively as it had sneaked up on her, but flanking the creature couldn't hurt.

She climbed up a bit farther and waited. Brian saw her, but didn't say anything. He looked at home up here in the branches, dodging the dragon's attacks.

"We need to go, son. Any minute they'll realize Dione's not firing on them anymore."

Oliver's voice had been the perfect diversion. The dragon had focused in on the new noise, forgetting her. She pulled up on the branch above her and swung her feet forward, catching the wretched little lizard square in its ribs. It flew out of the tree and thudded on the ground. She hoped it hadn't survived the fall.

"Let's go," Brian said.

She followed him through the branches as best she could. Oliver was already on the ground on the other side of the ring of fire.

"Come on!" he said. "They've gone to check on their friend."

Once they were all on the ground, the trio sprinted toward the sitac tree.

They're right behind us! Dione thought, breathing too hard to shout. Her legs burned from the exertion.

"We're almost there!" Brian had overtaken his father in the lead position.

When the first cerulean blur charged Brian, she felt relief. He swatted the parrot away with his hands. The next moment, they stopped attacking Brian and focused on a familiar foe, the dragons. The parrots began to sing in eerie unison. The dragons on her heels stopped abruptly, angrily thumping their tails and backing away. Moments later, they ran off into the woods to escape the beautiful, unrelenting power of the parrots' melody.

Oliver panted, bracing one hand against the sitac trunk. Dione collapsed next to Brian, who was laughing between deep breaths. Eyes sparkling, he pulled her into an embrace and kissed the top of her head.

"We found it, Dione. Drink it in with your ears. The dragon song."

23. CORA

Cora took a deep breath. They were waiting on her. She'd led them all out here, yet she wasn't sure what they expected from her. From the conversations she'd had with them yesterday, she got the feeling they were just as angry and heartbroken as she was. But did they have the stomach for what would come? Did she?

"Beautiful morning, isn't it, cuz?" Lithia tossed her a polla as she approached, Bel by her side. "Big day."

Cora bit into the fruit. Underripe and a little too tart, but still tasty. "Are you all right? I heard from Felix you didn't sleep well."

"Just some bad dreams. Nothing a cup of coffee can't cure."

Cora noticed Bel frown at that. She barely knew Bel, but she always seemed to be frowning.

"What kind of bad dreams?" Cora asked. She knew she was prying, but that didn't stop her.

"The kind I don't want to talk about." The smile vanished from Lithia's lips for a few moments before she changed the subject. "What's the plan for today?"

"Simple. Get to Raynor Farm, kill the Green Cloaks," Cora said, counting off the steps on her fingers.

"Are you sure you want to do that? Why not arrest them?" It was Bel who spoke.

"There can be no peace while the Green Cloaks are alive."

"And you think their deaths will bring you peace?" Bel asked.

"Yes, I do."

Lithia shifted to stand next to Cora. "I agree with Cora. It's the only way to be sure. Kill the Green Cloaks. Kill the Vens. Happy ending."

"I hate the Vens as much as anyone, trust me, but the Green Cloaks are human," Bel said. "With all of the lies and misinformation floating around this planet, can't you see how they were confused? Don't you think that learning the truth could change their minds?"

Cora stared at Bel a moment. The girl made an interesting point, but truthfully, she didn't give a damn how confused the Green Cloaks had been or if there was a chance to redeem them. They had set off the flaminaria mines prematurely. They had let the Vens into the settlement. They had earned the deaths that were coming for them.

Her hands curled into fists. "I don't care if they can be saved," she said. "They are responsible for killing Aratians."

"The Vens killed the Aratians," Bel replied.

"Someone lights a match in a barn, and you want to blame the fire for burning it down?" Cora asked. "The Green Cloaks are responsible."

"The Vens are more than an uncontrollable force, like fire. Remember, they came here to kill you. They would have found a way, with or without Green Cloak help," Bel said.

Lithia scoffed. "So we kill the Vens next."

"Bel, the Green Cloaks killed my father in cold blood," Cora said. "I don't have it in me to forgive that."

Bel had no response to that. Cora watched the girl rub the intricate, floral tattoo that snaked over her hand and up her wrist. She braced herself for the next argument, but it never came. Instead, Theo ordered everyone to break camp. If they left now, they'd reach the farm by late morning.

***

Cora's stomach churned with nerves. They were coming up on the farm, and Theo had taken his men to scout ahead. They had been gone for a while. Too long. Cora's heart pounded, pumping her anxiety through her veins.

"Try and relax," a voice said. Cora recognized it as belonging to a Ficaran. The big one. Colm. "Theo is a capable warrior. He will be back soon." Then he added in a soft voice, "You are making the others nervous. They look to you."

She turned to glare at him. Who was he, a Ficaran, to chastise her? When she looked past him toward the others, though, she realized he was right. Many who had joined her had their *pila* blades drawn or easily accessible by their sides. Lithia, who was standing next to him, nodded in agreement. She relaxed her shoulders and took a seat on a nearby rock.

It was strange to accept comfort and advice from a Ficaran, but it had been a strange and awful few days. She comforted herself by remembering that, soon, she would have closure. She and all the other Aratians that the Green Cloaks had betrayed would be able to heal.

She felt the tremble of the ground before she saw the brown and black fur of the maximutes returning. Controlling her impulse to jump up, she stood and walked calmly toward Theo. They met at the edge of where their group was waiting.

"How many are there?" she asked.

He exchanged a looked with Felix before answering. "Six."

"So few," she said, uncertain whether to be glad. Either there had been fewer traitors than expected, or not all the Green Cloaks were here. She was about to share her concern with Theo when she noticed how pale he looked. "What aren't you telling me?"

"They're dead," he replied.

"All of them?" She was glad that the others hadn't heard this revelation yet.

"Yes. The Vens beat us here."

"Show me."

"Cora, it's not a suitable sight for a young woman's eyes."

"I thought you were a man who could follow orders," she snapped. "Show me."

Theo nodded, though he seemed more sad than angry at the command. "The first body is in the field. He was killed trying to escape."

Cora paused a moment to scratch her maximute behind the ear, and he licked her face in thanks. He had been a gift from her father. No one had wanted to claim the pup because his fur was all black, a bad omen in Aratian culture, and so her father had found a solution. He had given the pup to Cora and taught her how to ride, though few women got maximute training. Cora didn't get to ride him often, so he spent most of his time with the cavalry, not as a war dog, but as a companion dog. *Even the fiercest warriors need a friend*, she thought.

She climbed atop the beautiful maximute and fell in next to Theo. She assured everyone they weren't in danger and ordered them to stay put. She could tell Lithia didn't like that idea.

Once they were out of earshot, she turned to Theo. "Bring Asher to the front. Elijah's son. I want to see his reaction to the first body." Cora told herself it was to judge his innocence, but a large part of her wanted him to feel a piece of what she had felt as she watched bodies fall around her that night. In her heart she already knew he was guilty.

"A sound idea," Theo replied, gesturing to the Ficaran who had been keeping an eye on him. After the battle at the Vale Temple, Theo recognized and trusted some of the Ficarans he had fought alongside, including Colm and his men.

Asher was loaded onto Theo's maximute. His hands were tied behind his back. He tapped his fingers to his thumbs, and his eyes darted about as soon as the farm came into view.

"We have something to show you," Theo said to him. To Cora, he added, "We'll ride ahead, and come back for the others."

Cora climbed atop her maximute, and the three were off. She hadn't been out to the farms in years, but the slick, white barn was just as she remembered it. In the distance beyond it was a short row of five small farm cottages. The barn was built from the same pre-fab material as many of the Ficaran apartments, but the houses were made from local materials.

They walked down a row of the field. The crops here were new, barely ankle high and littered with weeds. This made the body easy to see at a distance, along with the two large carrion birds, omens of the state it was in.

The birds flew away at their approach, and Cora glanced toward Asher. His fingers stopped their twitching. Once his eyes settled on the body heaped on the ground, he couldn't look away. Once they were close enough, she lowered herself from her maximute. She wanted to hesitate when the smell hit her, but she resisted and breathed through her mouth. *This is what a leader would do*, she thought. *Right?*

Her inspection was brief. After seeing so much death in the past few days, she thought she would have become more inured to the sight, but it was just as gruesome as ever. This was the unmistakable work of a Ven. She had seen enough shredded bodies to know the aftermath of Ven claws. She thought the face was familiar, but she couldn't look at the body for long enough to remember the name.

Theo helped their prisoner down from the maximute. "Asher, do you recognize this man?"

The young man clenched his jaw, and for a moment, Cora doubted her conviction that he was a Green Cloak. Then, he broke. His chest heaved and his lip quivered. He clumsily fell to his knees, his hands still tied. Theo moved to restrain him, but there was no need. The boy was sobbing into the dirt.

Cora felt strange. Asher deserved this. A part of her was glad he felt grief, even if it was only a fraction of her own. The strange part was the connection she felt to him in the moment, the sadness of seeing someone in so much pain, even if he deserved all of the pain in the world.

They killed your father, she reminded herself. *They betrayed your people.*

Hot rage burned away her pity. Asher lay in the grass, silent tears running down his cheeks. She towered over him on her maximute. "So you are a traitor. Let's go see if everyone's dead. How many of you were there?"

He didn't answer.

"How many more bodies did you find, Colm?" she asked, her tone matter-of-fact.

"Five more besides this one."

A fresh sob escaped the boy's lips. "They're all dead?"

"How many were here?"

"There were six here when I left." His voice was lifeless as the corpse next to him.

Something about the way he phrased it nettled her. She put it together, but Theo was already speaking.

"Here. There are more elsewhere?" he asked.

"Yes."

"Where?" Cora demanded.

"You'll kill them, too," Asher replied.

"What do you mean 'too'?" Cora interjected. "Vens did this. You chose them over your own people, and this is how they repaid you."

"We chose truth, or at least a chance for it, but we were wrong. By the time we realized what the Vens were it was too late."

"What do you mean?" Cora asked.

"We thought that the Vens would recognize and appreciate our help, but they killed the ones who let them in. By then, it was too late to do anything."

"You never even talked to them?" She raised her eyebrows. "You assumed they were what you thought."

"Anything was better than the Farmer and Michael, or so we thought."

Cora balled her hands into fists, nails digging into her palms as she fought to keep control of her emotions. "Then what's your plan? Why not confess?"

"You would have rejected us. We just wanted to find a way to come back home."

"That's true. We don't want you back," Cora spat. "What were they doing out here?"

Asher was silent.

"Tell me!" she shouted.

But Asher wasn't listening to her. He was staring glumly at the farmhouses, no doubt thinking of his fellow Green Cloaks.

Wrong as it is, she thought, *even traitors can be mourned.*

24. CORA

Theo called one of his men with the communicator and ordered them to bring everyone to the farmhouses. He heaved Asher back onto his mount, and he and Cora headed to the nearest cottage. The other bodies were inside. She hesitated at the door, examining a smear of dried blood on the doorframe.

"Cora, you don't need to go in there," Theo said.

"I do," she replied.

Cora thought that she was prepared, but she was mistaken. In the field, the blood had soaked away, into the ground. Inside, it had coalesced into sticky, coagulated pools. She didn't try to reconstruct what had happened. All she could process was the blood and the smell and a pair of lifeless eyes that stared right through her.

Cora burst back outside, and though free of the metallic stench, she could not master the urge to vomit. She knelt next to a small bush and heaved, aware that most of her traveling companions had arrived and were watching her.

Jai hopped off his machi and hurried to her side. "Here," he said, offering her a handkerchief. She took it and heard Theo's men explain to the group what had happened.

Her eyes were watering. No, she was crying. She wanted Jai to leave her alone. She turned away, but he put a hand on her back, saying nothing.

"I wanted this. I wanted to kill them all." More death, more blood. If the Vens hadn't gotten here first, it would have been on her hands. "I know I would have killed the Green Cloaks if they'd been alive. If they'd resisted at all. I wanted them to die, but—" She took a shuddering breath. "Ever since my father died and Will died, there's been this hole in my heart, and I thought this would give me closure."

"But that hole is still there?"

Cora nodded. "This isn't justice. This is horrible. War is horrible. Will we ever have peace?"

"I think once the Vens are all gone, we stand a chance," Jai replied. "Do you really think they'll leave us alone?"

"We can't be sure, but the Icon works again, which will protect us. Plus, from what Lithia has told me, the Vens never sent out a message about this place. No others know we're here." Cora knew that they were safer now than before, but there was a fear in her heart that would never go away. Not after everything she'd seen since the Vens arrived.

"Then I do think we can have peace," Jai said. "We've got Ficarans here helping us, and a few weeks ago, I never would have imagined that was possible."

"If the alliance lasts."

"Make it last. You'll be in a position to do a lot of good once you become Regnator."

She raised her eyebrows at him. Had he not figured it out? "I don't think I can accept the conditions of becoming Regnator." He would understand her meaning. *I cannot marry you.* She would never marry him or anyone else. She thought he understood that.

"Then change the rules," Jai said.

Cora cocked her head, sizing him up. If he was saying what she thought he was, then Jai wanted to reform the Matching as well. Maybe he did understand.

A door slammed. Cora hadn't noticed Lithia or Bel enter the house, but she heard them leave. Bel turned back to the house and closed her eyes. Maybe she was praying, or maybe she couldn't get the images out of her head. Lithia kicked over a box of empty glass jars, causing them to shatter in a beautiful tinkling noise, then stormed off into the field.

"I'm going to check on her," Jai said, "but I'm here if you need anything. I want to be your friend."

"I know. Maybe we can be friends. Lithia needs a friend, too, especially with Dione gone. Make sure she's okay."

As soon as Jai left her side, Theo emerged from the next house. He looked troubled, but not like before. Concern, not disgust, wrinkled his brow. In another moment, he was by her side.

He spoke quickly, in a low voice. "There's something I need to show you," he said, leading her into the house. Once inside, he led her to a back room and opened a storage trunk.

Cora felt her pulse quicken. "The missing guns! What were they planning? Is that why they were out here? To collect these?"

"It looks that way," he replied.

"What did they need the guns for? You don't think they were planning a rebellion, do you? After everything we've been through?" Cora felt her anger returning, but the day's bloody images pushed back against the tightness in her chest.

"I do. I've already called Benjamin to warn him, but I don't think we should stay here much longer. We ought to return home. Hopefully Asher will give up his companions."

"Good. We need to tell Colm about the guns, too," she said. "They belong to the Ficarans, and I don't want to risk our alliance, especially in the face of everything that's going on."

Theo stopped her before she could leave. "There's more." He produced a small framed screen. An Artifact. She'd seen one of these before. It displayed pictures and played back video.

"Did the Green Cloaks leave a message? Is there video of their meetings?" Maybe they would be able to identify the rest of the traitors.

"No, it's something else. Look." Theo turned it on.

The first picture was a young woman Cora recognized. Her grandmother. But where was she? Behind her was a window that looked out onto the stars. Like a house in space.

Theo showed her the next picture. And the next. Some had gleaming towers in the background, others had too many moons. The clothes were unlike their own. Every face she recognized belonged to an elder.

These had not been taken on Kepos. Here was proof of what Lithia and the others had told her. She had believed them, yet somehow seeing these pictures made it real in a completely different way. Now she knew their tales weren't just wishful thinking.

"There's more," he said.

Now she was watching a recording of a beautiful young woman. Her face was familiar, and after several seconds, Cora placed her.

"She's the grandmother who arranged my hair for the Matching. Victoria's mother."

It seemed to be an interview. Off camera, Jameson asked why she had decided to join his expedition.

"I want to get out there. Explore! In all my life, I've never left the station." The woman laughed and grinned for the camera.

Cora couldn't watch anymore. According to Lithia, Jameson had taken away this woman's memories. She had been promised a new life, but Jameson took that promise too far when he brainwashed her and the others after he brought them to Kepos. Every Aratian and Ficaran needed to see this.

"Jameson really was lying," she said out loud. Theo just nodded. She looked at him closely. "He wasn't a god. I have no claim to rule." There had been some small part of her that hoped that Lithia was wrong about Jameson, but there was no disputing what she had just seen.

"Yet we need a Regnator," Theo said.

Cora shook her head. "No, we need a leader. I knew this was coming. This changes nothing, only makes it more urgent. When the others find out…"

What had she been expecting? She couldn't attack traditions like the Matching and still hope to preserve the ones that gave her power. Was it worth this to eliminate the Matching?

Yes! was the resounding response in her head.

"There will be chaos," Theo said. "Many people are confused, questioning what they know about the Farmer. The attack has shaken them, and many don't want to believe that the outsiders are telling the truth, that our whole way of life is a lie."

"It's not our whole way of life. Just the Matching and the Regnator."

"And the reason for our conflict with the Ficarans."

"If our conflict is based on lies, that's all the more reason to strengthen our alliance."

"And who will do that?" he asked.

They walked back to the front of the house. Cora thought about the implications of this video. She would have to step down. "I know that I cannot take over my father's position, but—"

"You have to. Without succession, there will be chaos. Power-hungry wolves like Elijah will step in. Your father had flaws, but he was a fair leader. You are like him."

They emerged into the bright daylight, and she blinked a few times as her eyes adjusted. She looked around for Elijah's man— no, his spy—Gavin, but didn't see him with the others. It made her uneasy.

"I'm just a girl to them," she said. "Especially now that I'm not the granddaughter of a god. No one will allow it."

"You fought alongside us. You're out here now. Look at these other women who follow you. These things were unthinkable before the Vens came."

"I'm not sure even that's enough. But there's something else." Cora hesitated, looking up at Theo. "I feel relieved, knowing that I won't become the Regnator. Once I show these images to our people, all doubt will be gone. The Farmer will be established as a liar."

"We need a plan before anyone else sees these pictures. For many on the fence, confused about who we are and where we come from, it will be proof enough. But if men like Elijah get a hold of it…"

"There will be rebellion," Cora finished. She closed her eyes, glad that Elijah didn't have the display. What if that had been his plan all along? Between the images and the guns, he could do some real damage.

Theo nodded. "More fighting and more death."

Cora needed to put a plan in place. Her people's doubts about the Farmer were strong after the Ven invasion, but faith could soothe doubt away, especially at such a painful time.

"Theo?" She turned over the Artifact in her hand. "What if there's another copy?"

25. ZANE

Zane was in the *Calypso*'s common area taking a break by himself. Oberon was "in the middle of something" and had promised he would be up soon, but that was half an hour ago. Zane didn't mind. He had gotten used to spending time by himself when he lived on the freighter with his parents. In fact, it was overwhelming being around so many people all the time. Dinner with nothing but his thoughts was a welcome break.

An incoming call on Zane's manumed surprised him. It was Bel. Had they made it to the farm already? His fork clattered onto the half-empty plate.

"What's wrong?" he asked, heart pounding.

"Nothing's wrong," she replied. "I just missed you. I wanted to hear your voice."

Zane smiled. This admission did nothing to reduce his heart rate, but calmed away his anxiety.

"I miss you, too."

"How's your arm? How are things on the mountain?"

"Arm's doing okay. Hurts a lot, but I can move it pretty well. Oberon's too caught up in the *Calypso*'s death to think of much else."

"Right. Poor Oberon," she said. "Don't tell him, but Dione and Brian found his dad, and now they're going to try and fly the colonizer off the island."

"Didn't she say the dragons lived near the colonizer?"

"Yup." Bel offered no additional information. "That's why I don't want you to tell Oberon."

"Interesting." It was the nicest thing he could think to say. After spending time with Dione, he was beginning to doubt how smart she actually was. Or maybe Lithia's impulsiveness was rubbing off on her. Dione had been growing on him, but her selfishness—running off to the island without a thought of how it would affect the rest of them—had stopped that. Either way, Zane had nothing nice to say at the moment, and Bel didn't like it when he shared how he really felt, so he was glad she changed the subject.

"Any news on the translation of the datacore?" she asked.

"Nearly complete."

"Have you checked my hypothesis? Do the Vens have a predator?"

"No. Until the datacore is completely translated, I can't really do that."

"What do you mean?" Bel asked.

"The program translates in passes rather than going straight through. It's kind of like an antique printer. Instead of printing the whole image, it lays down all the cyan ink first, then magenta, yellow, and finally black. If you're missing a layer, the image won't look right. Same with the program. Afterward, it tries to smooth out the translation, like an artist adding highlights and shadows. We could look at what she has now, but it wouldn't be very readable."

"Well, I wouldn't presume to look at your masterpiece before it's ready," Bel teased. He could hear the smile in her voice, and that made him miss her even more.

"She'll be finished once you're back, and we can look at it together."

Bel laughed. "You know what, Zane?"

"What?" he asked, pushing his food with his fork.

"No one has asked what the Vens are up to. They escaped. Are they going to live in the forest now? Take up residence in the Forest Temple?"

"I don't think the ragtag group you've described to me should go hunting them down," he said.

"I agree. The Vens killed the Green Cloaks at the farm we were investigating before we arrived."

"Aren't the Aratians taking precautions?" Zane asked.

"They've got guards, but the Ficarans wouldn't leave them any guns," Bel replied.

"Victoria keeps going on about how the Aratians stole them. She's in a bad mood. Keeps threatening Benjamin."

"Well, we found the guns, so that crisis should be averted. She was sort of right. The Green Cloaks had them here."

Zane furrowed his brow. "What were they planning?"

"Nothing good. But now I'm more worried about the Vens. Why come all the way out here if they were just going to attack the Aratians again? I looked at the maps, and this farm is in between the Vale Temple and the Marauder."

Zane pushed his plate away and pulled up a map. He shook his head. "That's technically true, but it's not the most efficient route. Why would they swing so wide?"

"Maybe killing their comms has interfered with their sense of direction, too," Bel offered.

Zane pursed his lips. He didn't think that was right. There was a much more direct path for them to return to the Marauder. "What if they're regrouping before another attack on the Aratians?"

"We shouldn't underestimate their desire to kill us. Can Sam track them?"

"Not a chance," he said. "Integrating the *Calypso*'s hardware into the base is going smoothly so far, but Sam is taxed. The translation's almost done, but even if I stopped that, she'd have to do a lot of communicating with the space station and run a lot of simulations with the data. Basically, it would be a mess."

"I see your point." Bel sighed. "I know you wanted to wait for me, but this is too strange. See what you can find out from the translation, even if it's a blurry image. It might give us some hints on what they're up to. Alliance intel hasn't been as accurate as I would have hoped."

"I already explained, the translation isn't complete," Zane said.

"There has to be something to look at, even if it isn't pretty."

"This isn't going to be fun," he warned her.

"I never thought it would be," she replied.

***

Zane and Oberon had spent the better part of the previous night and the morning working on migrating the *Calypso*'s heart and soul over to the Mountain Base.

Oberon put a hand on Zane's shoulder after they made the final adjustments, just in time for a late lunch. "Thank you, Zane. You were right about the *Calypso*. She never would have flown again. At least this way, she'll get to do some good."

Zane gave him a sad smile. "I know what it's like to love a ship. I really meant it when I said it was like an organ transplant. She'll live on in this base and do a lot of good."

"Thank you, professor," Sam chimed in. "It makes it easier to say goodbye, knowing that the Icon will remain functional."

Though Zane was tired, there was a new task on the docket.

"Oberon," he said. "I was talking to Bel, and she wants to know what the Vens are planning. They attacked the Green Cloak hideout."

Oberon stroked the short beard that was growing on his chin. "I would have thought they'd attack the Vale Temple again, but with their communications disrupted, they might have a different directive."

"Bel thinks the Alliance intel is misleading," Zane replied. "She thinks we might be able to find something in the datacore. The translation is still rough, but we might get lucky."

Oberon's expression grew dark. "She's probably right. Things haven't been adding up. I'll make sandwiches and brew us some coffee. Download what we've got so far on some tablets and meet me in the common area."

Zane did as he was told. Tired as he was from the long hours they'd put in, he was ready to look into what they had found. He wasn't like Dione. He didn't trust the Alliance to share important information with the masses. He knew what power did to most people, and it seemed to him that the people who sought power were often the ones who didn't deserve it.

Like he'd predicted, most of it was gibberish—bad translations that didn't make much sense. He was one and a half cups in to the pot of coffee when he found something. A list of conditions. If this, then that. They looked like contingency plans, or recommendations for how the Vens should react to certain conditions. "Oberon, take a look at this."

They didn't have the entire list, but it looked endless. "This explains when they can use their armor and weapons," Zane said. "They didn't use armor at the Field Temple—probably because there was such a small number of Ficarans, based on what I'm reading."

"What's the point of all this?" Oberon wondered aloud, skimming the list. "Why preset these conditions rather than let commanders make their own choices?"

"Maybe the Ven commanders aren't the ones calling the shots," Zane said. He knew what it felt like to be micromanaged, but this was an extreme.

"What conditions cause them to retreat, like they did at the battle for the Vale Temple?"

They both perused the list, but Zane figured it out first.

"If long-range communications get disrupted, they prioritize reestablishing communications over anything else. That allows them to transmit combat data back to the citadel ships." He looked up at the professor. "This must mean they're heading back to the Marauder."

Unlike the Invader, which Sam had blown up with the Icon, the Marauder was still in one piece, out in the field where the Vens had landed it. Brian and Dione had disabled its transmissions array. Zane was still bothered by the knowledge that the Vens hadn't gone straight there. What had they been doing in the meantime?

Oberon was already making plans. "Victoria's got some people at the Marauder, but they're techs, mostly. Enough fire power to fend off Aratians, but I'm not sure about Vens." The pair looked at each other, at once giddy from their discovery and terrified by its implications. The general consensus had been that the Vens would try attacking the Aratians again. Now, that seemed extremely unlikely.

"How long do we have?" Zane asked. "What do we do?"

"Warn the Ficarans and the Aratians. Tell Victoria to send reinforcements to the Marauder."

"She'll never believe us. She'll think it's some ploy for us to get a shuttle."

"I know, but we've got to try. She remembers what happened the last time she didn't heed our warnings about the Vens."

"I can assist." It was Sam. "I'll tell her that I've detected Vens approaching, but she'll need to send out scouts in Flyers, as well as reinforcements."

"But you can't do that kind of surveillance right now," Zane protested.

"She doesn't know that," Sam replied.

Zane smiled. He was glad Sam was on his side now. He would miss her when she was gone.

***

When Zane reached the top of the stairs, he glimpsed a tall woman with dark brown hair in a high ponytail walking in the opposite direction.

"Victoria!" he shouted, jogging after her. She stopped long enough to turn, make eye contact, and continue walking. "Wait!"

"Like I told your professor, I'm not going to lend you a Flyer," she said.

"That's fine, Dione and Brian are idiots, anyway," he said. "We've got a real problem. The Vens."

Her mood shifted in a moment. She beckoned him into a room off the hall and closed the door. "Who told you?" Her voice was low and the down-turned corners of her mouth twitched. Up close he could clearly see the dark circles under her eyes.

"Told me what?" Zane asked.

Her eyes widened, and she stepped back, now angry she had given something away. Zane thought it was best to continue before she said anything else. "We were reading up on the Vens and discovered that they're going to attack the Marauder to reestablish communications."

Victoria frowned at him. "Your information is wrong."

Zane hesitated. He had pulled the info prematurely, but this wasn't a translation error or a misunderstanding. The simple language of the list he'd found had probably made it more translatable than some of the gibberish he and the professor had skipped over.

Then it hit him. "You know where the Vens are. You've gotten word. Not from Colm. Bel would have mentioned it. Not from your people at the Marauder, or you'd believe me." It took him a second to piece things together, but he figured it out before Victoria could leave the room. "They're at the Field Temple, aren't they? I know you sent teams to scavenge the settlement."

She pursed her lips, but nodded. "You might be the only clever one in your group. The Vens came back to the Field Temple. One of the teams stopped checking in, and I've withdrawn the others until we can send a group that is prepared to take them on."

Zane had no idea what the Vens were doing at the Field Temple, but he knew where they were headed next.

"Trust me, the Field Temple is just a pit stop. They're headed for the Marauder. They can't be allowed to reestablish communications."

Victoria peered at him, clearly skeptical. Finally, she nodded. "I'll send support to the Marauder."

"Call the Aratians, too. You'll need all the help you can get. All of Kepos is at stake."

She paused in the doorway before leaving him alone in the room. Zane wasn't sure if he had gotten through to her. He might have to make his own calls.

26. CORA

Cora finally felt like she had a moment to relax. Her uncle knew to be on the lookout for a Green Cloak rebellion, and they would be heading home soon. She felt confident that they would learn something useful from Asher. She wouldn't become Regnator. She had proof that the Farmer was a liar. *Jameson. Call him Jameson.* Names had power, after all.

Cora had shown Lithia the images of the original colonists, including their grandmother, Miranda Min. "What do you think people will do when we show them?"

Lithia scoffed. "Freak out. But that's normal. I think after the Vens, people will be receptive at least. They're looking for answers."

"If we don't have a Regnator, though, what do we do?" Cora asked.

"You can still have a Regnator. Maybe have an election? Draw names out of a hat? I'm not the best person to ask. There are a lot of options."

Cora opened her mouth to ask more questions, but the girl running toward them gave her pause.

"Lithia!" Bel was shouting. "Lithia! Oberon called."

"What's happened? Did he fix the *Calypso*?"

Cora could tell from Bel's expression that the news was grim.

"The Vens are approaching the Marauder. He needs our help. Cora, Oberon is requesting maximute support," Bel said.

"My uncle is still in charge, not me."

"He couldn't reach your uncle."

"That's strange," Cora said. She tried calling Benjamin, but there was no answer. She called Moira, who had been in her lab all day and hadn't seen him. She tried one of his aides, but they said her uncle was busy.

"Whoever Oberon talked to refused to let the Flyers land in the settlement," Bel said.

"Some alliance you've got there," Lithia muttered.

"I'll go," Cora said. "We have a few maximutes. Theo, will you and your men join us? It will take us some time to ride there. How long do we have?"

"I'm with you," Theo said. "I doubt the others will hesitate."

Bel nodded and stepped to the side to call Oberon and update him.

Theo put a hand on Cora's shoulder. "These others, though…" He gestured to the people who had come with them. Most were talking among themselves, looking a little scared.

"Does anyone want to join us?" Cora asked the group. "You're under no obligation to come."

Jai and Amber readily agreed, but the others had seen enough. "I'm sorry, Cora," said one of the girls. "We just can't. I thought we could help, but that was against Green Cloaks, not the Vens."

Cora gave her an understanding smile. "No one can fault you for that. Thank you for your support."

"Riding will take too long," Bel interjected. "Victoria's sending five Flyers, one for each maximute and rider, and whoever else can fit."

Cora looked around.

"So what happens to us? It's not safe to be out here." It was Gavin. He sounded angry. "Is your uncle sending a Flyer for us?"

"If you're so worried about safety, I wonder why you volunteered for a potentially dangerous expedition. As for my uncle, I haven't been able to reach him," Cora said. Repeating the fact set her stomach roiling.

"He picked a bad time to lock himself in his lab, then," Gavin replied.

Cora relaxed a little, despite the barb at her uncle. That certainly sounded like him.

"I'll ask Moira to go find him," she replied.

"I can take care of that. I have some friends in the labs, too."

Cora frowned at the spy. "Go ahead, then." He was up to something, but she didn't have time to figure out what. She needed to speak with Theo, coordinate the Ficaran pickups, and learn as much as possible about what was happening at the Ven ship.

"Theo, can one of your men return with the machi on his own? Maybe Taylor and Lena can help? Colm can ride his maximute, if that's all right." If Gavin did get the Flyer to pick them up, they would be leaving their machi behind. A single Flyer was not large enough to transport the rest of their group and their machi. A maximute and a couple of passengers would be a tight fit when the Ficaran Flyers came for them.

"Shouldn't be a problem. Machi are far easier to corral than humans." He gave her a grim smile. Taylor and Lena nodded in agreement.

Gavin approached her and spoke again. "I can take custody of the prisoner, too. No need to drag a liability into a fight with the Vens."

"No," she said. "He stays with me."

Gavin pursed his lips, but didn't argue the point further. She didn't trust him, but she supposed there couldn't be much harm in letting him catch a Flyer here. With only two of Theo's men remaining, she had to admit she would feel better if their Flyer retrieved everyone and took them to safety.

The Green Cloaks had murdered her father, and now several of them were dead. The rest would be taken care of when she returned home. She returned to her volunteers, her stomach in knots. She would have to face the Vens again, hopefully for the last time. The Vens had killed Will, but they had run. They were not omnipotent demons. Like all creatures, they had weaknesses. Like all creatures, they could be killed.

27. LITHIA

Lithia's head was swimming.

Distracting herself had worked too well. She'd been focused on helping Cora and rescuing Dione, and she hadn't bothered trying to anticipate where the Vens might go. She was so used to defense when it came to the Vens that offense hadn't crossed her mind.

Now here they were, on defense again.

She and Bel did not have maximutes. They did, however, have the guns they'd found. Since they were heading to help the Ficarans anyway, she figured it couldn't hurt to use them once they got there. Victoria would be happy to know that the missing weapons had been recovered, and she could have them after the battle.

When they won.

Much to Lithia's surprise, Gavin had pulled it off. The Aratian Flyer arrived first. Those who had chosen not to face the Vens again filed on board, but Gavin approached Cora for one more argument.

"Are you sure about taking Asher?" he asked.

"Yes, he'll stay with us for now," Cora replied.

"You would take him to the fight with his hands bound?"

"Relax," Lithia said. "He can stay in the Flyer. I don't want this Ven-loving Green Cloak jerk getting anywhere near them."

"Elijah will hear about this!"

Lithia rolled her eyes. "We know. That was the whole point of you joining us, wasn't it? I'm sure you've been telling Elijah our every move."

The man's lip curled in anger, but Lithia didn't care. There would be a reckoning when the battle for the Marauder was over.

Soon after, the Ficaran Flyers showed up, Oberon co-piloting one of them. Apparently the threat was dire enough that Victoria had relented and let him use a Flyer. More likely, she didn't know, and he was piloting this craft under her nose.

She and Bel squeezed in with Cora and her maximute. The other Flyers each took a maximute on board. Without ceremony, Oberon closed the shuttle and took off.

He spoke without turning to look at them. "One of the lookouts in the woods sent a warning. It gave us some time to get prepared, but the Vens are already there. If we hadn't known to look for them... I just hope we're not too late."

Lithia felt a strained hum as Oberon pushed the Flyer to its limits, so it was no wonder that they beat the others to the battlefield. They landed a short distance from the fight, but close enough that when the Flyer opened, they were met by shouts and gunfire. A howl pierced the air, as Canto welcomed Cora's maximute to the fight.

Lithia held a real gun in her hand this time, one recovered from the Green Cloaks. It felt heavier than her stun rifle, even though it was just a handgun.

She stood, ready to follow Cora on her maximute out onto the battlefield, but the second the light hit her, all of the sounds—the yelling, the cracks of gunfire—grew impossibly loud. She struggled to breathe. She leaned against the shuttle's frame and coughed, trying to catch her breath. Her head grew fuzzy, and nausea overwhelmed her. Leaning was no longer enough. She sank to the ground and turned all her focus onto breathing.

Not another battle. She couldn't do it. She wasn't built for it.

Get up, a voice inside her screamed.

"Lithia?" Bel was by her side. "Oberon, I think she's having a panic attack."

Lithia shook her head. This wasn't a panic attack. She was fine. She just needed a second, and she'd be fine. She tried to tell them, but she couldn't get the words out. The other Flyers were arriving now, each setting down at the edge of the battlefield.

"Go on," Bel said to Cora, who had hesitated when Lithia fell to the ground. "We'll be right behind you."

"Leg's asleep," Lithia managed, as she put all of her mental effort into breathing in, then breathing out, each breath slower and more controlled than the last. "Just need a minute."

"Bullshit," Bel said. "You're panting. You can't even stand. Stay here. We don't need you getting yourself killed."

Oberon was by her side now, picking up the gun that she had been holding. "It's okay to sit this one out," he said. "No one doubts you or your bravery."

Lithia took several deep breaths as she listened to Bel and Oberon talk.

"Where is he?" Bel asked. "I don't see him."

"Zane's inside the Marauder," Oberon replied.

"You're kidding! That stupid…" Bel's words were unintelligible as she ran toward the fray.

"Stay put. Don't get yourself killed. I've got to keep an eye on Zane and Bel." With that, Oberon was off.

Tears stung at the corners of her eyes, and her chest felt tight again.

Get it under control, that same internal voice said.

Even though she dreaded not being able to see what was going on, she closed her eyes and counted out her breaths. In for two, out for two. Then three, and four, and five, until she was back under control.

She stood slowly, but felt shaky on her feet. She had no weapon. She would be useless in the fight, and as much as she wanted to help, she couldn't. Every time she started walking toward the others, she stopped short, her chest gripped by some invisible squeezing hand. After minutes, she had only advanced a few meters.

She couldn't do it. Her body was refusing to cooperate. Her body was rejecting her mind's greatest desire, to kill the Vens.

Burning alongside her hatred for the Vens was rage at her own impotence. These monsters who had maimed and killed so many would accomplish their goal. Fly off, send a message to their kin, and rain down more death on Kepos. Fear locked her muscles even as she tried to will herself, then coax herself forward.

She failed. But maybe she could help in another way. As long as she kept her distance, she could breathe.

For the first time since landing, she took stock of the battle. The two dozen surviving Vens had their armor on, protecting their back plates, but they were also closely packed in formation, holding what looked like shields, as green as they were. Since when did the Vens use shields? Where had they gotten them?

Realization hit her as suddenly as her panic had. Their shields must have been fashioned from Ven plating, and where else would they have found that much plating than their dead? Had they truly looted the bodies of their brethren to create these shields?

Of course they would have no qualms about defiling their dead. They barely cared about preserving their own lives, let alone the bodies of their fellow Vens. It also explained why they had taken so long to arrive here, considering their head start.

They advanced slowly and steadily, careful not to break rank. It made them an easy target, but a powerful one. These were not the Ven tactics of the vids, but this was not a typical situation. Destroying their comms had significantly impacted their behavior. Now they had a new goal. It was no longer kill everything in sight. The Vens had to board the Marauder and restore the signal. Maybe even flee. Whatever their motivation in attacking colonies, it was only as good as their ability to share their experiences.

She couldn't let them broadcast the location of Kepos to more Ven ships. Lithia would prefer if the colonists didn't have to rely on the Icon to protect them against more of the invaders.

Lithia watched the battle rage around the mass of Vens, which easily stood a head taller than the human defenders. With their added shielding nothing could break through. The defenders didn't have a chance. The Aratians and Ficarans tried to draw out individual Vens, but their prior lapse in communication had been remedied. They were all of one mind, growling together in rhythmic steps toward their goal.

They're almost at the Marauder, Lithia thought. They'd moved through the defenders like a plow through a field. They were slow like this, but unstoppable, and far more deadly. Anyone who approached the column received a heavy blow to the head or abdomen. Though she was far away, she thought she could still hear the cracking of bones after each swing.

As the Vens approached the ship, the fighters' cries and charges became more frantic.

She saw a woman with a long, dark ponytail stand right before the Ven formation, firing a sidearm at close range into the green mass. Victoria. After a couple of shots, one near the front fell. Victoria stepped back, maintaining a consistent distance between herself and the Vens. Another Ven near the front stumbled. Victoria paused to reload her weapon, and suddenly, in a horrible, synchronized movement, the entire formation darted forward. One of the forerunners swung with its club, and Victoria crumpled to the ground.

A cry of anguish rose up from the defenders, but none of their efforts made a dent in the armored, green mass.

Lithia paced, fingertips at her temples. Even if she had the means to run in guns blazing, the last several people to do that were now lying on the ground, probably dead.

They must not get to the Marauder, she thought. *They cannot get to the Marauder.* She squeezed her eyes closed. *Think! They cannot get to the Marauder… if the Marauder doesn't exist.*

She opened a channel to Oberon, Bel, and Zane.

"Zane, can you fly the Marauder and have Sam destroy it?"

"I've been in here for hours trying to figure out how to do just that without triggering any fail safes," he said.

"And we can't blow up the ship?"

"No," Zane said. "I've already told you, this isn't some vid or holo. Self-destruct buttons aren't a thing."

"Understood. Is there some way to ruin the ship? So they can't fly it or use it to communicate?"

"Probably, but it will take more time than we have," he replied. "Dione and Brian tripped some fail safe in here when they disabled the transmissions array, and I don't want to rush and make things worse."

Worse? Lithia didn't think it could get much worse, but she was done arguing with Zane. That left one option. She wasn't entirely sure she could pull it off, but she didn't see an alternative.

"Zane, get out of there! Get everyone out now!"

She reentered the Flyer, empty except for her, and strapped in. She checked the emergency equipment, then did some quick math with the Flyer's help. If she crashed into the Marauder, it would be grounded, just like the *Calypso*.

"Lithia, what are you doing?" Bel shouted through her manumed.

"Helping," she replied, cutting Bel off. She needed to prepare.

You'll die. The thought came from the part of her brain that had kept her from running into the battle. The part that whispered her mortality into her ear over and over.

"Not today," she muttered to herself. "The math works out. I'll survive if I eject at the right time."

As she lined up her trajectory, she factored in the people on the battlefield. She wouldn't want to hit any of them. She'd need to make sure they were also out of the potential "splash zone." Maybe the Vens would be close enough that she could clip them on her way in.

Lithia's hands froze in the middle of their work.

The fighters couldn't make a dent in the Vens because they were in an impenetrable formation. If she broke their ranks, the fighters and maximutes could do their job.

She'd love to just drop a giant boulder on them, or blow them up with a case of flaminaria, but those were not viable options at the moment. She had only the shuttle, which she needed to be inside.

The Vens were like a battering ram, but so was she. Why destroy the castle when she could wreck the siege weapon? She could slam straight into them instead of the Marauder and eject, but that was even riskier than crashing into the ship. They were a smaller target, so she'd have to eject later. She ran the calculations.

She wouldn't be able to eject at all. In order to ensure she would hit her target, she couldn't leave the controls. She glanced once more at the Marauder, weighing her options. She knew what the better choice was.

She'd crashed these Flyers before. Several times, actually. The first time, the initial crash on Kepos, she'd gotten control back in time to moderate the speed quite a bit. When she'd skidded into the Ficaran hangar to rescue Dione, she'd also had a lot of control over speed. The lake hadn't really counted, since they had hovered over the water before abandoning ship. *Rest in peace, Nate*, she thought.

In every prior instance, she had been trying to mitigate the effects of the crash on the shuttle. Not this time. She took the shuttle up without another moment's hesitation.

"Sam?"

There was a several-second delay. "Yes?"

"I know you're weak, but make sure that my message gets through to everyone out there on the battlefield. Can you do that?" She took the Flyer up several meters into the air, just to get their attention.

"I… yes," Sam replied.

"Broadcast this message: 'Everyone, stand clear of the Vens! Make a path and give them room. Get back!'" she shouted. She saw confusion, hesitation, and finally compliance as they looked up to the Flyer in the air.

"Are you trying to get yourself killed?" Bel shouted through her manumed. "We talked about this. It's not worth it!"

"I'm not suicidal, Bel. This is going to work. Just get the maximutes ready to move in," Lithia replied. Her mother's voice popped into her head, reminding Lithia of her oft-repeated admonishment: *Brave and stupid share the same hospital bed.*

28. LITHIA

If it had been possible to rev a Flyer's engine, Lithia would have. Instead, she dropped back to ground level, plotting her course carefully, making sure she hadn't missed any changes in elevation. While a dive bomb might look more impressive, speeding along the ground, just meters above the earth, was a far more difficult maneuver.

But Lithia had more than acquired flying skills. She had an innate ability and acumen that she had been honing through practice, in sims and in actual flight. She took care to angle the shuttle to minimize the damage impact would have on her and the craft while still preparing a powerful punch for the Ven formation. She had never done this in a real craft before, but she felt confident as she accelerated straight toward the armored column.

Then, she crashed.

Straight into their formation. It was like running into a wall. She had certainly killed a few, but the sudden deceleration had truly tested the shuttle's safety restraints. She shouted in pain.

Oberon's panicked voice crackled out from her manumed. "Lithia, are you okay?"

She panted. "Still... in one... piece," she said between shallow breaths.

It was as if a white-hot poker had been shoved into her side. It was hard to breathe again, but this time it was because every deep breath she drew was accompanied by searing pain.

She tried to unfasten the safety restraints, but they were stuck. She tried to move and loosen her prison, but the second she strained against them, her ribs screamed in agony. She had certainly broken one or two. She was trapped, though she wouldn't have been any use in battle in her condition.

She watched the camera feeds to see what was going on. The late afternoon had faded quickly into evening, and it was getting hard to see what was happening.

Her gamble had worked, from what she could tell. The Vens had been scattered and disoriented. Many had even been killed. Even from inside her metal stronghold, she heard a maximute howl. Several others echoed the cry, and at first Lithia thought it had been Canto rallying the Aratian maximutes. Then, in the dying light, she made out a few massive, dog-shaped shadows bounding out of the forest toward the fray.

"Wild maximutes," she mumbled to herself. Now that the Vens were scattered, the furry beasts would be able to attack with ease. Apparently, the maximutes had been waiting in the wings until the opportune time. Dione had mentioned that wild maximutes had saved them once before, when they were looking for the professor.

Dione. What was her friend doing now? Was she in the middle of her own battle?

She could take this Flyer right now and rescue Dione. The thought energized her, and she ran a few checks.

She could probably—

She winced in pain. No, she couldn't. This Flyer would need serious repairs, and Victoria wouldn't let her so much as look at one after this. Better to wait it out and see if the Aratians would lend her theirs.

As much as she hated being trapped, she was glad to be out of the battle. She'd been surrounded by so much fighting and killing and dying that she didn't know how much more she could take. The chaos felt manageable from inside her broken metal box. She might be stuck, but she could still keep an eye out with the cameras. It was getting dark, but the cameras showed her the battle as clear as day.

It looked like her side was winning, thanks in large part to the maximutes. They were tearing apart the Vens, who lacked the numbers and coordination to efficiently take on the giant beasts. The Vens had planned for maximutes, but not for maximutes in combination with her shuttle.

When the last Ven fell, she didn't hear shouts of victory. Instead, she saw men and women going around with *pila* blades, systematically and decisively killing the last of the Vens on Kepos. They had learned well.

Something inside of her relaxed, a tension she hadn't realized had been there. Was it possible that the Vens were all truly dead? Were they really safe?

"Open up," Bel said from her manumed.

Lithia groaned as she reached for the release. Her relaxed feeling was giving way to a weak feeling. The adrenaline was wearing off.

Bel, Oberon, and Zane poured into the shuttle. Cora was conspicuously absent, but Lithia was surprised to see Jai with them. He cut her harness carefully with his *pila* blade.

Her newfound freedom felt good, yet everywhere the harness had touched her was tender. When she stood up, the room swam a little. She took Jai's outstretched hand for support as she got her bearings.

Oberon frowned at her. He opened his mouth as if to berate her, but sighed instead. No one spoke as he looked her over. "Damage report."

Lithia cracked a smile, careful not to laugh. He finally got her. No doubt there'd be some lecture later, but she had no regrets. She'd done what was necessary.

"Bruises from the restraints. Cracked ribs, probably, but I can breathe okay. It just hurts."

"You're still an idiot," Bel said.

"That makes two of us, where the Vens are concerned," Lithia replied.

"You may be an idiot, but you're one hell of a pilot," Zane said. "Who even thinks of doing that?"

"I appreciate that, Zane," she replied. "Mind if I list you as a reference once we get out of here?"

She forgot herself and laughed, then winced, leaning on Jai a bit more. They led her out of the shuttle, where a few curious Ficarans watched. A couple even clapped as she made her way out.

She was not the only one injured, but the death toll was astonishingly low. Some of the injuries would likely prove fatal in the coming hours. Victoria had already been taken back to the Mountain Base along with the other gravely wounded. Apparently the Vens had one-track minds. At the Field Temple and Vale Temple, all they did was kill. Here, they were only trying to get back to their ship, and they almost succeeded.

Theo handed her a drink, its steam visible in one of the Ficaran spotlights that had been erected for nighttime work.

She took a whiff. It smelled medicinal, and she recalled the last time she'd had some. Her ankle had healed in no time. Her ribs might need a few extra days, though. Everything was agony when she closed her eyes, but she closed them anyway. The conversation was moving too fast for her to follow, leaving her with her own thoughts.

The tea cooled quickly in the night air, and soon she was resting in the makeshift Ficaran camp, indifferent to where anyone else was, grateful that the pain might subside enough to permit sleep.

Before she nodded off, she managed to type out a few letters for Dione.

Alive.

Her friend wouldn't understand that this check-in was a little more meaningful than the others, but that was fine by Lithia. Sleep weighed heavily on her body. She had a feeling the nightmares would be too tired to come get her tonight.

29. DIONE

The parrots had settled down for the night, but Dione was wide awake. They'd been taking turns napping all afternoon and evening under the sitac tree, leaving the parrots and whoever was on guard to watch out for threats. Once the dragons had fled, the birds had squawked and sang, clearly irritated that she was in their space, but Oliver told them that as long as they didn't try to pick any of the fruit from the tree, or even off the ground, the birds would eventually calm down.

Despite the noise, she'd taken a very refreshing nap and was now wide awake in the late-night darkness. Brian stirred next to her when she sat up. She smiled.

It felt good that she didn't have to keep a wall up between them anymore. Being angry with someone was exhausting, especially when you still had feelings for them.

With a yawn, Brian rolled to his back and stretched his arms. He opened his eyes sleepily and grinned at Dione before sitting up next to her.

"What are you thinking about?" he asked in a low voice.

"You."

"And how cute I am when I sleep, right?"

"Yeah, the way you drool is adorable," she teased.

"I know," he replied, leaning in for a kiss.

His lips felt familiar, like they belonged on hers, and she lingered before breaking away. She nodded to his still-sleeping father, but he just laughed quietly and shrugged.

"He doesn't care," Brian said.

"I do." She rested her head on his shoulder, enjoying the peaceful moment.

"Fair enough." Brian instead took her hand in his. "Your hands are cold." His were warm, and she snuggled closer to him. Even though the air was relatively warm, nights on this island were much cooler than the days.

"I know. According to Lithia, I'm cold-blooded. She's not exactly precise with her biology vocabulary."

"Cold-blooded?"

"When an animal can't produce enough heat internally, they rely on external sources like the sun."

"Oh! Ectotherms," he said. "My dad taught me out of some of the biology books we have."

"Yeah, like snakes or lizards."

She and Brian exchanged a look, like they'd just had the same idea.

"The dragons are lizards. What if they're ectotherms?" Dione said.

"That's strange, though. Wouldn't a dragon be an endotherm, since they can create fire and all?"

Dione shook her head. "It actually makes more sense for it to be an ectotherm. Think about it. If you need an external heat source to survive, what's better equipped to live this way than a creature that can make its own heat source?"

"Check the listing," Brian said.

Dione pulled up the list of nightmares on her manumed. "Yep. Ectotherms. You know what this means, right?"

"They're slower when they're cold, like at night," Brian said. "Unless their fires keep them warm enough."

Dione nodded. "Even with the fires, it's nothing like the heat of the sun. It would also limit their range at night. They wouldn't stray far from their fires."

In their excitement, they had failed to keep their voices down, and Oliver woke up.

"What's all this noise about?" he asked, rubbing his neck.

"We think that the dragons will be slower at night since they're ectotherms," Brian replied.

"I think I know where you're going with this, but I hope I'm wrong," Oliver said.

"If we go now, we might be able to catch them sleeping, or at least lethargic. That, combined with the song, could give us enough of an edge."

Oliver grimaced.

Dione didn't blame him. She was anxious about encountering the dragons again, but this had been the plan all along. Why was Oliver so hesitant now? "What's wrong?" she asked.

"That encounter we had a few hours ago. It's the first time I've seen a dragon in years. I'd forgotten how vicious and clever they are. Even with the song, I don't see how we can do this."

"Aren't you curious?" Brian said. "Don't you want to get off this island?"

"Of course. But I'm not eager to get myself killed right after I've been found," Oliver replied.

"That ship is our only way home," Brian said.

Dione smoothed the goose bumps on her arms. If it still flew, that statement was true for her as well. "We've come this far," she said. "Isn't it worth it to check it out?"

Oliver nodded. "It is. These dragons are not to be underestimated, though. They're smart and ruthless, far beyond any other animal I've encountered."

The trio set out, walking slowly in the dark. With no flashlight, and hesitant to use a continuous source of light like a glowglobe that was impossible to turn off, they followed Dione, who led the way by the light of her manumed.

"The good news is that I doubt we'll run into any dragons out here at night," she said. "Based on our experience this afternoon, I'd say they're daytime hunters. Like most lizards, they're probably sleeping at night during the colder hours. Is there anything else we should be looking out for?" She directed her question toward Oliver.

"I don't go out at night if it can be avoided, and we're outside the region where I've spent most of my time. I can't give you many specifics, but the usual suspects, like snakes, spiders—oh, there are glider tree frogs, too."

"Glider tree frogs?" Dione asked.

"I don't think we're close enough to water to see any, but they like to pounce out of the branches. Had one land on my face once. Instant numbness wherever its hands and feet landed. It walked down my neck before I brushed it off, but it got the side of my mouth. I couldn't eat right for a week."

"Got it." *Snakes, spiders, and dive-bombing frogs. Oh my.*

"It's getting lighter," Brian said.

Dione looked up. Sure enough, moonlight spilled freely onto the forest floor.

"The undergrowth is thinning out," she said. This was not what she had expected as they neared the center of the island. Everything should have been getting thicker and wilder, but knowing what lay at the island's interior helped her piece it together.

"Look," she said, pointing to a blackened patch of earth. The scorch mark confirmed her hypothesis. "The dragons keep the jungle thin here."

"We're getting close," Oliver said.

After that revelation, their conversation ceased and Dione turned her manumed's light off. Not only could the moonlight reach them through the sparse canopy, the underbrush, a tripping hazard, was not as thick, undoubtedly thinned by periodic dragon fires.

An orange dot appeared in the distance, which she soon recognized as a fire. It was well into the night, but they had finally reached their destination. The orange dot flickered, and the hairs on her arms stood on end. A dragon had crossed in front of the flames. They were awake.

Oh, no. They lounged by the fires they had made. They were *warm.*

She tapped Brian, who was leading the way, on the shoulder, and whispered. Even though the fires were still distant, there could be others patrolling the woods.

"Those fires will keep them warm," she said. "I've got a bad feeling about this."

"We can't turn back when we're so close," Brian whispered. "Even if they're awake, we can still do this."

Oliver sighed. "We've come this far. All right. Let's go for it."

Dione grabbed Brian's hand and squeezed it. He was too much like Lithia. Headstrong and reckless. That was why they made a good team. On the other hand, she was naturally cautious. That was one of the reasons she'd come with him to this island despite being mad at him. She'd been worried about what he'd do if he came here by himself.

Still, she felt Kepos changing her, wearing away the part of her that hesitated, that looked before she leapt. She was beginning to doubt their decision to find the colonizer.

She pushed these thoughts aside and followed Brian and Oliver toward the fire. Dione pushed back against the tightness balling up in her chest by mentally singing the digits of pi to the tune of the dragon song.

They had the song. It was enough to banish the little pack of dragons that had found them earlier. It would protect them long enough to get inside the colonizer.

She had always imagined seeing her name followed by the letters *Ph.D.,* but now she imagined a new epithet to complement her name.

Dione Quinn, *Dragon Slayer.*

30. DIONE

Dione marveled at the sight before her. They had stopped just before the forest thinned into a mere smattering of trees. The earth ahead was charred and mostly bare, except for some small shrubs and clusters of weeds. The colonizer loomed in the background, clearly visible across the expanse.

The ship was massive. They had approached perpendicular to its body, near one of the ends. She couldn't see the other end, which stretched into the trees. Apparently, the dragons were concentrated on this side.

The area the dragons occupied was a wasteland, and everything smelled burnt. *Like Lithia's baking.* Dione smiled. Soon she'd be back with her friends. And Oberon. She'd have to own up to what she'd done, but she wasn't worried about that anymore. Helping Brian had been the right choice.

There was one large bonfire that burned bright enough to leave spots on her vision. A handful of dragons were retrieving sticks and branches that had been stacked in piles throughout their... camp? She didn't know what to call it. Then, with a flick of their heads, they tossed the sticks onto the fire.

They were watch fires, probably intended to keep them warm and alert at night.

Fascinating, she thought before catching herself. *No, terrible. Very bad news for us.*

The dragons were both terrible and fascinating. She would focus on surviving, but what a great subject for a paper—no, thesis—these dragons would be. Try as she might, she couldn't turn that part of her brain off.

Dione furrowed her brow and scanned the landscape. Dark shapes dotted the expanse in front of her, none of them moving. Only a few were awake and keeping watch, and they were on the opposite side of the colonizer. Why? Did they have predators? Dione hadn't seen anything in the wild or in Jameson's records that could stand against the dragons. A rival dragon clan? No, this had been the only bald patch on the island from above.

Brian was studying the dragon-peppered expanse before them. "What is it?" she asked.

"I'm not sure yet," he answered, still distracted.

She followed his stare, watching the dragons pace this way and that. "Do you—"

He cut her off. "They're guarding something."

"Yeah, but I don't know what they're guarding against. I doubt they have any predators here," she said.

"No, it's not that. The way they move. They're not focused on the outside. I mean they are, but not exclusively. They're *protecting* something. Can't you see it?"

Dione could not see it. Whatever subtle behavior or pattern he was observing was for his eyes alone. As curious as she was, she was also tired and so, so close to seeing Lithia and the professor again. She had been rehearsing what she would say to Oberon on their walk here.

"We should wait somewhere safer while we get our bearings," she said.

Father and son didn't seem to hear her. They were wrapped up in their own conversation.

"I see it," Oliver said. A moment later he gasped. "Brian, it's a nest!"

"Exactly!" Brian said. "It's not a typical patrol of the perimeter. They're guarding that specific area."

After another minute, Dione saw it, too. "The nest is inside the end segment of the colonizer," she said softly.

"We need to get out of here." Oliver's excitement shifted into fear. "However violent they were in the jungle, they'll be even more tenacious in their attack if they catch us this close to their nest."

"Dione says this ship is a colonizer," Brian said. "It brought the original colonists here. Jameson had a way of coming back to it safely, and we just found that. The song. We can do this. We'll never have a better chance, and even if we did wait days, maybe even weeks, for more people to come, do you really think a large-scale, assault-style attack would yield better results? Reducing or eliminating engagement with these creatures is the way to go. I'm going to check it out by myself."

"Brian—"

"No. Victoria will come in here, guns blazing with what little ammo she has left, and get a bunch of people killed. Or she won't come at all."

Dione disagreed. "I think she's learned her lesson. If we explain the nest to her, she'll exercise caution. She's not stupid."

"No, but she's too stubborn to take recommendations. I have a better chance if I go alone. This is stealth work, and I've spent years avoiding the Aratians while smuggling. I know I can do this," he replied. "Before any Ficarans come here and get killed because of my intel about the colonizer, I have to make sure the fabricator is here. I won't be gone long."

Dione bit her lip. She did not want to go near that colonizer, especially if the dragons had a nest inside, but Brian was important to her. He had risked a lot to help her and Lithia when they first arrived on Kepos. Since then, she had gotten to know him better. Despite his flaws, he had the best interests of his people at heart. Sometimes it made him stupid, though, like Lithia, always charging off on some idiotic plan. And just as she looked out for Lithia, she'd be there to help him.

She put her hand in his. "You don't even know what to look for," she said. "I'm coming, too. It'll go faster with me there."

"You don't have to," he said.

"I know," she replied.

"I'm going to stay here," Oliver said. He was watching the dragons with that same intent stare Brian had earlier.

"What?" Brian asked.

"Just while you scout things out. I can keep an eye on the dragons and let you know if anything changes. Watch your backs, in a way."

"Are you sure?" Brian asked.

"Yes, I'm sure."

Brian pulled something from his pocket. "Here's my communicator. Be careful."

Dione couldn't read Oliver's face in the moonlight, but he took the communicator from Brian's outstretched hand and hugged his son once more.

Brian and Dione headed into the woods, moving parallel to the massive ship. They were going to the opposite end. Based on the thickening vegetation, there would be fewer dragons there. Or maybe the entire ship was filled with dragon eggs.

Or baby dragons, she thought.

How many eggs did a dragon lay? Were baby dragons any less dangerous? Though her general anxiety about traveling the island had diminished since they found Oliver, she felt the tightness in her chest return.

To get her mind off that feeling, she turned her focus to the stimuli around her. The hazy quality of the predawn light. The sound of Brian's breathing. The textured exterior of the dark, metallic ship. It was divided into segments, and they had just passed the smallest one. The dragon-infested one.

Soon they passed the place where the dragon segment was joined to the next. The dragon-infested segment was smaller than the middle segment, though it had the same dark, textured exterior. Often colonizers had identical, self-sufficient segments so that different locations in a system or on a planet could be colonized, but Jameson had chosen specialized segments. The middle segment was longer and much bigger, but it was eclipsed by the first segment, which was larger still. She had seen it when they first arrived at the island via Flyer, but she had been so focused on the dragons, she hadn't realized how big it was. It made sense. Jameson had brought a few hundred people with him.

She glanced back at the smallest segment. She hoped that the separation between each segment had kept the dragon nest confined to that one, and that the fabricator wasn't in that section.

A twig snapped, and Brian stepped in front of her, as if to protect her. Dione resented that instinct for a moment, until she realized Lithia would have done the same.

A single dragon walked by, closer to the ship than their hiding place. It hadn't seen them. Something was poking from its mouth. Dinner?

No. It held a small bundle of sticks. *Incredible*, she thought. *They're gathering kindling for their watch fires.*

"Brian, the fire and claws aren't what make these dragons so dangerous. They're more than vicious. They're intelligent. I'll bet they make plans and anticipate what their prey will do. Back when they had us surrounded in the tree, I thought I was keeping them distracted with my shots, but now I'm wondering if it wasn't the other way around. They were keeping me distracted while their friend crawled around to the back of the tree to attack."

"That doesn't surprise me," he said. "I may be good at recognizing patterns, but you definitely have more experience with animal behavior."

"The good news is that there aren't many dragons over here," she said. They all seemed to be clustered at the end of the colonizer where they had left Oliver. She had only noticed a few sleeping at intervals near the ship on their walk.

"That's what worries me. The ones who are awake are probably out scavenging for kindling. It will be harder to spot them and avoid them. And the rest will wake up soon."

"You're right," she said, looking to where the ombré sky was fading from black to navy to light blue. "We need to get inside the ship."

Dione should have been worried about access, but she had a strong feeling that Jameson's hubris had taken over so that he hadn't programmed some key or passcode, relying instead on his magnificent and terrible dragons to take care of anyone who ignored the warnings about this island and discovered the colonizer.

She and Brian walked around the front of the craft to the opposite side, where they saw a clearly marked door. A few dragons slept along their path, but they crept silently around them, never getting close enough to startle the beasts awake. Few creatures would be foolish enough to invade their space.

As Dione had suspected, the door opened with no resistance. It creaked loudly, and she heard the dragons stir behind them, but they were inside before she could tell if any had woken and seen them.

The lights automatically came on, along with life support. The ship used very little power in the absence of its crew, but Jameson must have programmed it to maintain certain settings. Dione was unimpressed with the cold metal and industrial feel of the passageways, but Brian was awed. Though they were presumably safe, they continued in silence, whispering when necessary.

"What's it like to be here?" she asked.

"Well, on the one hand, this place pisses me off," he said. "Everyone lied to us about this island. Jameson because he parked this colonizer here, Sam because she knew how dangerous it was. But my dad survived here for years. We could have handled this place. We could have used the materials on this ship. We needed a fabricator. This ship would have settled the question of the Farmer long ago. The Aratians would have admitted the truth."

Dione sighed. She'd listened to her father and his friends complain about the steadfast ignorance of their political opponents too often to have that much faith in proof. "There will always be some who ignore the evidence in front of them. There's no guarantee."

"Yeah, but a massive space ship is gonna convince most people."

"You might have a point there."

They wandered a bit, opening doors and exploring the ship. This first section was huge. The first thing they noticed were all of the doors and branching hallways. They opened a few, and each revealed a tiny cabin that would have housed one of the original colonists that Jameson brought. A few contained personal effects, though most were bare.

"This level is just cabins, I think," Dione said.

There were five levels in this segment, and they had to climb a few ladders in order to get to the main one. This housed a conference area and a few larger cabins, probably intended for senior crew. Again, there was a maze of hallways, but they stuck to one of the two central hallways until they found the bridge.

Though the controls were not as confusing as on a Ven ship, the interface was old. It was familiar but clunky to her, like when she tried to use one of the school computers that ran a weird operating system that only tech nerds like Zane knew how to navigate. Once she got the hang of it, though, she had access to all of the unrestricted systems. Thankfully, that was most of them.

"Looks like this segment is safe. The doors haven't opened for decades, see?" she pointed to the display. "I assume that was Jameson's last visit."

"What about breaches?" Brian asked.

"None. Hull integrity in this segment is good. There are a few weak spots in the next segment and some weakening near where it joins to the final segment, but those won't be an issue in atmosphere. The final segment is… compromised, to put it lightly. "

"What's that?" Brian asked.

There were some warning lights flashing on the screen.

"That's the last segment. The hull has been breached, and there's a fire."

"That's not good."

"Could be worse. The sections of a colonizer were designed to detach. They can be piloted independently. We just need to hope that nothing vital is in that last section, and considering its size, we just might get lucky."

"So we can detach the last section?" Brian said.

"I think so."

"What about the fabricator? Is that in the last section?"

Dione did a little digging. This first segment was the primary one. It contained the bridge, cabins, and the jump drive. The final segment contained mining equipment and other gear. Jameson had probably had some grand plan for introducing more and more of that tech. The middle segment contained more cabins, the med bay, the mess hall, and Brian's holy grail, the fabricator.

"It's in the middle section."

"Good." Brian sighed in relief. "Let's detach the dragon nest and get out of here."

31. DIONE

The computer kept spitting back error messages.

Dione slammed a fist onto the console. "Come on! Can't we catch one break?"

"It won't detach, will it?"

"No, it won't. I could separate this segment from the middle one, no problem, but the fabricator's in the middle one. The middle segment won't separate from the dragon-infested one."

"Can we move the fabricator? How big is it?"

"Too big. The only way to bring it back is to take the whole middle section with us. The dragons must have done something to the separation mechanism, maybe damaged the wiring, fused the hull, I don't know."

Dione backed away from the console and sat in one of the many unoccupied chairs.

"Let me see," Brian said.

He was a natural. Sure, colonizers were supposed to be idiot-proof since they were often filled with hopeful farmers and miners rather than experienced space-flight personnel, but those people would have received weeks, maybe even months, of training.

Brian had no training, but he dove right in. He'd been watching her closely, and he had an intuition with tech that she could never hope to learn. Dione pulled her legs up into the chair and rested her head against them, closing her eyes. She would let him figure it out.

Her mind was buzzing with the new discovery she'd made while in the ship's systems. She'd checked the jump drive, and it worked. She could go home. They all could.

She sent a message to Lithia. *On the colonizer. The jump drive works! We can go home!*

Brian interrupted her thoughts. "I got it to run a diagnostic. The problem is fixable. It's just some damaged or faulty wiring."

Dione hopped out of her chair. "Great, I'll message your dad."

"Hang on," he said. "There's more. The bad news is that this can only be done from inside the last segment."

Dione scoffed, but Brian's expression remained earnest. "You can't be serious. There's no way we can pull that off," she said.

"I don't see another option."

"It's a pretty obvious one. Leave the fabricator here. There's nothing wrong with the mechanism that detaches this segment from the middle one."

For a split second, Dione thought about just detaching the first section, refusing to entertain any argument from him. It was what Lithia would have done.

"We need the fabricator," he insisted.

"No, you don't. This section is more than enough evidence of the colony's origins. Plus, the jump drive works. We can go home and tell the galaxy about you. Once people know you're out here, you'll be able to buy and trade for what you need. You could even get a fabricator. I bet I could find a way to get you one for free. A grant or something. My dad could pull some strings. A week ago, you didn't even believe this fabricator existed. Why is it so important now?"

"I thought no one would come out here. What about that Bubble you mentioned? Even assuming you're right, how long will it take?"

Dione didn't answer. Bureaucracy moved slowly, even she could admit that.

Brian continued. "I like this alliance with the Aratians. I like this peace. I like knowing that there's another meal coming for my family and friends. This is our chance to convince them all, beyond a doubt, that the Farmer was a liar. We can repair their tech. Even with Moira's help, our land won't be clean for years."

There was so much uncertainty in his eyes. "I think I understand why it's so important to you," Dione said, "but this is way too risky. The dragons are defending their nest. You'll have to walk right into it to pull this off. And we don't know how long it will take you to fix it. Or if you even can. If anything happened to you—"

"You're leaving me anyway! Why do you care?" Brian's eyes flashed. "If I die, you can take this first segment and jump back home. Win-win." He lowered his gaze back to the console.

Dione took a step back. "Is that really what you think? That I'm desperate to leave you behind? I don't want to lose you."

"I saw your message to Lithia. This ship will get you home."

Couldn't he see that this wasn't about leaving him? It was about returning to the life she'd been ripped from. "I don't want to leave you. But I. Don't. Belong. Here." She slammed her open palm on the console as she spoke those last words.

A long silence hung between them. Dione didn't know what to say next. "Brian, please. It's not personal. You get that, right?"

"I do." He wouldn't look at her.

She did not want to lose him, not to dragons, not by leaving Kepos. "Come with me."

Instead of speaking, Brian closed the gap between them and cupped her face in one hand. He kissed her, pulling her close with the other hand on her waist. She wrapped her arms around him in response, crushing her body and lips to his, wishing there were a way to get closer.

When they finally parted, she was breathing heavily, reluctant to let go. The austere gray interior brought the reality of their mission crashing back.

"I don't know if I can," he said softly, kissing her forehead. "But I want to."

Even that gentle kiss sent warmth tingling all through her body.

"Help me come up with a plan," he said.

Dione took a few deep breaths to focus her thoughts on the problem. "You need access to the attachment mechanisms. Where, exactly?"

Brian pointed to the ship map. "Here."

Dione studied the map alongside him. All of the segments were connected on the second level. There were two main corridors that ran parallel down the length of the ship on either side, and one segment separated from the next by a door that joined the corridors. The other levels within the first and middle segments were not connected.

"Okay, that's near the starboard entrance." Dione traced her finger along the starboard corridor. "If we follow this corridor down the whole ship, we'll be able to use the starboard door that joins the middle and final segments." She stopped and tapped the location on the map.

Brian frowned. "That's the issue. The starboard door is malfunctioning, but the port door works."

"If you go in through the port door, you'll have to head into the last section until you reach this cut-through," she said, pointing. "Here."

Brian cocked his head. "That doesn't look so bad."

"That cut-through is one of the more open areas of the ship. You'll be exposed."

"Only if the dragons find me."

"That's the other thing. See this?" She motioned to a flashing red icon; he nodded. "It's a fire indicator. There's a fire burning in that room."

"That doesn't mean they're in there. It could just be—"

"It has to be recent," she said. "There's not enough flammable material for a fire like that to burn unassisted."

"You think the dragons have been bringing in sticks and logs, just like we saw them stoke their watch fire outside."

"It would explain the fire. Maybe their eggs need to be warm," she said.

"So, if they are in that cut-through, how do I get past them? What about the maintenance tunnels? I'll need to use them to get to the attachment mechanisms anyway."

"Those are a death trap. I'd spend as little time as possible down there. If you meet a dragon in those close quarters, you can't run or maneuver away from them."

"And meeting one in the cut-through or corridor will be better?" He raised an eyebrow.

"You can run there, maybe even close some doors to buy you time to escape."

"If you say so. There's the dragon song, too."

"It won't work on all of them." After their last encounter with the dragons, she needed to be prepared to defend herself, even if that meant using lethal force.

"It might. If it was enough for Jameson, it will be enough for me."

"We can't count on it. Let me think," Dione said, closing her eyes.

She was a dragon slayer. What did she need? Claws that could rip through their hides. Maybe they could find a sharper weapon. She lacked the strength necessary to wield that kind of weapon, though. Were there guns on board? A chemical weapon? Would the medical bay have anything?

She was a dragon slayer. She would need thick, protective skin. Fireproof, just like the dragon hides. Ship work could be dangerous. Emergency response gear? Work gear?

I am a dragon slayer. Dragons were fire. She would be ice. No, she would be the absence of fire. A fire extinguisher?

"Dione?" Brian asked.

She opened her eyes, mind filled with ideas and questions. They needed to do a little scavenging. "I am a dragon slayer. Follow me."

32. CORA

The darkness suited Cora just fine. She was standing out in the field where her father had been killed, glad to be left alone. Unable to sleep, she had wandered out into the emptiness, a comfortable distance from the Marauder and the small camp that had sprung up around it. The grass rubbed against her ankles, making them itch, and a moon owl hooted in the forest.

The Vens were dead. The Green Cloaks were dead—at least, the ones who were at the farm, but that only lifted some of the weight from her shoulders. She knew there must be more, hiding among her people, and she had no clue how to find them or what to do about them.

They had blindly sided with the Vens because the Farmer hadn't told them the truth, and instead of answers, they had received the same violence as every other inhabitant of Kepos. There were gaps in Jameson's story that most people overlooked. Unpleasantness that people dealt with. That was life. The Green Cloaks had only been searching for truth, and that search had led them to do terrible things. She could almost understand their motivations. Could she bring herself to pardon them? Could her people forgive them? Should they? She didn't know.

A pale glow lit the horizon. Dawn was coming, and it was nearly time to interrogate Asher. Without Gavin around, she was hopeful he might betray some of Elijah's plan. The man was up to something. The more she thought about his words at the memorial dinner, the more uneasy she felt.

She took a deep breath and returned to the camp. In a few hours, they would return to the Vale Temple, once she knew what to do. The pictures, along with the knowledge that there were still Green Cloaks in her home, gave her plenty to consider.

Lithia had stumbled off to rest before she'd had a chance to thank her. As much as she wanted her cousin's input right now, she would have to trust Theo.

He, along with the other Aratians, had set up a little ways from the Ficarans. He was having a few words with his men outside one of their tents. She was hardly surprised they were already awake. Duty and discipline were Aratian virtues.

"Has Asher told you anything, yet?" she asked. Before they returned home she wanted to know as much as possible about the Green Cloaks still in the town, and what Elijah was planning. Many of his actions didn't make any sense to her. If he was against the Farmer, why was he so intent on keeping the Matching? Before she went back with the photographic evidence, she needed to anticipate how he and her other opponents might react.

"I wanted to wait for you," Theo said.

"Thanks."

The two entered the tent where Asher was now asleep. Or pretending to be asleep. Theo woke him, and he made a big show of yawning.

"Time to go home?" he asked.

"Not quite," Cora replied. "I have some questions for you."

219

"I don't have any answers for you," Asher said. "Just take me home."

For a second, Cora pitied him. She remembered his grief earlier that day, how, in a moment of anguish, he had confessed and given them more information than he had probably intended. "We need to know what your father is planning," she said. "He's the one leading the Green Cloaks, isn't he?"

Asher just frowned at her.

"He's the one who challenged me at the memorial dinner. He's your father. No one remembers seeing him during the battle," she explained.

"The battle was chaos. That's hardly proof," Asher replied.

"Here's what I don't understand. If he was so opposed to the Farmer and his teachings that he would sacrifice his friends and neighbors to the Vens, then why is he fighting me on the Matching? Wouldn't he want to eliminate such a strict tradition that the Farmer established?"

Asher opened his mouth like he wanted to reply, but just as quickly stoppered it. "Why should I tell you anything?" he finally said. "What good will it do me? I'm just going to end up like them."

Cora raised her eyebrows as she understood. "You think we're going to kill you."

He glared up at her, his face a dark mix of anger and pain.

"A day ago, that would have been true," she admitted. "I wanted to kill every last Green Cloak left on Kepos. You all would have deserved it. You still deserve it. You murdered my father. You murdered our people. *My* people. You are guilty, and have earned death as a punishment.

"But yesterday, I saw what that revenge would look like, and I couldn't stomach it. Maybe it means I'm weak, but after seeing those bodies, I realized that I want them to be the last." Tears stung at her eyes, but she reined in her sorrow. "You will be punished. Your comrades will be punished. You will have to earn your place back in society, but we will find you a place."

"You don't have the power to do any of this. You are not the Regnator," he said. "You should never become the Regnator."

"Because of this?" she said, holding up the digital image display. She let him watch as it cycled through the pictures, but he barely looked at them. He had seen it before.

He glared at her. "Yes."

"I agree. There need to be some changes around here, but Elijah isn't the one to make them. I get why he wants to get rid of me, but why has he aligned himself with a pro-Farmer group, a pro-Matching group, when belief that the Farmer is a liar is the one thing that unites us?"

There was a pause, but Theo's voice, not Asher's, filled it. "The enemy of my enemy is my friend," he said.

Asher didn't meet her gaze, and she took that to mean that Theo was right. After she'd halted the Matching, she had alienated a portion of her people. They needed somewhere to turn, and Elijah had taken advantage of that, even if he, too, hated the Matching. It would be worth it to pretend just long enough to secure power.

"So what's his plan? How is he going to take over?" Cora posed the question out loud, but she was almost asking herself rather than Asher, who had not been forthcoming. She would have to find a way to subvert Elijah while they found proof of his involvement with the Green Cloaks. His support made him dangerous to confront.

One of Theo's men popped into the tent. "Colm is about to leave, but he wants to speak with you first."

The man changed places with Cora and Theo, who met Colm at the edge of their camp.

"I wanted to thank you for helping today," Colm said. "Victoria is not doing well, and I need to return to the Mountain Base. Thank you for finding and returning the missing guns as well. Now that we know it was the Green Cloaks who took them, I think our alliance is stable."

"Thank you for helping us find them. It feels good to work together for a change," Cora replied. That was one crisis averted, at least. By returning the stolen guns and proving that it was the Green Cloaks, not her uncle, who had taken them, she had eased that tension. She had foiled Elijah's plan by disarming him, and she had also helped stabilize the alliance.

Colm left, and shortly after, she heard the gentle hum of a Flyer in the night. She stood in the open air for a few minutes and took a several deep breaths.

"We're getting nowhere," she said to Theo, once she'd gotten her bearings.

"We have to think like them," he said. "How would you take over if you were Elijah?"

She didn't want to think like Elijah. "Shoot everyone," she replied half-heartedly. "But we took his guns."

Theo clucked his tongue. "He's a weasel, not a lion."

Cora thought about what he had done so far: garnering support from those who opposed her and her uncle; stockpiling Ficaran weapons. He preferred to line up the pieces, but let someone else push them into place. "Discredit and remove the current Regnator. Challenging me at the memorial dinner was a start."

"But you're not the Regnator. Your uncle wields that power right now."

Cora snapped her head to look at him. "That's right. I've been thinking about this all wrong. I'm not the one in charge. Half the people won't recognize my authority without a husband, and the other half are beginning to doubt the Farmer and my family's right to rule anyway. Rightfully so," she added under her breath.

"So how would you weaken Benjamin's position?" Theo asked.

"Force him to balk at tradition. Let his niece abuse power she doesn't have." What else had Uncle Benjamin been complaining about? She'd been too involved in her own feelings and problems to pay much attention.

She gasped. "The guns!" She looked at Theo, eyes wide. "That was the plan. They took the guns, but maybe it wasn't to rebel. Maybe it was to frame my uncle. The alliance with the Ficarans gets more strained, then Elijah comes in, returns the weapons, and puts the blame on my uncle by claiming *he* was hiding them!"

"If the Ficarans already have their guns back, or at least most of them, what is Elijah planning to do?" Theo wondered aloud. "If the guns were never for rebellion, what is he planning?"

Cora thought about her uncle's failure to send maximutes and return her calls. She gulped, and the knots in her stomach tightened. "I think we need to ask ourselves what Elijah has already done?"

33. LITHIA

Lithia woke up in pain. This was nothing like her ankle, which had healed miraculously fast after the tea. Instead, she felt like she had run a marathon. Or at least, what she imagined she'd feel like if she ever ran a marathon. She was more of a contact sports kind of girl. It was still early, but the sheer exhaustion that had allowed her to sleep through the pain had worn off. When she read the message waiting from Dione, her good news took the edge off.

She hobbled out of her tent to find Cora already awake, speaking with Theo. More like murmuring, really. The makeshift camp was small, and it took almost no time to hobble over to her cousin.

When Cora saw her, she grinned. After such a rocky start to their relationship, Lithia found herself happy to be on such good terms with her long-lost cousin. She had gone from adversary to confidante in a short time.

"You look terrible," Cora observed, her lips pursed in concern.

"Everything hurts. But that's expected." Lithia pulled the collar of her shirt, revealing a dark purple bruis, as wide as the safety restraint that had kept her from slamming into the shuttle's console.

She recognized the guard she had spoken with the night she'd screamed herself awake from the nightmare. "Got any more of that *vigo* stuff?"

He chuckled and handed her a full bottle. "Keep it."

Lithia took a long drink. Everything still hurt, but now she didn't care as much. She felt awake and ready to take on the rest of the Green Cloaks. She stretched, then winced. Maybe not physically, but mentally, for sure.

"So what's the plan?" she asked, carefully taking a seat.

"We know that Elijah is a Green Cloak," Cora said. "I've been trying to reach Uncle Benjamin, but I can't. I'm worried that Elijah's up to something, and I don't want to walk into a trap. Still, I need to return home."

She didn't need to accompany Cora. Lithia glanced at one of the Ficaran Flyers, unguarded and begging to be flown. She could go rescue Dione, except Dione had found her own way off the island. Apparently she'd found a ship with a jump drive. She might already be on her way back. It was hard to believe they might soon be going home themselves.

"Lithia?" Cora was looking at her expectantly.

"Sorry. Zoned out for a sec. What was your question?"

"What's your government like?" Cora asked again. "Do you have something like a Regnator?"

Lithia sighed. She hated politics. "No Regnator, but we've got a council of core magistrates from the core planets. Those are the most important ones in the eyes of the Alliance. Then we've got planetary delegates who form the Congregate—really, it's a complicated mess."

"How do you choose the council?"

225

"Very long and annoying elections."

"Like the Ficarans?" Cora asked.

"I guess. I don't know how they do it, to be honest. We vote, and—"

Lithia stopped mid-sentence. Cora was frowning at her communicator.

"It's Evy," she said, accepting the call. "Who gave you a com—"

A young, frantic voice cut her off. "They have my mom and dad!"

At once, the banter around Cora stopped. Lithia leaned forward on the edge of her seat. "Who does?" she asked.

"They're Green Cloaks. But they're not wearing green." Evy's voice was hushed now. "But I heard them talking about the people on the farm you were going to. And how they're all that's left now."

"What do they want?" Theo asked.

"I don't know." Evy sniffed. "They're trying to find me."

"How could the people let this happen?" Cora whispered, more to herself than anyone else.

"It's a secret. No one knows yet. I think they got my dad yesterday because he didn't come to dinner. Then they came here in the night. Please come back. I don't want them to find me." Lithia heard Evy sniff again. She was definitely crying.

"We're going to figure this out and help you," Cora said. "Keep hiding. Type in messages if you need me so that you can stay quiet."

"I love you, Cora," Evy said.

"I love you, too," she replied.

She ended the call, and Lithia watched waves of emotion wash over Cora. She felt them, too. Evy was the bravest ten-year-old she had ever met.

Theo was already in motion, rounding up his men, speaking with the remaining Ficarans about transport. Cora was by his side, offering her opinion where appropriate.

Lithia sat, clenching and unclenching her fists. *It never ends*, she thought.

"What's going on?"

The voice startled her. She turned to see Oberon, trailed by Bel and Zane.

"The Green Cloaks have Benjamin and Amelia. They're looking for Evy, but she's hiding. Some sort of coup," Lithia said.

She was trying to wrap her head around the implications. Were the Green Cloaks trying to take over and somehow offer up Kepos to the Vens? No, they'd finally seemed to realize the Vens were bad.

"There's something else," Lithia said. "Dione found the colonizer. She says the jump drive works."

Before the others could react, an angry shriek echoed through the camp. *Cora.*

Lithia hurried off to find her cousin, wincing as she moved. The others followed, along with Jai. "What happened?" she asked when she arrived at Cora's side.

Cora showed her the message. It was from the same communicator Evy had been using: *I have her. Bring me my son, and we can trade.*

Lithia watched Cora's trembling fingers tap out a response: *Elijah?*

A response came: *Yes. Come at midday.*

Cora didn't reply. Next to her, Theo massaged his knuckles as he thought.

"What do I do?" Cora asked those around her. She sounded tired.

"Discredit Elijah publicly," Lithia said. Her brain went straight to confrontation. "His son is a Green Cloak. People will believe you when you say he's one, too."

"He's made a point of vocally siding with the Farmer's traditions, like the Matching. Maybe this is why. He was planning this all along, and wanted people to doubt anyone who called him a Green Cloak."

"Anticipate him then," Bel said. "He wants to be in charge. You're in his way. Benjamin's in his way. Remove yourself as the enemy."

"What are you saying?" Cora asked.

Lithia saw where Bel was headed with this. "Give up the title of Regnator," she explained.

"But if I do, I won't have the power to stop the Matching," Cora said. "I have proof that our ancestors had lives on other worlds. That the Farmer lied." She held up the storage device.

"And soon, Dione will have the colonizer," Lithia said. "More proof. The Matching will be dealt with, but you need to catch him off guard."

"I think I can help with that," Zane said.

"How?" Cora asked. "I can't exactly pass around this image device to one person at a time." She waved the small device to emphasize her point.

"While I was working in the Graveyard before the battle, fixing up those lights and the tiller, I saw a holoprojector in there."

"Graveyard?" Oberon asked.

"Yeah, it's a building full of broken Artifacts. One of the guys I was working with kept asking about it, so I took a look. I think with a few minor repairs, I can get it working."

"Are you up to it?" Bel asked. "How's the arm?"

"Still hurts a bit. I'll need some physical help, but I can walk someone through the repairs."

"Then I'll help you," she said.

Zane nodded. "We can show everyone at the Vale Temple what you've got there. As long as it's good enough to make an impression."

"It is. This will prove I have no right to rule. If Elijah has a copy of these images," Cora said, " then I definitely need to beat him to the reveal. Since we found this at the farm with the Green Cloaks, I wouldn't be surprised if he does."

"My men and I can get you in via the secret gate. It's guarded, but they can buy you enough time to slip in," Theo said.

"I can guide you to the Graveyard," Jai said. "There are some less traveled routes through the city that I know."

"I'm going with Zane," Bel said.

"Zane, Bel," Oberon spoke up. "Need another pair of hands?"

They looked as surprised as Lithia felt.

"Sure," Zane said.

Was Oberon doing this just to keep a closer eye on them? It didn't matter. These were things Lithia had to do. She had obligations. "Cora, I'm going with you. I think Theo should come, too. Everyone else can either stay here or help Theo's guys get Zane into the settlement."

Oberon crossed his arms. *Oh boy,* Lithia thought. *Here it comes.*

"You're still injured," he said. " I know that you're struggling with the aftermath of the battles you've seen. No one expects you—"

"I'm going with Cora," she repeated.

"You won't do her any good in your condition. You don't have your stun rifle," Oberon said. "You need to rest."

"It might be safer if you went with Zane," Cora agreed.

"We look too alike," Lithia said. "I'd endanger the mission. People will be looking for you, not them. As soon as she said the words, though, her wheels started turning. "I have an idea. We can give him what he wants."

Cora folded her arms, clearly impatient to get a move on. "And what is that, exactly?"

"People who crave power love to feel like they have you right where they want you."

"What's your plan?"

"Submission," Lithia replied. "Turn yourself in."

"Seriously?"

"Kind of."

Cora raised an eyebrow. "What exactly do you have in mind?"

"I'm glad you asked, cuz. We're going to get him to confess."

34. BRIAN

B rian followed as Dione led the way to the armory. She was so focused on looking for weapons and gear and supplies that she didn't seem to notice the splendor of the ship around them.

Flyers were one thing, but they weren't that much larger than some of the giant tillers and tractors he had seen the Aratians use. This ship, on the other hand, was huge. He struggled to wrap his head around the fact that ships like this were common. The factories that built them had to be massive.

He couldn't wait to show his dad. Not for the first time since entering the colonizer, he doubted his decision to leave his dad outside the ship. At the time, it had seemed safer, but now he wasn't so sure.

It was too late to change that now. They needed his father to keep an eye out. He knew the dragon song. He was hidden away from their view. He had survived on this island for three years, and Brian was going to bring him home.

They made it to the armory, but the racks were completely bare. Jameson had cleared out the guns long ago.

"It was worth a try," Dione muttered.

"Maybe we'll find something else we can use," Brian said.

They went down to the second level and walked down the long starboard corridor that connected all three segments, opening a door or two at intervals, until they reached a set of much larger and thicker doors. These were airtight. When the segments separated, a hull segment would extend and cover the the area.

"This is it," Brian said.

"The next segment is smaller," Dione said. "The first segment had five levels, but this one only has three. We're entering on the second level, which contains the med bay and mess hall."

They crossed into the middle segment to search for protective gear. There were several closets throughout the ship that contained maintenance equipment, including some fire-resistant work coveralls.

"I don't see any helmets," Dione said, looking around. Brian laughed when she pulled out a suit and held it up against herself. It was way too big. "Here," she said, tossing it to Brian. "Might fit you."

Brian stepped in and pulled the zipper all the way up. "Like a glove," he said.

He handed Dione the smallest suit he could find, but even that was too big. She tried it on anyway.

"I can't wear this. I'll trip over the loose material. Look!" She stretched her arms out in front of her, but the gloved sleeves drooped where they extended past her hands.

"Good thing you're staying here, then," he replied.

"I'm coming with you," she said, poking her hand through the cuff. "Arguing will just waste time."

He sighed, but smiled. "It was worth a try." He inspected her coveralls closely. "There's no time to hem it..." He looked around the closet.

"You can sew?" she asked.

"Of course I can. What kind of backwards world do you come from where people can't hem a pair of pants?" He didn't wait for an answer. "Give me your knife. I'll cut away some of the excess fabric. You won't have full body protection, but it's better than nothing."

Brian cut the sleeves and legs to length for her. When she tried the pants on, they still hung a bit loosely on her body. "At least I can move now. Let me see that," she said, gesturing for the knife.

She sat on the floor with the suit remnants and carefully cut the excess material into strips. She used the strips to secure the baggy suit to her body at her hands and ankles where the cuffs had been cut off.

They both managed to find gloves that fit, and Brian found some work boots. Dione decided that her own hiking boots would be enough.

"What about this?" Brian asked, holding up a piece of gun-shaped equipment.

"A nail gun? It might distract them, but it will be about as damaging as throwing rocks at them."

"Can't hurt," he replied, slipping it into the belt of his suit. He wished he had brought a gun with him, but there had been no time. If they hadn't stolen that Flyer when the Aratians were packing it with supplies, he never would have gotten the chance to come here.

Dione kept picking at her piecemeal outfit, then looking at Brian. "I look ridiculous," she said, tucking the gloves into her pocket. "You look like those coveralls were made for you."

"Yep, completely ridiculous," he said.

Dione rolled her eyes. She slipped her hand into his before leading him away to their next stop, the medical bay. The med bay had been cleared out, too, except for a small cabinet that Jameson had left stocked with a spray to treat burns.

"Lucky for us," Dione said. "I guess he kept this here in case he got a few burns on his way in."

"I don't see anything here that can slice through a dragon, though," Brian said.

"Nothing chemical either." Dione seemed disappointed. "And fire won't do any good against them. I don't think we can focus on trying to kill them. We need to keep them away from us altogether, but I'm hesitant to rely solely on the dragon song."

"What if we adjust the temperature controls on the last section? Freeze them out?" Brian suggested. "If they're ectotherms, it will definitely slow them down. Maybe even stop them."

"That's... actually a great idea," Dione said. "I bet we can do that from the main bridge."

As they were leaving, a fire extinguisher caught Dione's eye. It was wearable and not too bulky, with a short hose. "We should grab that, too," she said, removing her pack so the extinguisher could take its place.

Brian dutifully put her pack on his free shoulder, removed the extinguisher from the wall, and strapped it to her back. Though compact, it was still quite heavy, and he watched her shift her weight from one leg to the other.

Once they reached the bridge, Dione went immediately to the console to adjust the temperature in the colonizer's last segment.

"Can I borrow your manumed?" Brian asked. "I want to update my dad."

When his father picked up, he filled him in on all they'd learned. "They're focused on that last segment," he said. "You should be able to safely come on board."

"No, you still need someone to keep an eye out. I'll bet that once you start poking around, the dragons out here might try something. If they do, I'll be able to warn you."

"It's safer inside the ship," Brian replied.

"I've found a good spot, son. I'm well hidden, but I can still see them."

"Dad, please," Brian begged.

"I've avoided these dragons for a long time. I can manage one more morning. Just don't leave me behind once you get the ship running."

He could hear the smile in his father's voice. "There's no danger of that," Brian replied.

He relented in the end , but he still wished his father would come inside the safety of the ship.

By the end of their conversation, Dione was still trying to access the climate controls. Brian took a look, but he also came up with nothing.

"Time to call someone?" he asked.

"I can't call the professor," she replied.

He nodded. "Sorry, that's my fault."

Dione scoffed. "Hardly. I made this choice. I came here with you of my own free will. Maybe Zane can help."

Brian returned her manumed to her outstretched hand and waited as she spoke with Zane.

"Zane, do you have a minute?"

"Uh, sure. But be quick."

"Why, what's going on?" Dione asked. "Is everything okay?"

"Bel and Oberon are with me. We're on our way back to the Vale Temple now. Lithia's doing well, considering the broken ribs."

"What?!"

"She didn't tell you?" Zane sounded surprised.

"No, she—we—have mostly been doing check-ins. Last night's was the usual message: 'alive.'"

"So I'm guessing you didn't hear about the coup?"

"Are you messing with me right now?"

"Nope. That's why we're headed to the Vale Temple. Elijah and the Green Cloaks have taken over."

"Who's Elijah?" Dione asked.

"The bad guy. Look, I don't have much time before I need to go silent. If you want help, ask now."

There it was again. Brian wondered what Dione had done to this guy to make him treat her this way.

Dione explained the problem. "So how do I access the environmental controls?" she asked.

"You won't be able to do it," Zane said.

"Why didn't it have a problem when I tried to detach the last segment then?"

"It can detect it's damaged, so the safety protocols allow anyone to detach it so it doesn't compromise the other segments," he said. "But environmental controls are finicky and vital. I'm not surprised they're one of the restricted systems."

"So if we were in space, I could jettison the entire compartment, but not adjust the AC?"

"Yep."

"That's ridiculous."

"Welcome to Systems Design 101. Check your logic at the door."

Dione groaned. "What now?"

"You can adjust the environmental controls from within the compartment."

"With no access code?"

"Yep. If it's 'in distress,' anyone can fix it," Zane said.

"What if I was a saboteur?"

"There are a few other safeguards, like a lockout from someone with access codes, but I'm guessing there's no one there to lock you out. In case there's an emergency, like a fire, the people who are closest and best poised to help don't have to worry about getting access. They can just fix the problem."

"Still seems weird to me," Dione said.

"Yeah, it was just a style of ship back then," Zane said. "Colonizers, where there was some degree of trust and community, were more likely to have this setup."

"Where would the controls be?"

"Probably right at the entrance to the segment. Look for an access point when you go to the second segment, and the final segment should have one in about the same place."

"Got it. Thanks," Dione said.

"Anything else? I'll be out of contact soon."

"Nothing except for good luck, Zane. Bel and Oberon, too."

"Thanks," Zane replied. He hesitated for a few seconds. "You, too."

Brian cocked his head as she closed out the call. "Why does he hate you?"

Dione shrugged. "He doesn't hate me, but he doesn't like me either. In fact, since we've been on Kepos, he's warmed up to me."

"That was warmed-up?"

"Yeah, it's a long story. Part of it is my fault, but part of the reason he dislikes me is something I have no control over."

Brian nodded. He could relate. Victoria had always taken her anger at his father's departure out on him.

They reached the door to the final section. "You ready?" he asked.

Dione took a deep breath. "Yeah, let's do this."

35. DIONE

So much had happened since that first Ven attack on the *Calypso,* and Dione had defied the odds time and again. When she and Lithia had crashed on the planet, she had defied her own expectations. She had learned so much, had grown so much, but this fear she felt was becoming her new normal. In fact, the line between fear and exhilaration was beginning to blur a little.

Zane had left her with so many questions. No one had filled her in on the problems they were facing. She couldn't help from where she was, but they still should have told her. Lithia especially. *A coup.* She could hardly believe it.

She looked at Lithia's message from last night. *Alive.*

Not good enough, she thought, and sent a reply to her best friend: *Be careful. Stay more than alive. Stay safe.*

"You can leave my pack here," she told Brian. "I'm leaving the stun rifle, too. It won't do any good against the dragons and might get damaged in the heat."

She had her knife and the fire extinguisher. Brian had his nail gun and machete. She nodded. From here on out, they would have to be quiet. Brian opened the door, and a wave of heat washed over her, stinging her eyes. She blinked and tried not to cough from the smoky air. The ship's environmental systems had filtered out most of the smoke, but the scent remained strong, like the smell of clothes after a bonfire.

The two segments were like night and day, and she and Brian stepped out of their safe, well-lit hallway into the final segment's dark corridor. The main lights were out, and the red emergency lighting gave the illusion of unseen fires glowing against the walls.

Dione was heartened, however, by the lack of blackened and melted materials. She suspected that the dragons didn't spend much time near the door they had just come through. She quickly identified the access panel, located just inside the door. They would only have to take a few steps into the dragon-infested section in order to crank the environmental controls and freeze out the reptilian pests. The corridor was dragon-free, so Dione went immediately to the panel. It would take some time for the environmental controls to cool such a large ship, especially if there were breaches.

"That should do it," she said. "I'm dropping this section to five degrees Celsius. That's enough to immobilize most cold-blooded creatures. The dragons are so large we'll have to wait a bit for the cold to take effect. Let's wait where it's safe." She eyed the next set of closed doors down the corridor, wondering what lay behind them.

The two went back into the middle segment to wait for the final segment to cool down.

Brian sat against the wall, eyes fixed on the door they would soon head back through.

"If this works, and we manage to get this ship flying, what will happen?" he asked.

Dione sat next to him, close enough that their shoulders touched. "I don't know. I guess we'll take the fabricator to the

240

Field Temple, so you can rebuild. I don't think there's enough room at the Mountain Base."

"But what about after that? Will this ship really get you home?"

Dione turned to look at him. She had been trying not to think about the "after" very hard.

She would go home. That hope filled her a sense of purpose that made her feel like she could face down any obstacle, even dragons. But so much had happened in the past couple of weeks that she felt a connection to this place. More importantly, she felt a connection to him.

"I'm sure Zane and Lithia and Oberon will want to do a bunch of checks on the colonizer before we leave," she said.

"Before you go home," he said.

Dione nodded. His former anger was gone, and he didn't say what they were both thinking. She would be leaving. Whatever was going on between them would end. Her heart ached a little as she realized something for the first time.

She would never return to Kepos. This planet was outside the Bubble. It didn't exist, according to Alliance records, and she imagined there was a reason for that. She suspected that no private citizens would be making trips here. No colonizers bringing supplies. No trade, no infusion of genetic diversity. Her earlier thoughts on the matter had been wishful thinking.

She would find a way to protect Kepos. To provide for it. She'd talk to her father.

Dione shivered. Though the temperature of the middle section remained constant, the thought of what they were about to face unnerved her. Brian put an arm around her, and she rested her head against his shoulder. He was warm and comfortable. She would miss him.

The sentiment suddenly seemed silly to her. "I may be leaving, but I'm not gone yet. Let's make the most of our time without worrying about that for now." It was something Lithia might say.

Brian smiled. "You're right. Who knows? We might not survive the dragons anyway."

Dione rolled her eyes and returned his grin. Without further warning, he kissed her. He wrapped his arms around her, and she felt like she belonged in his embrace. His kisses were familiar and comforting.

An annoying chime sounded, signaling that it was time to go, and they broke apart. Brian gave her one final kiss on the cheek before getting up and offering her a hand. She took it and held on, even after she was on her feet.

"There are some warmer spots, but most of the segment is at or near five degrees."

"Then let's get this over with," Brian replied.

She squeezed his hand in earnest. "Be careful," she said.

Brian squeezed hers back before releasing it. "Tired of saving me?"

Dione didn't laugh, the lightness of the previous moment already gone. "Yes. I've got your back, so don't do something reckless."

Brian nodded. "Understood. Let my dad know we're headed in. If he notices anything outside, he can tell us."

"Got it." Dione sent Oliver a quick message.

The pair reviewed their plan one last time. Go down the corridor, cross the ship at the cut-through, then go back up the other side. Enter the maintenance tunnel near the starboard door and manually override the mechanism locking the two segments together. Avoid dragons. They would avoid the first level, which the dragons had completely claimed. They would also avoid the maintenance tunnels, except to repair the separation mechanism. The second level was their only way in and out of this segment.

They reentered the final segment, now much colder, and proceeded down the corridor to the first set of doors. Brian paused in front of them, looking to Dione. She nodded her assent and readied her fire extinguisher. Brian brandished the machete.

When the doors opened, they saw two dragons just on the other side. They had rolled onto their sides like dogs, sleeping. Or comatose. The frigid air had done its work.

But what were these two doing here? Dione glanced down the corridor and realized she could see all the way down. None of the other doors were closed.

"I think these were on guard duty. What if they heard us when we came in to adjust environmental controls, but got stopped by this door?"

"Doesn't matter now," he replied.

"I guess you're right. Should we... take care of them?" Dione knew the answer. Yes, they should kill them. It would be foolish to leave threats at their back; she had learned that lesson already. But killing a dragon, an intelligent creature whose ferocity was born of protective instinct, felt much different than killing a Ven. Dione and Brian were intruders, invading their nest. Threatening their offspring. The choice to kill in this case was more difficult to make, but no less necessary.

Get a grip. Kill or be killed, she thought.

"I'll do it," Brian said. He probably sensed her turmoil. "They may be sleeping, but we don't want to deal with them if they wake up."

She expected him to raise the machete, but instead he pulled the nail gun from his belt loop. He put it to the dragon's head and pulled the trigger, quick and painless. Brian dispatched the other dragon in the same way, and they continued on down the corridor.

As they neared the cut-through that would take them to the other side of the ship, Dione felt the air around them grow warmer.

She put a hand on Brian's shoulder to stop him.

"The fire," she said. "It's probably enough to keep the ones near it mobile. If we can sneak by unnoticed…"

She got a call from Oliver.

"What is it?" she whispered, cuing him into the need for quiet.

"The dragons out here are acting strange," he said. Dione strained to make out his words. "They've stopped patrolling, and are piling sticks and other kindling at the entrance they've been using. It's a dragon-sized hole in the side of the ship. Others are taking the sticks inside."

"More fires," Brian whispered. "Trying to raise the temperatures."

"A few that came out of the ship looked off, stumbling a bit, but they've recovered," Oliver said.

"Must have gotten out before the cold got them," Brian said.

"I think they're trying to heat a path back to the nest inside. They're working double time."

"Then we need to get over to the other side of the ship and detach the segment before we get swarmed," Dione said.

"Thanks for the heads-up," Brian said.

"Of course. Let me know if you need a distraction."

"Got it," he replied.

Dione ended the call, and they forged ahead, pausing only at the entrance to the cut-through. It was markedly warmer here, and she could hear the crackle of twigs in the fire. A glance around the corner told her only that the fire was large. A trough of dirt formed a ring around the blaze. She could make out eggs packed into that dirt. There was also a bulkhead halfway across the space that looked like it had once been part of a kiosk.

She whispered what she had seen to Brian. He took his own look, then spoke so quietly that she could barely hear him. "There are five that I see. Two are adjusting the dirt on the eggs, and the other three are on the far side."

Only five? It seemed too easy. Were the others frozen in place in some other part of the ship? Had they miscounted?

After one more check, Dione came up with the same number of dragons, as well as a plan.

"That bulkhead in the middle," she whispered. "If we get there, we can use it to block ourselves from view, at least for a little bit. But then we'll be a lot closer to the other side."

Brian nodded in agreement. "Those dragons by the eggs may move soon. Let's go before they're facing us."

No more waffling. Time to act, ready or not. Brian looked at her, waiting for her to take the lead. She carefully made her way to the cover of the bulkhead. Her ill-fitting protective suit made it difficult, but she and Brian reached the bulkhead.

She couldn't even sigh in relief for fear of making noise. The crackling of the fire and roar of the environmental system working overtime to cool the room provided some cover, but Dione wouldn't push it.

Brian moved past her to the other edge of the bulkhead. She was grateful for his sense of urgency as he peeked once more around the corner. He beckoned for her to follow.

With unparalleled grace, he picked his way across the expanse and disappeared around the corner. She did her best, and thought she was in the clear until her boot caught on a loose thread from her unraveling pant leg. She stumbled noisily around the corner.

She pressed herself against the wall, holding her breath while her heart pounded painfully against her lungs. Neither she nor Brian dared to look, certain the noise had caught the attention of the dragons in the room. She heard the clank of claws on the metal floor grates.

Brian grabbed her hand and led her down the corridor toward their goal, the separation mechanism. "Back to the cold," he said.

Even if the dragons pursued, the frigid corridor would afford the pair some protection. Dione shivered. At that moment, a dragon appeared in the corridor and sniffed the very spot where she had stood moments before.

Its large yellow eyes found them easily, exposed in the barren hall. It wasted no time, spitting its pungent accelerant and whipping its tail with a crack and spark. The liquid caught fire, and the metal grate warped in the heat. The flames disappeared, but two more dragons filed in behind the first, and all three raced down the corridor.

Dione stopped and turned, keeping her breath steady as she sang the dragon song. Two stopped and hissed, but the lead dragon seemed unbothered. She looked back at her comrades and hesitated before resuming her charge.

Time to run. Dione heard Brian pick the tune up, so she sprinted until she reached him, where he was waiting much farther down the hall. Here in the narrow corridor, the heat from the fire in the nest room could not reach them. The dragon had halted and was sniffing the cold air, tail flicking angrily in the air. The immune dragon was mostly light brown, but had pale green scales around her eyes.

"She won't follow. It's too cold," Dione said, no longer bothering to lower her voice.

"Good, let's go."

They could get to the separation mechanism and detach this segment, but how would they get back? She glanced back, and immediately regretted it. The dragon paced in the corridor, hissing, as if restrained by some invisible force field.

Dione reminded herself that there was nothing except the cold roaring through the ventilation system to keep the dragons at bay, and that dragons knew how to keep a fire burning in this ship, given the proper motivation. Intruders so close to their nest? There was no better motivation she could have provided.

They didn't have much time.

36. DIONE

"Can you go any faster?" Dione called down to Brian. She had stayed in the corridor to keep watch while he worked in the maintenance tunnel beneath the floor. As much as she hated watching the dragon pacing, she couldn't see it at the end of the corridor anymore. That, she found, was worse.

"Seriously?" Brian asked, eyes never leaving his work. "I've got the instruction manual pulled up as I work around this heavily damaged mechanism. Even with this thing constantly running diagnostics and telling me what to do, I'm still out of my element. When was the last time you repaired a ship within hours of seeing it for the first time?"

"I get it, I'm just worried. I can't see Toasty anymore."

"You did not name the dragon."

"I did. Toasty. It makes her seem less terrifying." Dione paced up and down the corridor.

"How do you know it's a she?" he asked.

"I can see it in her eyes."

"How scientific of you."

"Just keep working," Dione said. She stared down the corridor waiting for Toasty to return, but there was no sign of her or any other dragon. Maybe they were lying in wait, just out of sight.

"I've got to access another panel a little farther down. I'm almost done, I think," Brian said.

"Understood." Soon they would need to get back to the other side, and while Brian was busy working on the separation mechanism, she was planning their escape.

They would use the maintenance tunnels underneath the floors. It was obvious, and at this point the only solution. She called up the ship schematic on her manumed, trying to memorize as much as possible. They would need speed along with every other possible advantage. She still worried they might run into a dragon down there, but their only other path had a one hundred percent chance of dragons. She didn't need to be good at statistics in order to figure out what option the odds indicated.

She was so lost in thought that she didn't realize Toasty was back. She had brought friends. They were piling up twigs in the corridor.

"They're bringing the heat to us," Dione whispered to herself. When she tried to estimate how long they had until they built enough fires to make it down the hallway, she relaxed. The corridor was long, and the cold air pumping out of the vents would force them to light and maintain frequent fires.

But before Toasty and company could light their little pyre, a loud bang echoed through the ship. Everything grew eerily silent.

Brian poked his head out of the floor. "What was that?"

Dione soaked up the silence before answering. "Listen."

"I don't hear anything," he replied.

"Exactly. There's no more cold air coming from the vents. The environmental control unit has stopped." They exchanged a look. "Hurry."

Dione faced down the corridor once again and watched Toasty light the pyre. She was still cold, but their timeline for making the repairs and getting out of there had just shrunk.

A constant parade of dragons created the next pyre, closer than the first. Toasty lit it. Dione could feel the numbness leaving the exposed skin of her face. Her shield of frigid air was dissipating so quickly, she doubted Toasty would even need her third fire.

Dione sang the dragon song, but Toasty and another dragon were unaffected. They hissed and continued their work, while the affected dragons piled their sticks as close to their adversary as they could stand. It was like a twisted bucket brigade, passing kindling down the line rather than water. At best, the song would buy them a few more minutes.

Toasty moved forward to light the next fire, but stopped, sniffing the air. She took a cautious step beyond the unlit pile of twigs. Then another. Dione stopped singing without realizing it.

She barely had time to react when she saw the dragon sprinting toward her. Toasty balked for a moment when she hit the cooler air. The last thing Dione saw before closing the flooring grate above her head was Toasty rushing straight for her. She practically fell down the ladder into the crawlspace, where she landed on her back. She groaned at the rough landing. Before she could register Toasty's hiss and click, she saw burning droplets of accelerant raining down on her.

Her suit might have offered protection against a regular fire, but the fire droplets, fueled by whatever was in that accelerant, burned a few small holes in the suit before dying out. Strong arms pulled her out of the splash zone.

"Thanks," she said. "These suits aren't as fireproof as I'd hoped."

"Considering it burns hot enough to warp metal," Brian said, "I'd say this suit did okay. Better than nothing."

"Fair point. How's it going? We're out of time."

"Just finishing up," he said. "Assuming the dragons don't undo all my hard work." He pointed to the molten metal hardening on the ground under the grate.

They were so close. There was only one thing she could do, even though it made her sick with fear. When she and Lithia played at the holos, she was the one solving the puzzle or finding the key while Lithia held off the hordes of minions coming their way, but not this time. She hadn't spent her childhood fixing Artifacts like Brian. This was not her kind of puzzle. She would have to channel her inner Lithia.

She saw the fire extinguisher on the floor next to Brian. Another piece of her plan clicked into place.

"When you finish up here," she said, "go back to the other side and wait for me in the middle section where it's safe."

"Like hell I will," Brian said.

"You need more time, and I have an idea of how to give it to you. Once you're done here, head back to the port door. I'll meet you there."

"No, I'm not going to leave you in here."

"Splitting up is the only way I can get them away from you. Just finish up, get to the next segment, and prepare to detach. I need you to be ready."

She didn't wait for a response before turning and crawling parallel to the corridor. At the next exit, she climbed up, popped off the grate, and shouted in the direction she had come from. The dragons were clustered at the opposite end of the corridor around the grate she had disappeared through. "Hey! This way!"

Toasty and her dragon friends snapped their scaly necks in Dione's direction. As they ran toward her, she ducked back into the safety of the crawlspace.

If these dragons wanted war, she would bring it to them. She crawled along noisily, making sure they could hear her. When the path branched, she clunked down one direction and left her gloves there.

As quietly as possible she backtracked, took the other path at the fork, and crept forward. She wasn't sure if she had fooled them, but even a few extra seconds would make a difference.

If this plan even works. The cynical part of her brain whispered doubts. *What if it's not enough to stop them?*

She shook her head. Based on the behavior she had observed so far, she had every reason to believe it would.

Her knees and wrists ached from crawling under the weight of the extinguisher, but she was almost there. She took slow, deep breaths, trying to bank as much calm as possible before the chaos. She mentally went through her repertoire of tools: the dragon song and fire extinguisher.

Just a little farther. She heard scrambling from a side tunnel. They were on their way. She picked up her pace, her knees banging painfully against the floor. There it was, the ladder.

A dragon poked its nose into her tunnel and bounded toward her, but her hand was already on the ladder rungs. She started singing, and the sounds of the advancing dragon stopped. Her heart thumped against her rib cage as she scrambled up the remaining steps and shoved the grate aside. She was still singing, but a bit out of breath.

The heat from the fire hit her, like leaving an air-conditioned building on a hot day. The dim red lights still flashed all around her. She had emerged into the large room where the dragons were incubating their eggs. The central fire roared larger than before, and only the very tops of the eggs were visible in the ring of dirt.

The two dragons that had been stationed there were backing away, hissing and whipping their tails in anger. She could hear Toasty and the other dragons coming, claws scraping against metal in their haste.

She readied the fire extinguisher and kept singing. She strode to the center of the room and aimed the hose at the fire, which was surrounded by the dirt-covered eggs. She pulled the trigger, spraying foam on the fire.

It was too big. Or too hot. But it was getting smaller.

The scrambling, however, grew louder, until Toasty and her pack entered the room.

The others balked at the song, shaking their heads and backing away, but Toasty and the other immune dragon charged toward Dione. She directed the spray from the extinguisher at them, but they dodged, splitting off in opposite directions. They were going to flank her.

She felt something hit the back of her legs, but it didn't hurt. Accelerant soaked through the material of her suit, plastering it to her thigh and calf.

She gulped. Under no circumstances could she get too close to the fires around her unless she wanted to go up in flames. She doubted the efficacy of "stop, drop, and roll" in the face of dragon-accelerated fire.

The second immune dragon tried to spark her with his tail, but Dione was already moving out of range—and right into Toasty's path. She leapt at Dione, who let out another blast from the extinguisher just in time.

Dione choked on the fumes and dodged again, but the weight of the extinguisher threw off her balance. She stopped singing and toppled over, cheek pressed against the warm floor grate as she continued to choke and sputter. She felt the vibrations of the rest of the dragons swarming into the room, more than the few that had been part of Toasty's defense team.

She pushed herself up to her knees, but couldn't stop coughing long enough to start the song again. The other dragons should be on her. Then she heard a deep tenor echoing in the chamber all around her. The dragons that had stormed into the egg room continued past her, hissing as they went. A few stopped and snapped at her, but kept shaking their heads like they were trying to shake water out of their ears.

Brian? she wondered. A man rounded the corner. Oliver. He carried a large, thick branch. She didn't think it was much of a weapon, but now wasn't the time to complain.

Toasty and the other immune dragon moved toward him, the source of the song that had scared off their kin. Their tails flicked and clanged noisily as they approached him. She saw Oliver's eyes scanning the room for his son.

Dione managed to choke out, "He's safe," before another fit of coughing silenced her. Still on her knees, she tried to push herself up. One of her hands was covered in dirt. The eggs were right there. She still had a chance. Shrugging off the extinguisher with some effort, she scooped away the dirt, exposing two eggs. They were large enough to require two hands to hold, though she imagined a man like Colm, or even Oliver, could comfortably hold them in one.

She tossed the first toward Toasty. The shell shattered on impact, leaving a viscous smear and a small, limp lizard body. Toasty turned and sniffed at the mess before emitting a terrible, high-pitched screech. The other dragons waiting in the wings echoed back the screech.

The two immune dragons glared at Dione and would have rushed her way, if not for the other egg. She was holding it high above her head. Sweat dripped down her forehead. She couldn't wait to get away from this fire.

"Keep singing," she said softly to Oliver, trying to avoid triggering another coughing fit. She moved toward him, away from the ring of eggs. Toasty and her friend moved as well, putting their eggs at their back. They would not make the mistake of leaving the eggs unguarded again.

"We're going to go down that corridor and leave through the port door. Brian should be there by now, ready to detach this segment." She paused to recover, but talking was getting easier. "I'll give them back the egg before we leave this segment."

She carefully led Oliver down the corridor, past the corpses of the dragons they had killed earlier. A horde followed, and to an outsider, it might have looked as if Oliver was the dragon pied piper, leading them behind him rather than keeping them at bay. Toasty and her friend stayed much closer, snapping their jaws and clicking their tails, but never attacking.

They were at the door. When Oliver opened it, the two dragons on their heels lunged. Dione jumped, nearly losing her grip on the egg. There was no time to think. She rolled the egg down the corridor, hoping it would crack. The other dragon scampered after it, and Dione stepped across the threshold. Toasty, however, took her opportunity to attack with a flick of her tail.

Dione heard the door close before she felt it—intense heat, then pain. She screamed and collapsed to the ground, rolling in an attempt to quench the fire that was searing the skin, bearing it down to the muscle of her left leg. She scrambled to remove the suit.

Oliver's reaction was immediate. He beat the fire with his own jacket and pulled the suit the rest of the way off, exposing the burn. Dione wailed and banged against the floor with her hands. Her vision swam when she tried to lift her head.

"Help me get her to the med bay." It was Brian. She hadn't heard him arrive. "How bad is it?"

"I'll take her," Oliver said. "Get us home and away from these dragons, then meet me in the med bay."

Dione felt herself being picked up, followed by immense pain in her leg. She screamed, and then there was only darkness.

37. LITHIA

Three figures approached the Aratian gates. The central figure was bound and blindfolded, and the hood of his green cloak was down. He was flanked by Theo and a tall, dark-haired girl with a bandage covering half of her face.

This is never going to work. Lithia and Cora had traded clothes for the charade, but there wasn't enough time to do more. The bandage was suspicious, and Elijah would never fall for it. *Just make it inside the walls. It only needs to work long enough to get you in the room with him.*

At the gate, Lithia straightened her back and stepped forward to face the guards and put on her best Cora impression. She raised the pitch of her voice and let some of her own anger at Evy's capture seep into her words. "Elijah is waiting for me."

After searching them for weapons, one of the guards led them toward the Temple. The bustle Lithia remembered from her very first visit seemed subdued. While most carried on as if nothing was amiss, a few looked at her, eyes wide with concern.

Do they know about the coup? she wondered. *Or is it the bandage?*

The guard delivered them to the Temple. Elijah was waiting for them in one of the upper chambers that looked like it had been Michael's office before he died. Her chest still ached from the broken ribs, but it helped make her the perfect decoy. She was useless for much else. While they tied Theo to the chair, she took the opportunity to discreetly tap on her manumed. As the guard bound her wrists to the arms of the chair, she looked around the room.

There was a shelf with a few books and trinkets. The desk was small and practical, free from clutter. The window sill held a distorted figurine that she assumed Cora had made for her father many years ago.

Asher, already untied, went to join Elijah. They embraced, the father planting a relieved kiss on his son's forehead. Lithia was surprised that Elijah was capable of such an emotional display.

"The others, Dad," Asher choked out. "It was a slaughter. If I had still been at the farm…"

"But you weren't. You're safe. We'll all be safe soon."

A man appeared in the doorway and said, "Found her."

"Bring her in, then." Elijah turned back to Lithia, an arrogant smirk on his face. "The question you might expect me to ask is, 'Where's Cora?' but I already know the answer to that. You people really are predictable." Lithia could have kicked herself. He had barely looked at her, yet he knew. "You may have fooled the guards long enough to get in here," he said, "but I'm not deceived. It's shoddy work, really."

"Where's Evy?" Lithia gritted her teeth in anger, and her query came out almost as a growl.

"She's safe. Lithia, right?"

She exchanged a look with Theo. That had been fast. Too fast. Had he found Zane, too? Had there been enough time to get everything into place? She turned back to glare at Elijah.

"I have questions for you, too, so I'm glad you're here," he said.

"Great! We can take turns. I'll go first. Do you feel guilty?" Lithia asked. "All that Aratian blood is on your hands. You let the Vens in. Or was it Asher? Did you lead the Vens to your friends on the farm, too, then leave them to die? Remember how horrible the farmhouse smelled, Theo? That was probably Asher's fault."

Asher looked caught between grief and anger, but before he could respond, his father intervened. "Child, that's quite enough. Asher, why don't you get cleaned up?"

"Green Cloak scum," Lithia wrinkled her nose as Asher walked by.

"That's enough out of you," Elijah said. He waded up a ball of cloth and stuck it in her mouth. "I think I'll save my questions for another time. There will be plenty of it, after all." She tried to bite him, but choked on the dry cotton. He tied a scarf tightly around her mouth, and she gagged. Pain crackled through her chest. She had to calm down and focus in order to breathe, but the anger mixed with the pain made it difficult.

Through it all, Theo remained relaxed in his seat, almost as if he didn't register what was happening to her.

Cora was led in, also bound. Lithia's heart sank. She'd hoped their ploy would buy her cousin enough time to find her family, but they had failed. Another chair was set next to Lithia, and Cora took it, glaring at Elijah much like Lithia still was. She felt a pang for her cousin, trapped in her late father's office, a room full of memories, facing the Green Cloak leader.

"Where's Evy?" Cora demanded. "Where are my aunt and uncle?"

Elijah chuckled, looking from Cora to Lithia. "You two are quite alike, in more than appearance. They're fine. I don't plan to hurt them."

"Then why are you here, in my father's office?"

"Because I'm taking over."

"You can't do that," Cora said.

"Neither can you. Or your uncle. We have proof that the Farmer was a liar. You have no right to rule."

"I agree," she said.

Elijah tilted his head. "What game are you playing now?"

"No games," she said, turning instead to look at Lithia. "I have no blood right to rule. I'm not ready to take on the responsibility of Regnator. But one day, I hope our people will choose me."

"Well, that was a lot easier than I thought," he said.

"I'm not finished. You are a Green Cloak. You are unfit to rule."

"More fit than a petulant child like you," he replied.

"So you don't deny it? That you're a Green Cloak."

He smirked.

"Did you detonate the flaminaria mines early? Or were you the one who opened the secret gate after I sealed it?"

Elijah leaned forward, a sneer on his face. "Child, I handed Delia the knife she used to slit your corrupt father's throat."

Everything in the office went still, like the calm before a storm. Theo strained against his bindings, but they held firm. He spat on the desk in front of Elijah. Lithia turned to Cora with muffled pleas to keep her calm, but Cora already was. Her jaw was clenched, and her mouth twitched, but she was reining in her rage. "Justice will find you."

"Here's the deal I have for you," Elijah said, ignoring her threat entirely. "Give up your right to the title of Regnator, and let everyone know that you took care of the last of the Green Cloaks out at the farm."

"So they won't come for you?"

"Yes. I'll let you and your aunt and uncle desert to the Ficarans. I'd planned to buy their goodwill and further cooperation by returning their guns—"

"That you stole in the first place," Theo interjected.

"Yes, but since you already returned their weapons, I'll be keeping Evy here as collateral. Try anything, tell anyone, and we'll see how many bugs she can catch with a few missing fingers."

Cora was losing her control. "If you harm even one fingernail, I'll—"

"You'll what? Declare war? With what army? Your haggard recruits that wouldn't even fight the Vens with you? The Ficarans don't have the men or supplies to fight us, and they're enjoying the food shipments that are a part of the alliance your uncle brokered.

"I'll admit, we made a mistake believing in the Vens, but that doesn't change the fact that the Farmer lied to us. Our society is built on lies, and now someone has to dismantle those lies, starting with the Regnator's family."

"If you hate the Farmer so much, why do you support the Matching?" Cora demanded.

Elijah shrugged. "I needed the men's support. Not everyone helping me is a Green Cloak. Change will be incremental. The Matching will go eventually, once I no longer have use for it."

Cora looked at Lithia, eyebrows raised. Lithia nodded at her. Their part was over. Now if only Zane, Bel, Oberon, and Jai could hold up their end of the deal.

"Now that's over with," Elijah said, getting up and removing Lithia's gag, "I've got some questions for you.

"Elijah," a man called from the door. "We found more." Their captor left the office to have a hushed conversation in the hallway. Lithia was glad for the removal of the gag, but had nothing helpful to say. She had a feeling she knew what the man had meant by 'more.'

"A third group," Elijah crowed as he reentered the room. "That's more than I gave you credit for. I didn't find Jai's absence suspicious, but now I see I should have worried about him a bit more."

Lithia could see the concern in the downcast corners of Cora's mouth. She grimaced. If they had found Jai, then they had found Zane and the others, too. She checked the time. It hadn't been long. Zane was good, but was he that good? Had there been enough time? There was no way to tell if they'd finished what they set out to do.

"Thank you, by the way," Elijah said, "for returning the storage device with all the images. It will make this go faster. In fact, your friends even fixed the... holoprojector? I think that's what they told my men it was. Even showed us how it works, after a little prompting, of course. It's time that the Aratians knew the truth. And I'll be the one to bring it to them."

In another minute, two men came to escort Lithia, Cora, and Theo to a new location.

"I'm going to have my guards unbind your hands," Elijah said. "If any of your try to run or fight, just remember, I have Evy. I have what's left of your family. I expect your cooperation." He turned to Cora. "I hope you're ready to be unmasked."

Lithia discreetly tapped her manumed, though she couldn't know yet if Zane and the others had accomplished their mission.

38. LITHIA

The square was packed under a cloudy sky. Lithia thought there was a higher percentage of women in this crowd than at the Matching. The battle against the Vens had left a deep mark.

While they had been talking in Michael's office, Elijah's men had been gathering the Aratians. A small stage had been erected in front of the Temple, its backdrop of undyed, off-white curtains an obvious contrast to the colorful swaths of fabric the settlement had used during the Matching. Lithia could see the holoprojector on the opposite side of the stage, but she had been confined to the wings. She checked her manumed; she was unable to connect to the holoprojector.

She needed to get closer. When Elijah led Cora onto the stage, Lithia followed. The guard watching her was too slow to pull her back, and by the time he had regained control of her movement, it was easier to walk her to the other side. To the audience, nothing would seem amiss. Lithia cursed under her breath. She was still too far from the device to connect. Meanwhile, her guard was standing so close she could smell his stale breath.

Benjamin was already there. He looked paler than usual, but began to deliver a brief speech that had undoubtedly been written for him by Elijah. He paused before reading the final lines into the handheld amplifier: "And so, today, I step down as Regnator. Now, my niece Cora Bram has a few words."

Cora stood and spoke, reading off of a card Elijah had given her. In just a few sentences, she had also abdicated her role as leader of her people and called on Elijah to take over, since he had shown her the truth he was about to share with everyone else. That last bit left a bitter taste in Lithia's mouth.

Elijah grinned, but it only made his nose look more crooked. "I want to show you all what finally convinced me that the Farmer was lying, what convinced me that the Farmer was not a god. As you watch, you may be alarmed, but remember: there will be a way forward that honors both the truth and our traditions."

He nodded to one of his lackeys, who turned on the holoprojector. A crisp, three-dimensional image seemed to emerge out of the white backdrop. It was a smiling man, dining at a city cafe. In the background were cars and trams and the trunks of buildings taller than the Aratians had ever seen.

"Many of you remember this man as Miles," Elijah said.

Murmurs coursed through the crowd as they tried to make sense of what they were seeing. Lithia saw some nods, but also some angry faces. They did not want to accept this.

She felt afraid for Benjamin and Cora. Would the crowd become a mob? This seemed too hasty, not the best way to transfer power. Would the Aratians blame them, turn on them, thinking they perpetuated the Farmer's lies for their own benefit?

She might, in their position. That's what scared her.

"Show them Mary," Elijah said, nodding to his man at the holoprojector.

Another image came to life before the crowd. More murmurs. People were pushing up against the stage to get a closer look.

The next image, a laughing woman, appeared with no introduction, yet garnered gasps from the people.

Lithia watched heads turn, and cries of "grandmother" echoed through the crowd. It parted to let an old woman pass through, to get a closer look. She looked like she had been in the middle of preparing dinner when she was summoned to the square. A dirty, many-pocketed apron covered her clothes.

"What is this?" she asked, squinting at the holo-image. It was life-size, and Lithia immediately saw the resemblance between the old woman standing there and the young woman laughing. "I don't remember ever being there. What is that place?"

It looked to Lithia like the woman in the image was enjoying a carnival.

These must have been the personal photos of the colonists Jameson recruited. He had kept them hidden, but someone had found them. Someone had kept them. Someone had figured out a piece of the truth, and filled in the gaps with whatever else they could find. They had swapped the roles of villain and hero, making the Vens into a force for truth.

The Green Cloaks had been wrong about so much, but they knew that they were right about at least one thing. The Farmer hadn't swept them from a desolate universe into paradise. He had wooed them from full lives that they had lived on developed worlds, full of technology and wonders they would eventually forget.

The woman, the "grandmother," stared, mouth agape, at what she was seeing.

Lithia heard a throat being cleared beside her. When she turned to Cora, she was met with two impatient eyebrows urging her forward. "Oh," she murmured clumsily. She had been so wrapped up in the reveal that she almost forgot her part in their plan. Luckily, her guard had reacted in much the same way. His attention wandered enough for her to step toward the projector and establish a link. The Farmer might have done horrible things, but so had Elijah. He, too, would be exposed for what he was.

With a few taps on her wrist, the recording she had taken in Michael's office just a few hours earlier took the place of the grandmother's image.

The crowd rustled in confusion.

The angle of her camera had only captured a portion of Elijah's face, but his nasally voice was unmistakable. This was not a holo vid, but that didn't matter. The people didn't need to see it in three dimensions to understand fully what was going on.

Lithia allowed herself a momentary glance at Elijah's face. The would-be ruler gawked at the screen in realization. "Bet you're glad for Zane's help now," Lithia muttered under her breath. The moment she had stepped into Michael's old office, she'd begun recording. Elijah's words came flooding back through the holoprojector's speakers. Barely ten seconds of footage had played, showing nothing incriminating yet, but the murmurs of the crowd were mounting.

"Turn it off!" Elijah shouted.

Lithia's guard moved forward to assist the man at the projector, but she couldn't let them stop the playback. She shoved the guard, who fell off the stage and into the buzzing crowd.

"Let it play!" shouted Cora.

Lithia made a dash for the projector stand. Elijah's man tried to strong-arm her away from the Artifact, wrapping a hand around her wrist. Aid came from a stranger in the crowd who dug her fingernails into the tender skin at the back of his arm. He howled and released Lithia, who slipped past him to take up a defensive position at the holoprojector.

Now the crowd was curious. *It won't take long to reach the good part*, Lithia thought as she dodged Elijah's lackey. The playback continued.

Cora's voice was clear in the recording. "So you don't deny it? That you're a Green Cloak."

Everyone in the crowd fell silent as they saw Elijah's smirk, his eyes eerily cut off by the angle of the manumed. The Aratians waited eagerly to hear his denial.

Elijah's recorded voice boomed through the square: "Child, I handed Delia the knife she used to slit your corrupt father's throat."

When the revelation came, the crowd bristled. Their mood shifted as quickly as a cloudy spring sky turns dark and thunderous. Elijah saw his people souring against him and tried to find a way out

The crowd restrained him when he tried to leave the stage. His men didn't try to help him.

"Kill Elijah!" a voice shouted.

"Wait! He has my wife and daughter!" Benjamin shouted, but the angry mob drowned him out.

In the pandemonium, the woman who had marveled at her old holo image came to the stage. "I have a question for the traitor," she said, her voice as gnarled as her hands. She got up close, and Lithia was afraid she would not get to hear the question.

She saw Elijah's eyes widen, and she took a few steps toward the stage.

The woman fumbled in the pocket of her apron. She pulled out a kitchen knife, dull enough to be kept safely in a pocket. If

Lithia had been closer, she might have been able to stop it. The men holding Elijah in place had not seen it coming. The old woman was faster than anyone expected.

She plunged the knife, sharp enough for its task, upward into Elijah's gut and raised her voice. "Do you know how many of my children and grandchildren died because of Green Cloak traitors like you?"

Asher shouted and rushed to his father's side. The would-be Regnator collapsed to the floor of the stage.

A woman was let through from the crowd. A doctor, Lithia realized.

"He's having trouble breathing," the doctor said.

Lithia joined Cora in helping the old woman into a chair. Cora took the bloody knife from her hand. The old woman was breathing heavily, as though stabbing Elijah had taken a lot out of her.

"Grandmother," Cora said, "you didn't need to do that. We could have put him in jail."

"Your heart is pure, child. You would have made a good Regnator. I've known many good men in my years, and many more who've made mistakes, but that man would not have given up. Our prison could not have held him. Look at the minds he infected." She gestured to the men the crowd had rounded up.

"I agree, but haven't we lost enough?" Cora asked, looking hopelessly at the crowd.

"We have because of them. The Green Cloaks aren't welcome here," the old woman said.

The woman who had been tending to Elijah leaned back and shook her head. Asher sobbed. Theo was nearby, ready to restrain the boy if he tried something. For now, he seemed to be giving him a moment for his grief.

Lithia watched as the projector man she'd scuffled with tried to escape, concerned now for his own well-being. The rest of the Green Cloaks, at least the ones who had openly helped Elijah, were being rounded up by the crowd, and the Aratians were not gentle. They were mounting into a fury. Didn't Cora realize that she needed to do something?

"Cora, you need to say something." Lithia demanded. "They'll listen to you."

"I'm not the Regnator. Why would they listen to me?"

"Because you hunted the Green Cloaks to Raynor Farm. You helped the Ficarans kill the last of the Vens. You exposed Elijah as a traitor. You are Cora Bram, and that is all that matters right now. Do something!"

A wail of pain rose up from somewhere in the crowd. A Green Cloak was on the ground and at the mob's mercy.

Cora was already moving. Not into the crowd, but to where the amplifier lay forgotten on the stage.

"STOP!" Her voice boomed with strength and authority, stunning the crowd into a moment of hesitation. "Take the Green Cloaks to the prison. I'm angry, too—furious, even—but we can't give in to revenge. If we choose to condemn the traitors, then we will make that choice with our minds, not our hearts.

"When we were pursuing the Green Cloaks, I wanted nothing more than to kill all of them. When we found them, the Vens had beaten us to it. We found six dead Green Cloaks at Raynor Farm, and the sight did not fill me with the joy and relief I had anticipated. It made me sick to my stomach. All I'm asking is that we give ourselves time. A hasty decision where lives are concerned will leave us with regrets."

Cora still commanded respect and power, even after Elijah's revelation. The crowd softened and turned to listen.

"Elijah was right about one thing," she continued. "The Farmer lied to us. He was not a god. I am not a god's granddaughter, as I recently discovered myself. But I humbly ask that you allow my uncle to lead you just a little longer, as we set up an alternative form of government. Our people do not need more chaos right now."

Cora and Benjamin exchanged a look. It was clear to Lithia that her cousin had not had a chance to discuss this with her uncle, but even so, he nodded in agreement. It seemed that Elijah's proof had convinced him, too, stubborn as he was. Most of the crowd nodded along. Lithia got the impression, and not for the first time, that Aratians didn't like change.

One voice rose up above the others. It was Moira. Lithia hadn't noticed her before.

"When? When will you set up the alternative?"

"Within the month," Cora said. "I fully expect you to hold us to it. And give us input. Our numbers are fewer than they have been in quite some time, and every voice deserves to be heard."

Benjamin began directing people. Green Cloaks were taken to the jail. Others huddled in groups, discussing the day's events. Agitation was high, but the wild chaos had been subdued.

In the aftermath, Lithia got a call from Brian. "Where are you?" he asked.

"The Vale Temple. Where are you? Where's Dione? Let me talk to her."

"We're in the colonizer. We're about to land it near the Field Temple."

"Mother of the void," Lithia murmured, raising her eyebrows. *She actually did it.*

"The fabricator's on board, and I want to start negotiating terms of use before one side gets greedy or jealous. Complete

270

transparency. I want to preserve the alliance. Is Benjamin okay? Zane told Dione there was a coup?'"

"There's been a touch of a political upheaval here. Things are settling down, but I don't think it's a good time for Benjamin to leave."

She glanced over and saw him holding Evy on his hip and talking with one of the Aratians. Amelia was by his side. If they were free, her friends might be, too. She scanned the crowd and saw them—Bel, Zane, Oberon, and Jai—standing at its fringes.

"Could Cora come as a representative, then?" Brian's voice buzzed from her manumed.

If they had really brought back the colonizer, the Aratians would want to know about it. Lithia relayed the message to Benjamin and Cora, and Benjamin gave his niece permission to get things started.

She relayed this to Brian.

"I'll have Colm get you," he said. "He's apparently acting leader of the Ficarans for now."

Victoria's wounds must have been serious for that to be true, Lithia thought. She was about to end the call, but then she realized Brian had never handed the call over to her friend. "Wait. Where's Dione? I want to talk to her."

Brian paused long enough for uneasiness to creep into her stomach.

"She's resting," he said. "One of the dragons burned her pretty badly, but we patched her up."

Lithia was even more eager to go now. "Here are the coordinates. I'm bringing Zane and Bel, too."

"That's fine. I'll let Colm know."

He ended the call.

Time to round up the others and book it, Lithia thought. She had picked a location a little ways from the settlement for Colm's pickup point. She didn't think that a Ficaran Flyer should pop into the middle of the settlement after the day's excitement.

She headed over to collect Bel, Zane, and Oberon. Jai had already disappeared into the crowd, presumably to help.

"What happened to you guys?" she asked.

"They caught us, but we'd already fixed the holoprojector," Bel said. "They kept us with Amelia and Evy, but once our guards saw things were going downhill for Elijah, they ran." She grimaced. "I don't think they made it far, though."

"It's not up to us what happens to them now," Lithia said.

39. LITHIA

Lithia was glad it was Colm, not Victoria, who'd be at the initial briefing on the fabricator. He was a lot easier to reason with, and he and Cora had built up some rapport during the trip to Raynor Farm.

Bel and Zane were happy to come along and check out the colonizer. Oberon looked tired, but happier than she'd seen him since they blew up the Ven Invader. The ride was mostly silent, but Lithia gaped when Colm landed the Flyer next to the colonizer. It was huge.

"I can't believe they got this thing to fly," Bel said.

"I can," Zane replied. "They built these things to be idiot-proof. Normally the people on these things weren't well-trained. Everyone got a few rushed certifications before leaving, but really their skill sets were more focused on getting a settlement up and running once they hit the ground."

"These things are also pretty hardy," Lithia added. "They have to be when inexperienced people are flying them."

A tall, lean man with a beard emerged from the ship and waved at them.

"Who's that?" Zane asked.

"Must be Brian's dad," Lithia replied.

Colm clapped loudly and laughed. Lithia jumped and turned to see a wide grin spread across his face. "I can't believe it!" Colm crowed. "He's really back." He strode forward and wrapped the man in a strong embrace.

Brian appeared out of the colonizer in time to smile at Colm's greeting, but there was still no Dione. Lithia frowned.

Brian's dad made his way over to the rest of the group. "Oliver," he said, extending his hand to each of them. "Nice to meet you."

He studied Lithia and Cora closely, looking from one to the other, but didn't say anything.

Lithia figured someone would tell him soon enough.

"Where's Di?" she asked.

"In the medical bay, resting," Brian said. "Once she's awake you can see her. She's stable, and if any alarms go off, I'll get a notification."

"Once she's awake *she* can see *me*," Lithia retorted. "Why would her being asleep stop me? I'm going in there now."

Oberon put a hand on her shoulder. "Lithia, let her rest."

Lithia first bristled at the request and shrugging his hand off her shoulder, but then she nodded. She'd see Dione soon. Not even dragons could keep them apart.

Cora greeted Colm not with a handshake, but with a hug. This seemed to surprise him, but he smiled and hugged her back.

"We've been through too much to fight over whatever this is," she said, gesturing toward the colonizer.

Brian's face lit up. "I agree. It's the ship Jameson used to transport the original colonists. Inside there's a fabricator. With the right raw materials, it can make almost anything."

Colm pat Brian on the back, and Cora tilted her head, no doubt imagining the possibilities.

"Like farming equipment," she said.

Brian nodded.

"And medicines?"

"Some, I think," he replied.

She hesitated, then frowned. "Guns?"

Brian frowned, too. "Yes, guns."

"I can lock or remove the gun templates," Oberon offered. "With Zane's help."

Cora shook her head. "That's what the Architect did to the Flyers. She locked them because she didn't trust us to use them wisely. In doing so, she turned them into a weapon."

Lithia couldn't help herself. "But... these are guns. They are weapons."

"I know," Cora said. "The point I'm trying to make is that we need to make sure whatever agreement we come to makes us feel no need for an armed conflict. With each other, at least."

Colm nodded. "I understand where you're coming from. You want an agreement on moderation."

"Limitations on weapons and ammunition," she replied. "But I recognize that both sides will still need weapons."

"Victoria will not like this," Colm said.

Lithia scoffed, but turned it into a cough. Victoria was seriously injured, and derision felt out of place.

"This isn't about egos," Cora said. "Soon, my uncle and I won't be in charge of anything at the Vale Temple, and we want to put a framework in place with you that my people can build on. There's been so much change..."

Cora paused, and Lithia watched her take a steadying breath. The girl had grown so much in the past few weeks. When Lithia met her, she had been a trusting child. Now, she was negotiating the peace of Kepos. It seemed impossible to her, but she realized that her cousin had spent her whole life watching her father and uncle, learning the words and postures. After her experiences, she had learned the stakes, and what the words really meant.

Cora would actually make a good Regnator, though she was giving it up. This was perhaps her greatest sign of maturity yet.

"Colm, I'm tired," she said. "The Aratians are tired. We have an alliance, and with this fabricator, we can choose to strengthen it or tear it apart. If we do this right, no one will feel the need to fabricate a gun."

"Then let's do this right," he replied.

"We can start by drafting an amendment to your alliance right now," Oberon said, pulling a tablet from a nearby cabinet. "All I ask is that I have use of the first segment of this colonizer, the one with the jump drive. It's time my students and I made our way home."

"I don't think that will be a problem," Cora said.

"Nor do I," Colm agreed.

Lithia smiled. Negotiations were off to a good start.

40. DIONE

Dione was alone when she woke up. Pain shot through her calf. There was a giant note, impossible to miss, that Brian had left: "Call when you're up."

She sent him a message.

She tried to ignore the pain by walking through how the nervous system worked. An outside stimulus triggered a signal. That signal made its way through the nervous system like a game of telephone. Each neuron passed on the message—PAIN—to the next via chemical signals called neurotransmitters. Eventually the message arrived in the brain where it was somehow processed into the unpleasant sensation she was getting all too familiar with.

She distracted herself by picturing and mentally labeling the parts of a neuron while she waited for Brian to come to her rescue. Her lower body was encased in some sort of medical contraption that produced a sterile field to protect her damaged leg. She tried to wiggle her toes, but it hurt too much for her to assess the damage.

The doors to the med bay opened. Brian smiled at her as he entered. "Hey, how are you—"

"DI!" the voice that interrupted him startled her.

"Lithia?" Dione barely recognized her own weak voice.

Her best friend bounded into the room. "I'm here. You're an idiot. You know that, right?"

She wanted to respond, but one thought dominated her mind. "Brian, more pain meds?"

"You're almost maxed out," he said. "That's what the computer says, anyway."

"Almost?" she repeated back to him.

He hit a few buttons on the controls. "That's it, though."

The effect was nearly immediate. The sensation in her leg went from a sharp, biting pain to a throbbing ache. Habituation. Eventually, she'd get used to it. Dione smiled.

Lithia did not. She looked horrified.

"I'll be fine," Dione said softly. She felt very tired after just a few minutes. "This happened a few hours ago. I think. Jameson kept a bunch of really good burn meds and ointments on board. He knew he might need them one day. I'll be walking again in no time."

"I'll leave you two to catch up," Brian said before heading out.

Lithia nodded, but when Dione inspected her friend's face, something looked wrong. She saw dark circles under her eyes that hadn't been there before. The mirth that usually danced in her eyes, even in the face of a disaster like this, was absent. "Are you okay?"

"No, Di, I'm not okay. My best friend nearly got killed by a dragon. I've been fighting Vens. I've been crashing shuttles and breaking ribs. I've been watching people die. I just want to go home."

Dione reached out for her friend's hand, unable to get up yet. Lithia was sobbing now, and Dione squeezed her hand firmly, unable to embrace her.

"Does Oberon know?" Dione said, when the tears subsided.

"I don't think so. Everyone's upset with me except Cora. I crashed another Flyer into the Vens so they couldn't get to the Marauder. They think I'm crazy."

"I'm sure you didn't have a choice."

"It wasn't a stupid risk, though, Di. It was the only way I could protect them."

"You look exhausted," Dione said. "Why don't you stay here and rest a while?"

"I can't," she whispered. "The nightmares."

More silent tears streamed down Lithia's cheeks. Dione felt tears well up in her own eyes. She had abandoned her best friend when she needed her the most. Now, everything that Lithia had been bottling up was exploding under the pressure, and Dione couldn't even hug her.

"We're going to get you help. This ship has a jump drive. Brian checked it out. I think with a few repairs, we can make it space-worthy. We can go home. We can get you help."

Lithia shook her head in horror. "I don't think I can be fixed. I don't remember what it was like to be me before this planet. Before the Vens."

Sadness pooled in the pit of Dione's stomach. She had been feeling the same way. As things happened to them here, she had gotten a better understanding of Bel, of her quiet determination and the serious expression that nearly always masked her face.

This planet and the Vens, they had taken something from her that she would never get back. She had killed. It didn't matter that it was a Ven or that it was necessary. She didn't regret it, but it had changed her in ways she was still discovering.

Until now, Dione hadn't realized how much it had taken from Lithia. Lithia had killed, too. She had been in the thick of every battle on Kepos. She had seen death, she had dodged it by centimeters more than once since they crashed here. She had done all of this without her best friend by her side. Dione couldn't grasp the burden that was weighing on her shoulders.

While Lithia was fending off the Vens, she'd been looking for the professor, stopping communication on the Ven ships, and, most recently, looking for Brian's dad. Difficult and dangerous tasks, but nothing like the combat situations Lithia had faced.

Lithia sniffed and pulled her hand away to wipe away her tears. "I'd better go. Cora and Colm are still discussing how to share the fabricator."

"You don't have to go," Dione said. "Don't you think you've earned a break? There's a bed right there. I can tell you all about the dragons."

"I need to finish this," Lithia said. "You wouldn't even recognize Cora if you saw her now."

"Look at you, being a good influence. Wait until your mom and dad hear."

That got a small smile from her. "So you really think this thing will get us home?"

"I do," Dione replied.

She had to. That way she knew that everything would be okay.

***

A few hours after Lithia left, there was a knock on the door. Dione put down her reading, took a deep breath, and readied herself. She'd been expecting him, so by the time Oberon walked through the door, she had already planned out everything she was going to say.

He looked her over without a word, eyes stopping on the medical casing that obscured her ruined leg.

"I'm okay, you know. This machine is keeping the burns clean, and in a couple of days, I won't need to be in here anymore."

"You're not okay," Oberon said. "I've looked at the report of your injuries. You have serious nerve and muscle damage in your leg, and if this had happened anywhere else on that island except for the colonizer, you'd be dead. Do you realize that, Dione?"

The sympathy she'd felt for her teacher's anxiety slipped away. For the first time she could remember, she was mad at Oberon.

"Of course I realize that," she said. "But it's not like the rest of you were any safer. You're just mad that I left. I'm supposed to be the one who always follows the rules. You counted on that. It made you feel like you still had some control over us out here. Well, you didn't. I know you feel responsible for us, but when we arrived at Kepos, we thought you were dead. When I left you on that Ven ship, I thought you were dead. All we could do was survive. There were no more rules. Just because you came back doesn't mean that the rules did. This is not biology class. There are no do-overs. There is no room for mistakes, or you'll end up like me."

Dione didn't know when during her rant she had begun to cry, but she felt the tears dripping off her chin. "You think I don't understand that I'll be on crutches once I'm out of this thing? That I'll need special treatments and therapy if I'm going to walk pain-free? I've done my research, *professor*," she spat. "You should know me well enough to at least expect that of me."

Oberon looked down, and when he looked back up, tears were welling up in his eyes, too. "I didn't want this for you. Any of you. I'm so sorry."

Dione's voice softened. "I know. None of this is your fault, but you've got to stop acting like it is. You keep lashing out at us because of the choices we've made, but there were no good options. We did our best, and that's all you have the right to ask of us. We're all leaving here scarred, maybe me least of all. Bel nearly died, and she has that scar on her cheek. Zane and Lithia were in the thick of the battle against the Vens. I can't even imagine the things they saw. Lithia's not okay at all."

"None of this should have happened. You're just kids."

"We're more than that now. I know you don't want to hear this, but I've been thinking a lot about home now that we've got this colonizer. We can make it back to our world, the reality we left when we ended up here, but what if it's changed just as much as we have? I can't shake the feeling that there's something bad coming on the horizon. The Vens have been getting bolder, we knew that before we left. Then we were attacked inside the Bubble. War is coming, and we won't be the only ones affected by it."

"I hope you're wrong," he said.

"You know I'm right," she replied. "I've reviewed the old data we have on the Vens. We haven't looked at the datacore results yet, but I think we're going to find something."

"You should be resting, not reading about the Vens."

"Research keeps my mind occupied," she said softly, "and distracts me from the pain."

Oberon put his head in his hands and sobbed. She fought another round of tears.

It was hard to see her idol become a mere human being, but Dione tried to take heart. Professor Oberon was just a man, and if he was just a man, one day she could become like him. Intelligent, thoughtful, inspirational, all while still succumbing to human weakness. Oberon was a flawed human being, just like she was. That didn't make him any less worthy of her respect.

41. BEL

"Sam's dead," Zane told them. They were in the colonizer's med bay where Dione would stay for a few more days.

Bel reached out to hold his hand. She could hear the distress in his voice, even if the others couldn't.

"Technically, she was already dead," Lithia replied. Bel glared at her, and she lowered her gaze. "Sorry, Zane, I didn't mean it like that."

"She did a lot around here," he said. "Oberon and I were able to integrate a lot of the *Calypso*'s hardware into the base to improve the old AI, but it won't be the same."

Bel examined Zane's face, his red eyes and tightly pressed lips, and she gave his hand a squeeze. *I love you*, she thought. *I'm here for you*.

"She went through hell to protect these colonists, and she had a last wish. She wanted us to bury her," he said.

The room was silent for a few moments.

"Where?" Bel asked.

"There's a spot in the mountains where she liked to watch the sunset. Before she…" He trailed off, apparently uncertain how to finish the sentence. "She gave me the coordinates."

Oberon had something to add. "She gave me a petition to file that will give Kepos its own sovereignty. If the Alliance extends the Bubble to include this planet, the corporation that built this place won't be able to take it back. She already sent off a copy, but no one will get it for a very long time. That's why I'll file it as soon as we return to Lavinian."

"Creating the documents to give Kepos control over its own destiny were Sam's last act," Zane said.

Bel couldn't help feeling that Sam had overlooked something as she prepared for her death.

"Even with the Vens gone, Kepos still isn't safe," Bel said.

"We'll do our best. They might want some company after the isolation, but with the right filings, it will be on their terms," Oberon said.

Dione scanned the documents. "They'll have to set up a central government," she said.

"I've already approached Ficarans and Aratians, and they're taking care of that requirement with a co-council," Oberon said.

Bel was glad they were talking about the legal implications, but she had other, more tangible concerns.

"That's not what I meant," she said. "The island. Dione, you saw for yourself how dangerous it is. Some of those species have already made their way here to the mainland. Now that they've got the Flyers and they know what's over there, the risk is even greater."

"I've spoken with Moira," Oberon said. "She's going to work with both sides to develop precautions. She's also putting together a task force to root out the angler worms that have invaded."

Bel bit her lower lip. "I think I'll join the task force. We've got months before we leave, anyway."

Oberon nodded at her. "I'm sure she'd appreciate the help."

If Bel had her way, she'd blow up the whole island. She'd float that suggestion to Moira, she thought. Enough flaminaria would incinerate everything there. Even the dragons couldn't survive if the whole island burned. She might not get to decide what happened to Jameson's nightmare creations, but she would leave Kepos with as much information as she could, in case the island creatures became a threat.

***

Is this how you mourn a god? Bel wondered.

She had never been religious. She believed what she could prove, not what inspired her, but she closed her eyes anyway and wished peace for Sam's soul. When Bel died, she would decompose and live on only in the sense that the conservation of matter implied. She would not be destroyed, but changed in form. The electrical impulses that made her who she was would cease, and her sense of self would disappear.

She thought it was beautiful, and that Sam would have found it beautiful, too.

Though the Aratians had the capacity to cremate remains, Sam had requested burial. It was unusual on the core planets, but out on the Rim, it was common. Bel had attended a few burials.

The Ficarans had constructed a coffin and prepared a grave near the base itself. Almost every able Ficaran attended the service. Some of the older folks who had met Sam in person said a few kind words. Then, they sang. The music echoed through the mountains, and Bel felt awe at Sam's sacrifice and the way these people were honoring her. After the coffin had been buried, a few Ficarans came forward with young plants, sporting plump red buds that promised to bloom into magnificent, crimson blooms.

"It's a hybrid she created," Zane said, stepping into place next to Bel. "I found references to it back when I was up on the space station. She thought it was the best thing she'd ever engineered."

"Why? Is it medicinal? Edible?" Lithia asked.

"Purely aesthetic. Art for art's sake, in a way."

"Hmm. She never struck me as sentimental," Bel said.

"I think it was her way of coping with the inevitable. When she made the choice to merge her consciousness with Jameson's AI, she walled that part of herself off. In the past few days, as she lost control, I think those walls started coming down. Like asking for a burial. She finished the translation, though."

Bel hugged Zane, pressing her cheek hard against his chest. The translation. She had risked a lot to get that datacore. It had been stupid. Now that it was translated, she felt a strange sensation in her stomach. *Guilt.* Guilt that she had nearly died obtaining the information, and guilt that the translation had hastened Sam's death. What if the datacore turned out to be worthless?

"She sacrificed a lot so we could read what's on the datacore," Bel said. "We owe it to Sam to make the most of that information. Even if my hypothesis is wrong and the Vens don't have a predator, there's got to be something on there we can use."

"I used to be afraid that there wasn't." Zane rested his chin atop her head, holding her even tighter. "Now I'm more afraid of what happens if you're right."

42. DIONE

Lithia was cackling hysterically. "'Shuckers'? Are you kidding me?"

Dione grinned. It was good to hear Lithia laugh like that. "It makes sense, though. If your body was a hard exoskeleton, a Shucker would be pretty scary."

Everyone had come to the medical bay, where she would be trapped for a few more days, to discuss what Sam had translated from the datacore. Dione told herself the pain was getting better, but she wasn't sure if that was because it was true or because she wanted to believe it was true.

"And what are we gonna do when we find these Shuckers?" Lithia asked.

Bel rolled her eyes, but Zane laughed.

Even Oberon cracked a smiled. "The closest transliteration we have for their name is Sugians. Why don't we use that for now?"

"The rhyming options for that one aren't as good, but I'll roll with it," Lithia conceded. Dione studied her best friend closely, but the vulnerability she had displayed during their reunion was gone.

When the five of them began to pore over Sam's translation, they quickly discovered that Bel's hypothesis was right. Unfortunately, this meant that the laughter and smiles that had accompanied the start of this process soon evaporated.

There was no running from it anymore.

"The Vens have a predator," Dione said. "Everything we've observed about them, their behavior, tactics, all of it has a greater context that we've just discovered."

Oberon sighed. "You need to see this."

"Is it a picture of a Sugian?" Dione asked.

"No, not exactly." He cast it to the main screen.

Dione gagged, but Bel tilted her head and studied the image for a while before finally saying, "Huh, that's interesting."

"Is that a Ven... husk?" Zane queried.

"Looks like it to me," Lithia replied. "Is that what these Shuckers do? Sorry, *Sugians*?"

"Yes," Bel said.

"How does that work?" Lithia asked.

"They inject them with a poison that liquefies their insides, then they suck them out," Bel replied.

"Tasty," Lithia commented. "Bet those redundant systems the Vens have developed aren't very useful when they're all liquefied."

Dione called up a new picture. At the sight of the predator, all levity was sucked from the room like liquefied Ven viscera.

In general shape, it reminded her of a large jungle cat, but that's where the similarities ended. The creature was covered in a pale, thick skin. Its eyes were green with slits for pupils. It did not have lips; instead, its mouth was covered by thick flaps of skin. Another image showed those skin flaps open and extend to reveal a sharp bill.

"It must use the beak to pry open the Vens' back plates," Bel said. "Find a better picture of that," she said, pointing to a red blip on the image.

Dione obliged. She'd been through these before. She knew what Bel was looking for.

"Gross. Is that—?" Zane didn't finish the question.

"How they eat their Ven smoothie?" Lithia offered. Despite the joke, her nose was wrinkled in disgust.

"There are some images that have them walking upright on two legs, but they seem to prefer being on all four," Dione said.

"We've got a lot of information to go through before we get a picture of what's been going on with the Vens and these Sugians. Let's get to work," Oberon said.

He assigned them each a chunk of reading, and for a moment, Dione felt like she was back at StellAcademy. The nature of the reading quickly brought her back to reality.

Before she realized it, the time came for each to share what they'd discovered.

"I've been looking at loss reports, as in Vens lost to the Sugians. These numbers, though," Dione said, looking up. "They can't be casualties. These numbers are in the high billions. Do you think it could be your translation program, Zane?"

"It's possible," he said, "but it's also possible the numbers are right."

Dione blushed. She always seemed to say the wrong thing around him. "I didn't mean it like that. Your program really is incredible, I just—"

"I know what you meant." Zane nodded, and Dione felt relieved. "It's a valid concern. One wrong bracket or comma, and the whole thing goes to pieces. But what if it's right?"

"We don't know how the Vens reproduce," Bel said.

"The citadel ships are estimated to hold tens of thousands of Vens, not millions or billions. Even if our estimates are off, they can't be that wrong," Lithia said.

Dione frowned. "How long has this war been going on?"

"Hang on," Bel said. She tapped away furiously on her tablet, until finally casting what she'd found on the main screen. "The Invader belonged to one of the citadel ships, and this shows its movements over the last century. Lithia, can you overlay the Sugians' positions you were talking about?"

Dione saw it now. A game of cat and mouse, where the Ven citadel ship was the mouse.

"There's more," Zane said. With a few taps of his fingers, he had increased the size of the map. "This is the flight path for the last millenium."

Lithia gaped. "They've been at this for a thousand years."

"Longer," he said. "There's more data here, but I think you get the point."

"I've got the last known positions of the Sugians," Lithia said. A dozen or so red dots appeared on the screen. "They're close. Like, really close. Months out from the Bubble if I'm reading the Ven data right."

Dione tried to imagine what it would be like to be in constant flight. The Vens had arrived at her own corner of the galaxy decades ahead of these predators, but what was a decade in the life of a Ven? What was a decade in the face of millennia of running?

"Does the Alliance have this information?" she asked. 'I mean, our Alliance— the one with the capital A."

"I'm sure they do," Bel said. "They've captured a few Ven ships. They've had the same access to a datacore that we have, and they've got linguists and the most sophisticated translation tech around. They almost definitely have this information."

"I got into the Alliance database using Dione's dad's access, and I found some Ven data, but nothing like all of this," Zane said.

"Maybe her dad doesn't have the clearance," Lithia offered.

Dione nodded slowly. "He's pretty high up. If he doesn't know, it must be a small group at the very top controlling this info."

"About what I'd expect from the Alliance," Bel grumbled.

"We have the data now," Zane said. "We can do whatever we want with it."

"Like induce mass panic?" Dione asked. She and Zane might have made a lot of headway since he ruined her plants, but she wasn't ready to go full conspiracy theorist just yet. "We don't have any proof that the Alliance has some sinister plan. If they know about the Sugians, they must have a good reason for keeping it quiet."

Zane and Bel exchanged a look. Dione glanced toward Lithia and Oberon for support, but they remained silent.

Fine. That was their choice. But without good reason, she wasn't going to abandon faith in the government or her father.

"We'll cross that bridge when we come to it," Oberon said. "First, we have to get that colonizer back into shape. The ship is so large, and even though it's in working order, I'm creating a list of improvements, upgrades, and fixes to implement before we leave. It has standard comms, so we still can't get a timely message out to anyone."

"How long will it take?"

"A couple of months," he replied.

Dione glanced at Lithia, who did her best to hide her disappointment.

"We can't go any sooner?" Dione asked.

"I want to make sure everything is safe before we go," Oberon said. "This ship is our only way home, and I'm not taking any chances. Its jump drive is old, and it makes much shorter hops than the *Calypso* could. You got here in one jump, but it will take several in the colonizer to get us to the nearest colony. The charging time is longer, too."

Dione nodded and tried to shift her perspective. A few days ago, she thought she'd be stuck here on Kepos forever. A couple more months wouldn't be that bad.

43. CORA

Cora listened as her uncle delivered the speech. One week had passed since she first met with Colm, Brian, and the others about the fabricator, and in that week, there had been countless more discussions, both about the fabricator, and about how to choose a new Regnator.

"The Field Temple once belonged to all of us, before the Great Divide, and now it will again. We'll use the fabricator to repair the damage from the Vens, and we will set up a co-council of two Aratians and two Ficarans, to oversee the use of the fabricator," Benjamin said.

"We will set up our own government here—one Regnator whose power will be tempered by two Moderators. We will collect the votes for these positions in two weeks, after people have a chance to put forward their names and plead their cases." Benjamin's announcement was met with cheers from the crowd.

"I would like to announce my candidacy for Regnator," he continued. "If I am chosen, there will be no more Matching, though genetic testing for potential problems will be available to anyone who wants it. There is more to being Aratian than faith in the Farmer. I welcome any challenger and look forward to learning the will of the people."

Benjamin had spent the better part of the evening answering questions and making reassurances. Cora had made the decision not to run for Regnator against her uncle. She would not run to be a Moderator either. If elected, her uncle would end the Matching. That had been the only appeal the office held for her. Even if the new Regnator tried to maintain the tradition, they would fail. She felt it in the crowd. Aratians had only accepted the sacrifice of autonomy inherent to the Matching because they thought it was necessary. Now, it no longer was.

Her time working with Colm had convinced her to fill a different need. She would run for a spot on the Co-Council for the fabricator. By extension, she would have a say in re-establishment of the Field Temple. That was the future of Kepos: working together and sharing resources. No more petty fights over old traditions and false gods. No more deception. Just colonists working together to survive on a planet at the edge of an empire that she hadn't known existed a few weeks ago.

Lithia found her cousin helping rebuild a market stall later that afternoon. "Still not interested in Regnator?"

"No, my uncle is running. I'm considering a bid for Field Temple Councilor."

"I knew you were a power-hungry politician deep down," Lithia teased.

"I don't want to make decisions for the Aratians. I want to oversee the peace," Cora said. "I spent a long time hating the Ficarans. I'm ready to spend a long time keeping the peace between us, whether I'm on the Council or not."

She pulled Lithia into the biggest hug she could. Meeting her cousin had been the biggest reality check of her life, and she would miss her when she left.

"The repairs are already underway," she said. "I'll be moving to the Field Temple once the first apartments are complete. We're setting it up as a joint settlement since the fabricator is there."

"You won't be lonely?" Lithia asked.

"I promised Evy there would be lots of bugs, so I think she and Amelia will visit sometimes. With the Flyers, it's an easy trip. Some of the women from our expedition to Raynor Farm have declared their intent to move in once the infrastructure is there."

"You think a lot of people will move?"

"I don't know, but there's this feeling in the air when you go to the market now. People are talking about the Ficarans positively," Cora said. "They're telling stories, their own and ones heard from their parents, about what it was like before the Great Divide."

"That's great."

"Of course there are skeptics. There are separations of families. There is heartache. But the promise of change fills a lot of us with hope." Cora got quiet. "I think my father would have liked this. He was tough, but when he saw the pictures, he would have realized the truth. He would have embraced our new future."

"And I can promise you, Cora," Lithia said, "he would be so proud."

Cora nodded, though the comfort that reassurance brought her was eclipsed by her grief. This new Kepos, united in spirit, if not in body, had come at a terrible cost. In fact, grief had caused the unity felt by the Aratians and Ficarans. Everyone had lost someone. Some had lost everyone. Cora was glad for the peace, but she wished she could share it with her father. She wished she could share it with Will. She missed them both deeply.

"You said that Miranda left your grandfather," she said, "but that he never got over her."

"That's right," Lithia answered.

"Why do you think that is?"

"He always thought that one day she would walk back through the door. He wouldn't give up on that."

"Oh."

They waited in silence until Lithia spoke. "Will would have wanted you to be happy." Lithia produced something from her pocket. A white river stone, flat and smooth. "Here. Dione gave this to me. I'm not going to explain it as eloquently as she did, but it's a reminder that time will smooth over our grief, just like the river wore down the edges on this rock. The pain's never gone, but time takes the edge off."

Cora took the stone and rubbed the surface with her thumb. She couldn't imagine a day where it wouldn't hurt to remember her father and Will, but maybe Lithia was right. Maybe it would hurt less and less each day, until it became an ache in the background of her mind.

"Thank you," she said. "Think you'll ever come back to Kepos?"

Lithia grinned. "Of course! You haven't met the Min side of your family yet."

Cora returned her smile. Maybe today did feel a tiny bit easier, and that gave her hope for tomorrow.

44. BRIAN

Brian felt Dione's arms around his waist tighten as Canto negotiated his way up a gentle slope. It was her first day outside since her injury.

"I'm glad they let you out," Brian said.

"Me too." He heard her inhale deeply. "It smells alive out here."

The morning air was still fresh and cool, with a hint of floral aroma. "Nice after being cooped up, huh?"

Morning air made him feel like he could accomplish anything that day. But today wasn't about work. There'd been plenty of that recently, and there would be more coming. Today was about something else.

"Where are we going?" she asked.

"You'll see."

After a while, Brian brought Canto to a halt. "We're close," he said. "We can walk from here."

"You can walk. I'll hobble," she said, pulling her crutches from where they'd been fixed to the maximute's back. She tried to play it off, but he could see she was struggling with her new limitations.

"Hey, those crutches are state of the art on Kepos. Freshly fabricated from the newest decades-old designs we found."

She smiled, and Brian was glad for that. They dismounted, and he scratched behind Canto's ear as thanks.

"Right here," he said, spreading out a blanket. Dione winced as she sat. "You okay?" Maybe he shouldn't have dragged her out here.

After a few weeks of rest and medicine, her leg was usable, but for any real distance, she needed support.

"Yeah, it's just the nerve damage," she said. "It usually tingles a bit, like my leg has fallen asleep. After a while, though, the twinge feels more like sharp, hot needles."

Despite her pain, Dione settled in, and soon, they both enjoyed the panorama. They sat on an overlook that afforded them a spectacular view of Kepos. Rich, green trees stood against a bright blue sky. A gentle breeze rustled the leaves and drove away the late morning heat that they were just beginning to notice.

Brian could see a large, dark spot on the distant plain. The colonizer. Next to it was the Field Temple in miniature, tended by dots that were indeed moving, if he looked closely enough.

"It's beautiful," Dione said. "How'd you find this place?"

"Some people were foraging, and they liked the view. Here," he said, pulling some containers from his bag. "I brought breakfast." He smeared thick slices of crusty bread with tart, purple jam.

Dione took a bite, closed her eyes, and smiled. "Delicious." She leaned over and gave him an affectionate kiss on the cheek before taking another bite.

"Victoria has officially stepped down," he said. Her own injury had been severe. Brain damage left her functional, but with gaps in her memories both old and new. Brian knew it would be hard for a woman like Victoria, so strong and self-sufficient, to face such a new perspective on life.

"Is there hope for her recovery?" Dione asked.

"Some, though I don't think she'll ever take on a leadership role again. I may not like her, but without her, I think the Aratians would have stamped us out when we were at our lowest. I'll be glad for the change, though. It's time for someone to take over who can trust peace, rather than second-guess it."

"Who will that be? Nick?"

Brian laughed. "I doubt it. There are others who will be free to step out from Victoria's shadow. Those who appreciated her for what she was, but have ideas on how to be better."

"What about your dad?" Dione asked. There had been a lot of interest in Oliver leading the Ficarans after his return. He had survived the impossible and become something of a legend.

"No, he has other plans," Brian said, realizing his heart was pounding in his chest. He took a deep breath and looked Dione in the eyes. "I convinced him, Di. We're leaving Kepos and coming with you."

In her surprise, Dione choked on her crust of bread. Brian offered her a drink and patted her back. They had been through an ordeal on that island, and neither would have survived it without the other, but he felt like he was intruding on her real life, the one she really cared about, by leaving Kepos.

Dione took another sip of water before launching into a string of questions. "That's wonderful! What convinced him? Did your mom say anything?"

"My mom didn't say much of anything. She's a little better, but she's got a long way to go."

"There are incredible medical facilities on Lavinian. I'm sure they'll be able to help her."

"That was the deciding factor for my dad. He's surprisingly attached to this place, even if his curiosity about the universe beyond is killing him."

"What about Canto?"

Brian looked over at his golden friend, curled up in the sun for a nap, and fought back his emotions. "I'll miss him, but Melanie will take good care of him while I'm gone."

After a brief pause, she asked, "Are *you* sure about this?"

That was the moment Brian realized why he had been nervous. He'd worried about intruding on Dione's world, but more than that, he was afraid to leave Kepos. Here, he was important. He made decisions. He helped others. He had agency over his own life that people his age clearly didn't have in the world Dione came from. He also had a huge deficit of cultural knowledge. That scared him.

"I know you said you can't promise anything, but I don't see this as a one-way trip. I'm sure I'll come back to Kepos."

Dione beamed at him, then rested her head on his shoulder. It felt right to be close to her like this. He stroked her hair, then leaned down to give her a kiss. He pulled her close, holding her tightly against him. He was glad he'd be able to spend more time with her, but he still had his doubts.

"Promise me you'll help me get oriented?" he asked, gazing out at the vista. "Once we get to Lavinian, I mean."

As beautiful as this view was, he was eager to see what a core planet was like. He had trouble imagining a world covered in buildings and lives simplified by abundant technology.

"I promise," she replied. "We'll take care of you."

Brian believed her.

45. LITHIA

"Come on!" Lithia said. "We're gonna be late."

"I'm the definition of slow right now," Dione replied as she hobbled into the Flyer. "Not sure what you expected when you invited me at the last minute."

Since Victoria had given up her position, a little more trust had been thrown their way. Lithia and Oberon had retrieved a few more Flyers from the orbiting space station on the condition that they got their very own Flyer. No one objected. It was about time, too: she and the others were growing tired of hitching rides to and from the colonizer, since they were still staying in the Mountain Base.

Lithia landed outside the Aratian settlement, and she and Dione hurried to join the crowd. "The voting is over already," Dione said. "Looks like they're nearly done counting."

The votes had taken place out in the open. In a custom so ancient Lithia had forgotten all about it until Dione reminded her, stones were cast as votes into baskets. The stones were being counted publicly, so the vote could be trusted. With such a small settlement, things could be done this way.

The results were clear. Only those counting Benjamin's stones were still at work. Benjamin would remain Regnator. Lithia wasn't surprised. People preferred the familiar, and he had done a good enough job before the coup. The two runners-up, Theo and a man she'd never met, would be his Moderators. All men, still. No women had even tried to run. There had been so much upheaval, Lithia didn't begrudge the Aratians for sticking to this tradition—for the time being, at least. There was nothing in the new traditions to forbid women from running.

The results for the Field Temple Co-Council were a bit more exciting. When the stones were laid out for counting, it was impossible to tell who had the most. Lithia recognized the man with the most votes as a member of the maximute cavalry. When the second name was announced, the winner looked like she couldn't believe it. Cora, as a newly elected Councilor, joined the others on stage to make her oath to the people.

"She didn't want to be Regnator," Lithia whispered to Dione.

"Then why did she run for the Co-Council?"

"She realized that she could help. She spent some time with Colm, and they're the ones who negotiated the whole fabricator deal. She's actually pretty good at this. I never would have imagined that the whiny girl Zane and I tricked could become a competent leader."

"I think everyone on Kepos has changed," Dione said. "I mean, the Aratians and Ficarans are working together. They're even going to live together once the Field Temple is restored."

"Some of them," Lithia corrected.

Benjamin stepped to the front of the stage.

"Many of you came to me before the vote to ask about the pairs from the last Matching. I promised that if I was elected, I would honor my niece's wish and end the Matching. I reasoned that if people wanted to continue this tradition, they would not vote for me, so what better way to learn the will of the people?"

Dione turned to Lithia. "I can't believe Cora got through to him."

"I think it was Moira," Lithia said. "That woman has been against the Matching for a long time."

"We began the Matching in good faith," Benjamin was saying, "based on the Farmer's teachings and real science. It's true that there are risks of genetic drift in a small colony like our own, but now, we know that there are other colonies out there. Others who may one day come here, with our consent. The need to monitor and manage genetic diversity is no longer dire. We are not the only ones of our kind."

"Get to the point," shouted a woman near the front. Her short, blond hair made her instantly recognizable.

Moira, Lithia thought. *Right on cue.*

Benjamin smiled indulgently. "The Matches from this year are annulled. We will also begin accepting annulment petitions from those who have been matched in the past."

Murmurs pulsed through the crowd like waves. Some objected, but Lithia was surprised to see that most people didn't seem too bothered. Perhaps it was a weight lifted. After so many years of anxiety about the genetic health of humanity, it had to be nice for them to have that burden removed.

"Do you think a lot of people will take him up on it?" Dione asked.

"Honestly, no," Lithia replied. "There's too much baggage. Like kids. But I think anyone in a bad situation will at least have an out now."

Lithia surveyed the faces in the crowd. So much had been taken from these people, even if they were just beginning to realize it. She felt angry for them, but she was glad that changes were coming. For some Aratians, it would be like waking up from a bad dream. For others, she could already see they would question their new world order. It was a lot to process. It might not work. In fact, the only thing that gave her hope was that they were still so emotionally shell-shocked from their losses against the Vens that they were tired of fighting. They would go with the flow, and Lithia hoped Benjamin would lead them well.

***

There was another festival that night, set up in the newly rebuilt market. It reminded Lithia of the StellAcademy carnival, complete with booths and games, with small trinkets and treats for prizes. Giggling children were chasing one another, oblivious to the adults sampling savory dumplings and sweet fried dough. She even saw a few Ficarans in the mix.

Lithia noticed the joyful scene only as a backdrop at that moment. Her eyes focused on the large stone monument in the foreground. Cora's promised memorial loomed, scarred with the carefully etched names of those who died during the assault on the Vale Temple. Even the Ficarans who had lost their lives were given a side of the monument. Cora had made it clear that this was a memorial to the grief of Kepos as a whole. The only names missing were those of known Green Cloaks. It bothered Lithia that she couldn't match the names inscribed there to faces, because she had so many faces trapped in her memories of that night.

"Hey," called a voice from across the walkway. Lithia turned to find Jai smiling at her. "Can I join you?"

Lithia nodded, pushing her inner turmoil down. She liked Jai and was glad for the distraction. He had been nothing but kind.

"Come on," he said, waving her toward a nearby stall. "This is my favorite game."

It was a timed wooden puzzle. She failed it on her try, but Jai pieced it together in seconds, hands flying. He won a small trinket, a small maximute figurine, carved out of wood.

"Here," he said, offering her the prize. "To remember us."

"I'm not leaving yet. Plenty of repairs left to make." She cocked her head to one side. "Why are you being so nice to me?"

"Remember when I told you Cora needed a friend? You do, too," he said.

After more games and food, after all the lights except the glowglobes went out, he led her to the main square. Like many others had, he laid out a blanket so they could lie back and look up at the moon and stars.

Lithia lay next to him, enjoying the cool night air. He told her stories about the stars, but her eyes closed before even the first tale was over.

For the first night since the attack on the Field Temple, Lithia slept untroubled by any nightmares.

46. DIONE

Dione sat with her bad leg outstretched, waiting for the pins and needles in her calf to dissipate. She was finally off the crutches, but the pain came more quickly because of it. She found that if she stopped and took a break once the tingling began, she could prevent the pain.

She shouldn't have tried to help load up the ship, but sitting idly by while others did the hard work bothered her more than the pain. Now, she was tucked away, squeezed out of sight in a nook along the corridor.

Lithia struggled past her, hauling a wooden, Ficaran–made crate toward the living quarters.

"Crates go to the cargo hold," Dione said.

Lithia jumped, then laughed when she caught sight of her friend. She set the crate down and leaned against the bulkhead, panting. "Not this bad boy." She nudged the crate gently with her toe. Dione heard the telltale clink of bottles. "Don't tell Oberon." Lithia picked the crate back up and winked before continuing her march to her cabin.

"Secret's safe with me," Dione replied. Maybe she would help Lithia drink whatever was in that crate. Their journey home would be a long one.

She took it all in. This ship was darker than the *Calypso*, but much more spacious. She was grateful, because after so long in the fresh, open air of Kepos, she was dreading the sterile quiet of space. They had spent three months on this planet, from their first crash landing to the final repair of the colonizer.

It was hard to believe that the repairs were complete. The segment of the colonizer that contained the fabricator had been detached and situated right next to the Ficaran settlement. They had extended the newly fabricated walls around it, like a cell bringing in a particle via endocytosis.

In addition to Brian and his father, a few dozen colonists had decided to join them, but that was it. Everyone else was staying, ready to rebuild walls and repair relationships. The Aratians had also asked to send along the Green Cloaks, and Oberon had agreed, grudgingly. It turned out most of them wanted to leave, which was no surprise to Dione. They were outcasts, and in some cases, still prisoners, here on Kepos. Their only hope for a future lay elsewhere.

As eager as she was to go home, something heavy settled in the pit of her stomach. They had been out of touch with anyone in the Bubble for months. The Vens had been ramping up their attacks before they'd left, and she had no idea what they had been up to during her stay on Kepos. The Alliance was hiding information from the public, from officials like her father, but for what purpose? She wanted to believe that it was to protect humanity, but Bel and Zane's skepticism was infectious. Once they returned to civilization, they would have tough choices to make about what to do with the information they had found on the datacore.

And what about the Sugians? Could they be allies, or would they compound the threat posed by the Vens?

One thing was clear. War was coming. It was coming for the Vens, and it was coming for humanity.

Thank You

Thank you for reading! If you have a minute, I'd appreciate it if you could leave a review on Amazon or Goodreads. Every review helps me get the word out about my books!

If you want to receive updates on new releases and deals about my books, sign up for my mailing list. I send out emails when I have news: subscribe.ericarue.com/

If you want to learn more about the real creatures that inspired the dangerous island wildlife, you can read the blog post "About the Science: The Island Experiment" at ericarue.com.

You can also follow me on Facebook: facebook.com/ericarueauthor/

Acknowledgments

As always, without the support of my husband **Jacob** and my mom **Jane**, I couldn't pursue this dream. Their encouragement means the world to me. Thank you to my son **Valen** for being a good napper and letting me get in some writing time. Thank you to my wonderful beta readers: **Maggie Burnside, TR Dillon, Jane Eickhoff, Ralph Eickhoff, Adrianna Foster, Donna Royston, Bradford Karl Slocum,** and **Martin Wilsey.** Thanks to **Emma G. Rose** for helping me with my blurb. Shout out to *The Hourlings.* Thank you for the discussion, support, and excellent insights. I'd also like thank **Jessica Hatch** of Hatch Editorial Services for continuing to teach me the grammatical errors of my ways.

Most importantly, thank you, dear reader, for sticking with me this long!

About the Author

Erica Rue is a reader and writer of science fiction and fantasy, especially YA. Her abandoned biology major and handful of astronomy classes have prepared her well for writing sci-fi. She enjoys learning new words and promptly forgetting them so that she can rediscover them. When she's not writing, she forgets to water her garden, completes every side quest she triggers, and boosts her dog's self-esteem.

Also by Erica Rue

The Kepos Chronicles

The Kepos Problem
The Ven Hypothesis
The Island Experiment

Short Stories

"Trompe l'Oeil" in *The Curator* (anthology)

www.ingramcontent.com/pod-product-compliance
Lightning Source LLC
Chambersburg PA
CBHW031545240626
47153CB00002B/382